"I've been thinking...."

said shy little Olivia.

"You mean about getting my sister and your father together for real?" eleven-year-old Jenni asked excitedly.

"Exactly. They're already married. All we have to do is get them to fall in love."

"Easier said than done." Jenni sighed. "Any ideas?"

"Well, we can throw them together as often as possible."

"That's good," Jenni agreed.

"Then maybe it'll just happen naturally. You know, they'll do it on their own."

"We can't count on that." Jenni frowned, thinking hard. If Tess were to fall in love and stay married to Alec, it would be perfect. Tess was already like a mother to her, and Mr. Devereaux would make a really cool dad. Jenni smiled at her co-conspirator. "What we need is a plan...."

Dear Reader,

Welcome to Silhouette **Special Edition**...welcome to romance.

Bestselling author Debbie Macomber gets February off to an exciting start with her title for THAT SPECIAL WOMAN! An unforgettable New Year's Eve encounter isn't enough for one couple...and a year later they decide to marry in *Same Time, Next Year*. Don't miss this extraspecial love story!

At the center of Celeste Hamilton's *A Family Home* beats the heart of true love waiting to be discovered. Adam Cutler's son knows that he's found the perfect mom in Lainey Bates—now it's up to his dad to realize it. Then it's back to Glenwood for another of Susan Mallery's HOMETOWN HEARTBREAKERS. Bad boy Austin Lucas tempts his way into the heart of bashful Rebecca Chambers. Find out if he makes an honest woman of her in *Marriage on Demand*. Trisha Alexander has you wondering who *The Real Elizabeth Hollister* is as a woman searches for her true identity—and finds love like she's never known.

Two authors join the **Special Edition** family this month. Veteran Silhouette Romance author Brittany Young brings us the adorable efforts of two young, intrepid matchmakers in *Jenni Finds a Father*. Finally, when old lovers once again cross paths, not even a secret will keep them apart in Kaitlyn Gorton's *Hearth, Home and Hope*.

Look for more excitement, emotion and romance in the coming months from Silhouette **Special Edition**. We hope you enjoy these stories!

Sincerely,

Tara Gavin
Senior Editor

Please address questions and book requests to:
Silhouette Reader Service
U.S.: 3010 Walden Ave., P.O. Box 1325, Buffalo, NY 14269
Canadian: P.O. Box 609, Fort Erie, Ont. L2A 5X3

BRITTANY YOUNG

JENNI FINDS A FATHER

Silhouette®

SPECIAL EDITION®

Published by Silhouette Books
America's Publisher of Contemporary Romance

If you purchased this book without a cover you should be aware
that this book is stolen property. It was reported as "unsold and
destroyed" to the publisher, and neither the author nor the
publisher has received any payment for this "stripped book."

This book is dedicated to Ariel, who makes me laugh and
makes me cry—and always makes me proud.

 SILHOUETTE BOOKS

ISBN 0-373-09941-X

JENNI FINDS A FATHER

Copyright © 1995 by Brittany Young

All rights reserved. Except for use in any review, the reproduction
or utilization of this work in whole or in part in any form by any
electronic, mechanical or other means, now known or hereafter
invented, including xerography, photocopying and recording, or in
any information storage or retrieval system, is forbidden without
the written permission of the editorial office, Silhouette Books,
300 East 42nd Street, New York, NY 10017 U.S.A.

All characters in this book have no existence outside the imagination of
the author and have no relation whatsoever to anyone bearing the same
name or names. They are not even distantly inspired by any individual
known or unknown to the author, and all incidents are pure invention.

This edition published by arrangement with Harlequin Enterprises B.V.

® and TM are trademarks of Harlequin Enterprises B.V., used under
license. Trademarks indicated with ® are registered in the United States
Patent and Trademark Office, the Canadian Trade Marks Office and in
other countries.

Printed in U.S.A.

Books by Brittany Young

Silhouette Special Edition

Jenni Finds a Father #941

Silhouette Romance

Arranged Marriage #165
A Separate Happiness #297
No Special Consideration #308
The Karas Cup #336
An Honorable Man #357
A Deeper Meaning #375
No Ordinary Man #388
To Catch a Thief #424
Gallagher's Lady #454
All or Nothing #484
Far from Over #537
A Matter of Honor #550
Worth the Risk #574
The Kiss of a Stranger #597
A Man Called Travers #622
The White Rose #640
A Woman in Love #658
The Ambassador's Daughter #700
The Seduction of Anna #729
The House by the Lake #759
One Man's Destiny #807
Lady in Distress #831
A Holiday To Remember #885

Silhouette Books

Silhouette Christmas Stories 1989
"Silent Night"

BRITTANY YOUNG

lives and writes in Racine, Wisconsin. She has traveled to most of the countries that serve as the settings for her books and finds the research into the language, customs, history and literature of these countries among the most demanding and rewarding aspects of her writing.

Jenni's and Olivia's Plans to get Alec and Tess to Fall In Love

Plan One:

Wait until Tess and Alec are In their rooms. Knock flower pot off balcony. CRASH! They come running out of their rooms at same time, kiss each other and fall In love.

OH,TESS♥   Kiss   OH ALEC!   —CRASH ♭

Plan Two:

Get Tess out of her normal clothes and into spandex. Alec sees how gorgeous she is and falls in love.

ALEC   WOW! ♡   TESS In
← spandex

Plan Three:

Go on family vacation. Alec and Tess see how great it is to have a family and they stay together!

Alec
OlVia   +   TESS
JEnni   = Family

Prologue

He felt nothing. Not sadness. Not pleasure. Not hate or love. Nothing. Had he always been empty like that?

Alec Devereaux's hooded eyes stared blindly at the blue sky on the other side of the jet's window. For as long as he could remember, he'd been going through the motions of living. His entire life had been spent doing his duty. A boarding school had been his home from the age of five until he went to university. His absentee parents had remained virtual strangers to him until their deaths. His disastrous marriage had been arranged at his birth and accomplished when he was twenty. His wife's death ten years later had left him as emotionally untouched as their marriage.

And then there was Olivia, his daughter. She was ten. No—eleven. Every time he looked at her, he saw his wife.

It wasn't a pleasant association.

Of course it wasn't the child's fault, but still, he found himself avoiding her. It wasn't hard. His work kept him away most of the time. And on those occasions when he was at home, she was usually in boarding school.

A flight attendant stopped next to his seat, used tongs to pluck a hot, moist towel out of a basket and handed it to him.

"When will we be landing?" he asked.

"We'll be in New York in about forty minutes." She smiled at him in the suggestive way women usually did. "Will you be staying in the city long?"

"No." He offered her no encouragement.

"That's too bad. I'm going to be there for a couple of days before heading back to London, and I was thinking that we might get together for dinner. What do you say?"

Alec looked at her with unsmiling eyes so blue and dark they seemed black. "No, thank you." He could have made a polite excuse, but Alec never made excuses, polite or otherwise.

"Another time, perhaps," the attendant said as she straightened. She was still smiling, but her expression had grown stiff.

As she continued along the aisle, Alec wiped the steamy, lemon-scented cloth over his beard-shadowed face and tossed it onto the tray table. When the flight attendant picked it up a few minutes later, Alec didn't even look up. His mind was now thoroughly occupied by other things. He had a funeral to attend that morning. The dead man was Thomas Parish, an American who had once been a business partner of Alec's father. Alec personally had no use for the man. As far as he was concerned, Thomas Parish had been nothing more than a thief disguised as a businessman. It had taken Alec years to rebuild the family fortune that had been legally stolen by the man. So why was he going to the funeral? Mostly to make sure the bastard was really dead.

And because he'd been invited to the reading of the will by Parish's attorney. That could mean only one thing: the old man had changed his mind about Devereaux Hall.

That estate was one of the two things about which Alec felt passionately. The other was his loathing of Thomas Parish. Devereaux Hall had been the home of the Devereaux family for four centuries—until Parish had taken it as payment of Alec's father's debts.

And yet Parish had never lived in the home. It sat vacant year after year, steadily deteriorating. The grounds—thousands of acres—had been allowed to revert to near wilderness. As soon as Alec had the money, he'd begun the process of trying to buy it back, but Parish wouldn't even discuss it with him. For Alec, getting possession of that estate had become an obsession.

And now there might just be a chance. He'd find out at the reading of the will.

Once that was taken care of, Alec could focus on business. As much as he was capable of enjoying anything, Alec enjoyed his work.

But when he let himself really think about it, he recognized an emptiness in his life that even work couldn't fill.

Nothing filled it.

Chapter One

Alec stood in the background at the graveside service of Thomas Parish and watched the hundreds of people who had shown up to pay their last respects. They were among the most prominent businesspeople in the world. Alec knew most of them. But there was one woman in particular who caught and held his attention. Her hair, an unusual golden honey color, fell silkily to her shoulders. Medium height and slender, she was dressed in a black suit unrelieved by any touch of color save for the blush of her lips. Alec leaned toward the white-haired man standing beside him. "Who is that woman?"

Russell Kent, an old friend of the late Thomas Parish and a business associate of Alec's, knew instinctively who Alec was asking about. "That's Thomas's oldest daughter, Tess," he said quietly.

Alec was disappointed. He hadn't wanted her to be a Parish. "Why isn't she standing with the rest of the family?" He'd noticed early on that Tess was off by herself.

"She and Cheryl, her young stepmother, don't have what you'd call a close relationship. I suppose it would be more accurate to say that Tess is Thomas's *estranged* daughter."

Alec remained silent, watching Russell. "The young girl standing with Cheryl," Russell continued, "the one who looks just like Tess—is Jenni. She's Thomas's youngest child from his first marriage. He and Cheryl don't have any children together." A soft smile touched the older man's mouth. "Jenni's a charming child. But then so is Tess. It was just her misfortune to rub her stepmother the wrong way, so she got shut out. Rather the same way I did as his friend," he said sadly.

Alec watched Tess with his hooded dark eyes throughout the rest of the service. There was something about her that had caught his attention and wouldn't let it go.

Tess stood at her father's grave, lost in thought, unaware of Alec's intense scrutiny. When the short service was over, people quietly said their goodbyes to the family with promises to meet at the apartment for a reception. Only a few of her father's friends from the days of his first marriage were present, and they greeted Tess, though they hadn't seen her for years. The other people were friends brought into Thomas Parish's life by his new wife. Tess didn't know them, and they didn't acknowledge her.

Her stepmother of ten years, dressed in sleek designer black that hugged her voluptuous figure, gripped Tess's shoulder. Her long, bloodred fingernails bit into Tess's tender skin. "Don't forget to come to the apartment at two o'clock for the reading of the will."

Tess stepped away as she looked at the woman, only nine years her senior, through cool golden eyes. "You're not wasting any time, Cheryl."

"I see no reason to prolong the business end of things," she said matter-of-factly. "Just because Thomas is gone doesn't mean the world stops. Two o'clock. Don't be late."

She walked away, arm in arm with a man Tess didn't know and her stepmother didn't bother to introduce.

Jenni, Tess's eleven-year-old sister, slipped her hand into Tess's. Tess looked down at her and forced a cheerful smile to her lips. "How are you holding up, honey?"

Jenni's eyes were filled with tears. "I'm okay, I guess."

Tess wrapped her arms comfortingly around Jenni and held her close as she smoothed the child's long hair. "It's going to be hard for a while."

Jenni took a shaky breath. "I don't know why I feel so sad. I hardly ever saw him."

"You're sad because he was your father. It's that simple."

"I suppose." She sighed. "Do I have to stay with Cheryl?"

"I don't know." Tess certainly didn't want her to. When she'd heard her father was ill she'd tried to get in touch with him to ask if she could have custody of Jenni. Her phone calls had been rejected, and she'd had no way of knowing whether or not he'd received her letters. He'd never given her an answer.

"I won't stay with her, Tess," Jenni warned now. "I'll run away if I have to."

"Oh, honey." Tess put her hands on Jenni's thin shoulders. "Don't even think that. Running away is never an answer."

"That's what you did," she said accusingly. "You ran away and left me alone with them."

"I didn't run away. I was sent away. There's a difference. And I was only thirteen at the time. You were one. I could hardly have taken you with me to boarding school."

"You're not in boarding school now."

"No. Now I'm an artist struggling to make ends meet in a studio apartment barely large enough for myself."

Jenni wiped away her tears with the back of her hand. "I don't take up much room and I wouldn't cost you much, Tess." Her eyes suddenly lit up. "I could work! I could get a paper route. Maybe even two paper routes. One before school and one after."

"Oh, Jenni, I'd like nothing more than to have you live with me. What I need to do is figure out how we can manage it."

"You could get a real job," Jenni suggested, completely innocent of any offense in her words.

Tess laughed and ruffled her hair. "A real job, eh? Thanks a lot."

Jenni smiled back, her grief momentarily lightened. "You know what I mean. You're a teacher. You could teach."

Tess's smile faded. "Yes, I could." She studied Jenni's pretty face, so much like her own had been at that age. "Why are you so determined not to live with Cheryl? Has she ever hurt you?"

"She slapped me once, but I did kind of egg her on. Mostly it's what she says. I know she hates me. Before Dad died, she used to at least *pretend* she liked me, though. Now she doesn't bother."

It was amazing how clearly children could see things. Tess hugged Jenni again. There was no way she was going to leave New York without her little sister. "All right," she said softly against her hair. "I'll talk to her today when I come to the house."

"Jennifer! Come on. You're holding everyone up," Cheryl called from the long, black limousine parked nearby.

Tess kissed the top of her sister's head. "Go on. I'll be over a little later."

"When?"

"Two o'clock."

"Promise?"

"I promise."

"And you'll take me with you when you leave?"

"Yes." And Tess meant it. If she had to forcibly remove Jenni from that home, she would, and worry about the consequences later.

Jenni walked slowly to the limousine where their step-mother waited impatiently. She turned and looked at Tess just before climbing inside. There was no mistaking the pleading in her eyes. With a crunch of gravel under its tires, the limo pulled out and made its way down the winding road leading from the cemetery.

Tess turned back to the grave and looked at her father's casket, still above ground, waiting to be lowered. The moldy smell of freshly dug damp earth filled her nostrils. For the first time that day, her eyes filled with tears. She'd been angry with him for so many years. From the day he'd married Cheryl, just weeks after the death of Tess and Jenni's mother, everything had changed between them. She'd always felt that he'd chosen his new wife over his daughters. Whatever Cheryl wanted, Cheryl got. And when Cheryl had wanted Tess out of the way, her father had dutifully sent Tess away. From the time Tess was thirteen years old, she'd only returned home for holidays, and sometimes not even then. She'd blamed Cheryl, but more than that, she'd blamed her father. She'd adored him and he'd betrayed her.

And now he was dead. There would be no mending of fences. No expressions of remorse or forgiveness.

The anger had faded, but there was a deep well of sadness in Tess that couldn't be wished away. It was there, inside her, mixed with regret over all of those precious, lost years.

With a sigh that did little to relieve the ache in her heart, she walked over to her father's casket and placed a single long-stemmed rose on its shiny bronze lid. "Goodbye, Daddy," she said softly.

Alec watched the fleeting expressions that crossed Tess's lovely face as she leaned over her father's casket. The pain he saw was deep and real—and private. Feeling like an intruder, he at last averted his gaze.

When Russell started to approach her, Alec caught his arm. "Not now."

Russell had been Tess's honorary uncle since her birth twenty-three years before. He saw what Alec had seen and stopped without protest. "I'll talk to her back at the apartment," he said quietly.

Tess drove her cheap rental car past the exclusive New York apartment building where her father had lived. There were no parking spaces, so she continued on to the next block. She spotted one she could squeeze the compact into and managed it with the skill of years of practice.

She shut off the engine but didn't take the keys out of the ignition. She just sat there, filled with a dread that made her heart a leaden weight beneath her breast. More than anything at that moment, Tess wanted to be alone. She just wasn't up to having a confrontation with Cheryl, but she knew there was going to be one. There always was.

And there was Jenni. She'd promised.

Tess slid the keys out of the ignition, dropped them into her purse and climbed out of the car. When she shut the door, it didn't catch properly, so she opened it and closed it again, more firmly this time. Squaring her shoulders, Tess took a deep, strengthening breath and aimed herself at the apartment building.

"Tess! Tess, wait a minute!"

When Tess turned and saw the white-haired man walking quickly toward her, she almost laughed in relief. "Uncle Russell!"

"Hello, cookie!" He hugged her so hard he nearly lifted her off her feet. "How are you doing?"

"I'll be all right."

"I saw you at the funeral, but you looked like you needed to be alone."

Tess nodded. "Are you here for the reading of Dad's will?"

"That, and to see you and Jenni."

Alec, dressed in a suit as black as his hair, walked up behind Russell. He was a full head taller than the older man and looked at Tess with piercing blue eyes. This, then, was the daughter of his enemy.

Once Tess looked at him, she couldn't look away; the man was stunning. He stole her will.

"This is Alec Devereaux, Tess. His father and yours were in business together many years ago."

Tess's slender hand was engulfed by the man's much larger and stronger one. "My condolences on the loss of your father." His cultured British accent was unexpected—and so was the hostility she sensed behind his smooth manners.

"Thank you."

His eyes burned their way inside her.

"Are you coming to the apartment?" Tess was surprised at how unsteady her voice sounded to her own ears. She cleared her throat. "I understand my father's widow is having a reception. I'm sure she'd welcome you."

"I'll be at the reading, not the reception," he said coolly. Alec released her hand and turned his attention to the older man. "I have a stop to make first. I'll join you shortly."

Russell nodded.

Without realizing it, Tess rested the hand he'd held between her breasts and covered it protectively with her other hand as she watched him walk away, his broad shoulders straining at the material of his jacket.

Russell looked down at her flushed face. "Interesting man, don't you think?"

Tess felt as though she'd been caught doing something she shouldn't and quickly averted her gaze. "I suppose."

A smile curved his mouth, but he let the subject drop. "Well," he said as he took her hand in his and gave her fingers a squeeze, "shall we go slay the dragon?"

Tess sighed.

"Perhaps it won't be all that bad," he said.

She arched an eyebrow in his direction.

"All right, it probably will. But it'll be over soon enough."

They walked under the outside canopy and into the cavernous lobby of the apartment building. "It's strange coming here without Father," she said quietly. "Strange knowing that he'll never be here again. I remember him as being so strong. I thought he was immortal."

Her honorary uncle smiled sadly.

They announced themselves to the security man seated at a round desk slightly off to the side. He placed a call and spoke to whomever answered. "Go on up," he said as he hung up. "Do you know the way?"

Tess smiled. She hadn't been here for quite a while. The doorman had no reason to know she was Thomas Parish's daughter. "Yes, thank you."

She looked up at the older man and flashed him a wavering smile.

He took her elbow firmly in his hand. "Come on, cookie. Let's get this charade over with."

They took the elevator to the penthouse. The doors opened directly into the apartment. Cheryl was standing right in front of the elevator bidding goodbye to some people Tess didn't know and regally accepting their condolences. Tess stepped aside and out of the elevator as the others moved past her. Cheryl looked pointedly down her perfect aquiline nose at Tess and her husband's former partner. "You're five minutes late," she said without bothering to glance at her watch. "The others have already gathered in the library."

Tess literally bit her lower lip to keep from responding as they followed Cheryl through the apartment.

Jenni was sitting on the winding staircase looking sad and lost, but when she spotted Tess, she raced down and threw herself into her sister's arms. "You came!"

Tess hugged her tightly. "I told you I would."

"Can we go now?"

"I need to hear what the attorneys have to say about things first, but afterward we'll leave."

"Are you going to ask them if I can live with you?"

"Yes."

"What if they say no?"

"We'll worry about that if and when it happens."

Jenni wrinkled her nose. "I hate waiting."

"You're eleven. You're supposed to hate waiting."

"Great."

Russell ruffled Jenni's hair. "Hi, baby."

She smiled up at him. "Hi, Uncle Russ."

"There's a present for you in the car. I'll bring it in later."

"Thanks."

He cupped her face in the palm of his hand. "You get more grown up and more beautiful every time I see you."

"Oh, you always say that, Uncle Russ," Jenni said, obviously pleased that he'd said it again.

"It's always true."

Then, as though sensing Tess's reluctance, he put his hand in the middle of her back and guided her with gentle pressure toward the library.

Jenni watched them until they were inside, then dashed down the hallway and into a half bath that was attached to the library. Closing the hall door carefully behind her and locking it, she went to the door leading into the library and cracked it open so she could hear what was going on. She could see a little bit, too. There was her sister....

Tess looked around the room. Cheryl was there, of course, in a high-backed chair beside her father's desk. The man she'd seen at the cemetery with Cheryl sat in her father's chair behind the desk with the will in front of him. He was apparently the attorney. Jefferson and Matilda, the butler and housekeeper Cheryl had hired after moving in, were also in the room. Tess smiled at them and they smiled back. There was no family left on either her father's or her mother's side.

When her stepmother made no effort to introduce Tess to the attorney, Tess walked up to him and extended her hand. "I'm Tess Parish, Thomas Parish's eldest daughter."

The attorney politely rose and shook her hand. "I'm Curtis Connack, your father's attorney. My sympathies on your loss."

"Thank you."

He looked around the room as Tess went toward the couch. "We're still missing Mr. Devereaux."

"He'll be here in a few minutes," said Tess as she sat down.

Russell stood beside her, his hand comfortingly resting on her shoulder.

The attorney removed his glasses from his inside jacket pocket and put them on. "I suppose we can get through some of this business before he arrives. There are a number of specific bequests here," he said as he flipped through the first few pages. "The usual charities and special causes that Thomas had close ties to, of course." He went through a number of small bequests, several of which, such as antique books, were for his old friend and former partner. That was why Russell had been invited. There was money for the servants and several other people.

While everyone else was looking at the attorney, Tess watched her stepmother. And in watching her, realized with some surprise that Cheryl's control over Thomas Parish hadn't extended to his finances. It was obvious to Tess that her stepmother had no more idea than Tess did of what was in the will and was more than a little nervous about it.

The attorney removed his glasses and looked around the room. "To those of you who've been named as beneficiaries, I want to assure you that disbursement will occur as soon as reasonably possible. I would now appreciate it if everyone would leave except for Cheryl and Tess Parish."

Above the low rustle of people rising and speaking in whispers, Russell leaned toward Tess. "Do you want me to stay with you?"

Tess considered it for a moment, then shook her head. "Thank you," she said, genuinely grateful for his concern, "but I've been handling things alone for quite a while now. I think I can handle this."

"I can wait outside...."

"No. Whatever happens in here, I'll be fine."

The man, nearly seventy, looked at Tess. She sounded strong, but there was such an air of vulnerability about her. It was with great reluctance that he finally left the room.

No sooner had the door closed behind Russell than it opened again and Alec walked in. "I'm sorry I'm late," he apologized.

The attorney looked up. "You must be Alec Devereaux."

"Yes." Alec strode to the desk to shake the man's hand.

The attorney rose. "I'm Curtis Connack, and you're just in time. Take a seat, please."

Cheryl extended her hand. "Hello. I'm Cheryl Parish." Her tone was more flirtatious than grief stricken. "Were you and my late husband close?"

His look of distaste was fleeting, but Tess saw it clearly. "Hardly."

Cheryl looked at the attorney. "I don't understand...."

"Everything will soon become clear," the attorney said in a businesslike tone.

Alec looked toward Tess and inclined his head, then sat down in a chair halfway between the two women.

The attorney put his glasses back on. "All right, this won't take long. Quite simply, what Thomas did was divide his liquid estate three ways. You have access to your third, Cheryl, but Tess's and Jennifer's thirds are to be placed into a trust until such time as they reach the age of twenty-five. The remaining nonliquid assets will be sold, and revenue from those sales will also be divided equally among the three of you."

"What about the apartment?" Cheryl asked.

"I was just getting to that. You get the apartment, Cheryl. Tess, you get the beach house in Maine." He looked at Alec. "And then there's the estate in England."

"What are you talking about?" asked Cheryl in surprise. "What estate in England?"

Alec waited in silence.

"You know what I'm talking about, don't you, Mr. Devereaux?" the lawyer asked.

"That's why I'm here."

The lawyer let out a long breath. "Cheryl, I'd like you to leave now."

"But..."

"What comes next has nothing to do with you. It's a private matter between Mr. Devereaux and your stepdaughter. You may return when we're through."

Cheryl was furious. She rose abruptly and swept from the room leaving behind a trail of expensive perfume.

The attorney waited until the door had closed behind her. Picking up a video cassette, he crossed the room, put it into the VCR and turned on the television. The screen flickered to life and the face of Thomas Parish looked out at them.

Tess's heart caught.

"Hello," he said with a slight smile. "I had some things to say that translate better to the spoken rather than written word. This concerns Alec Devereaux and my daughter, Tess. I assume you're both present to hear this.

"Devereaux, for years you've tried to buy back your family's estate from me, and even though it's been sitting empty in the two decades since I became the owner, I've refused to entertain any of your offers. The simple fact of my possession of that property—your heritage—has been a great source of contentment to me. Or perhaps more accurately, your family's loss of possession is what brings me pleasure. Your father was a stupid, greedy and arrogant man. In the years of our business partnership, I was good enough to make him money, but not good enough to sire a daughter worthy of marriage to his son. Tess wasn't aristocratic enough for you, apparently."

A frown creased Tess's forehead. Where was this headed?

"Well, times change. So do circumstances." Thomas leaned back in the armchair he was sitting in. "I'm now willing to part with it—for a price. That price is your marriage to my daughter Tess."

Still in the bathroom, Jenni, her eyes huge, clamped her hand over her mouth to keep from making a noise.

Tess gasped. "What?"

"You can, of course, decline. But if you do, the property will go into a government trust. Four hundred years of Devereaux history gone, with a single stroke of the pen." Thomas Parish smiled. "I'll give you the details of the marriage in a moment. First, though, I must turn my attention to my daughter, who I'm sure is saying to herself that she would never agree to something like this. Well, Tess, let's see if I can change your mind. You've made a gallant effort over the years to stay close to Jennifer. She adores you."

Jenni, peeking through the slit in the slightly ajar door, nodded.

"It was your letter asking for custody that gave me the idea for this, shall we say, *transaction*. It's quite simple really. If you marry Alec Devereaux, Jennifer is yours—as long as you and the young Devereaux abide by certain conditions. Those are as follows: the wedding will take place in my apartment immediately after the viewing of this tape. Arrangements have already been made. The marriage must last for a minimum of twelve months. One day short of that and all bets are off. Tess will live with Alec Devereaux in the home he currently occupies in England. Jennifer may live there also. How you maintain your living arrangements after complying with what I've specified is entirely up to the two of you. My attorney will use whatever methods he deems necessary to make sure the two of you are living under the same roof. And, Tess, papers have already been drawn up giving custody of Jennifer to Cheryl in the event that the conditions I've set forth are not met."

He stared steadily into the camera lens. "I suppose you're wondering why I'm doing this, reaching beyond the grave, as it were, and manipulating your lives. The answer is because I can. I have what you want, and you must do as I ask to get it. Of course, you can always decline to play my little game, but you won't. Let's think of this as my final gesture to the British aristocracy—among whom my daughter will number shortly." He smiled. "Goodbye."

The screen went blank.

The attorney turned off the television and removed the tape while Tess and Alec sat in stunned silence. At least Tess was stunned. She had no idea what Alec Devereaux was feeling. His face seemed carved in stone.

She looked at the attorney. "Can he really keep me from getting custody of Jenni if I don't marry Mr. Devereaux?"

"Yes."

Her heart sank into a well of confusion. "Why would he do something like this?"

Alec turned his cold eyes toward her. "Revenge. Your father set out to ruin my family, but he couldn't quite wipe us out completely." He studied her face for a long moment. "Did you know about this?"

The attorney spoke for her. "She didn't. No one did, except me."

Alec didn't believe it for a moment. This whole thing smelled of conspiracy to him. But Alec was a logical man. He wanted that estate back in his possession. Marriage meant nothing to him. If he had to marry the woman to get his ancestral home back, that's exactly what he'd do. But not for one minute longer than twelve months. He looked at his watch. "How quickly can we get this farce over with?"

"Immediately. There's a judge in attendance who was a friend of the late Mr. Parish. He's been apprised of the situation and is prepared to perform the ceremony."

"What about the paperwork?"

"Red tape was cut. Everything has been taken care of except for signatures."

"Then let's do it," said Alec.

"No!" The one-word protest was out before Tess could stop it. "This isn't right. I can't marry you!"

"I don't see that you have any choice," he said coldly. "Your father has seen to that."

She looked helplessly at the attorney. "Please, this can't be legal. There must be some way I can have Jenni without having to marry."

"I'm afraid not," said the attorney. "I drew up the agreements myself. They're airtight." There was a note of pride in his voice.

Her heart sank further. "I can't believe this is happening."

"Don't be melodramatic," Alec said impatiently. "It's only a piece of paper. We don't have to like each other. We don't even have to know each other. We'll just get married, wait out the twelve months and go our separate ways."

"Unless, of course, your father misread your intentions toward your little sister," said the attorney. "If you're willing to give up custody of Jennifer, there's no need for you to marry."

Jenni, still behind the door, held her breath.

"I want my sister with me," said Tess.

Jenni exhaled.

"Then it's settled." The attorney started putting papers back into file folders. "I'll get the judge."

Jenni tiptoed across the bathroom floor, quietly opened the door and closed it behind her. Running into the living room, she spotted her Uncle Russell.

"Hey," he said with a smile, "I've been looking for you."

She smiled back, looking at him with innocent eyes. "I was in the bathroom." Sitting on a stair, she folded her hands in her lap and looked around the room. She was so glad she wasn't going to have to stay with Cheryl. And yet she didn't want her sister to be unhappy. She looked up at the man standing beside her. "Uncle Russell?"

"Umm?"

"How important is it for someone to love the person they marry?"

He looked down at her, a frown creasing his forehead. "I'd say it's very important. Perhaps the most important part of the marriage."

"What happens to people who aren't in love and get married?"

"I suppose that depends on the reason for the marriage. And, of course, it's possible for people to fall in love afterward. In the old days marriages were often arranged with remarkable success between men and women who'd never even met before the ceremony." He looked at her curiously. "Why do you ask?"

She looked away and shrugged. "I was just wondering."

Cheryl, looking elegant but angry, passed the two of them without acknowledgement and strode into the library, slamming the door behind her.

Russell and Jenni looked at each other and pulled faces. "Uh-oh," they said in unison.

"I've waited long enough," said Cheryl. "This is my home and I demand to know what's going on."

Alec's eyes locked with Tess's. "Your stepdaughter and I are going to be married."

Cheryl was clearly shocked. "What?" She turned toward Tess. "What's he talking about?"

Tess stared straight back at Alec. "My father has left us no choice but to marry."

"I don't understand." Cheryl turned to the attorney. "I don't understand," she repeated. "What's going on?"

"Your husband is giving custody of Jennifer to Tess, but first she must marry Mr. Devereaux."

"But I thought custody of Jennifer would automatically go to me, along with control over her trust fund."

"That's exactly what would happen if no marriage were to take place."

"So are you saying that Tess will have control of Jennifer's trust fund?"

"I'll have control of the trust fund until Tess gets legal custody of Jennifer—which should be in a year," said the attorney. "Not a single penny from it will be distributed, however, until Jennifer reaches twenty-five."

"But I'm sure my late husband would have wanted Jenni to stay with me. After all, I'm the only mother she's known for the past eleven years."

That caught Tess's attention. "Oh, please, spare us your brokenhearted mother act. I'll never understand what my father saw in you."

Cheryl pulled her shoulders back. "You'll never understand a lot of things. You thought your parents had such a perfect marriage before your mother died."

"They did."

"Grow up, Tess. Your father and I were having an affair two years before your mother died, and she knew it. I wasn't the first. He had affairs all the way through their marriage. Thomas was weak, like all men when it comes to beautiful women."

"That's enough, Cheryl," the attorney snapped.

Tess felt as though she'd been punched. Her father had cheated on her mother? And her mother had known? How could he have done that to her? And how, knowing it, could her mother have stayed with him?

Cheryl stepped in front of Tess. "As you get older, pet, you'll discover that men see what we as women want them to see. Nothing more and nothing less. Men like to think they're in control, but the fact is if you give a man an attractive woman and a promise of sexual pleasure, he'll turn on everything and everyone he loves. You should know that firsthand. I told your father that I wanted you gone, and a week later you were in boarding school." She flicked Tess's cheek with her red nail.

Tess didn't flinch.

"Your father's need for what I could give him outweighed his responsibility to you. In that, he's no different from any other man." She looked at Alec. "And I do mean any other man. You'd be wise to remember that, Tess."

"If you don't mind, I think I'll find another role model for my lessons in humanity."

"Don't be so naive. It doesn't become you. Furthermore—"

The attorney walked to Cheryl and grasped her arm. "I said that's enough."

"It's time she knew the truth."

He steered her toward the door and rather ungently escorted her through it.

Tess stayed rigidly where she was, her stepmother's words ringing in her ears.

Alec watched quietly. He didn't know this woman who was about to become his wife. He didn't *want* to know this woman. And yet there was something about her that he couldn't ignore. She looked more wounded than he'd ever seen anyone look. "She's wrong, you know," he said quietly. "Not all men are like that."

Tess raised her eyes to his, so lost in her pain that it took her a moment to focus on his words. "I wonder," she said sadly.

Alec wanted to go to her; to comfort her. That feeling caught him off guard. Instead, he rose abruptly, walked to the window and stood looking outside. "There are things that need to be discussed before they return with the judge."

Tess stared at his back without saying anything.

"Are you prepared to leave for England today?"

"Today? Of course not. I have to get Jenni packed, my apartment sublet and furniture stored. And I've got to do something about finding a job in England. I don't have any money at all."

"You'll be living in my home as my wife. You won't need a job."

"I understand that part of complying with my father's demands requires that I live in your house, but I don't want your charity. I can take care of my sister and myself without financial help from you.''

He shrugged his shoulders. "Have it your way. Your father's the one who made the rules.''

Tess was humiliated. Her father had put her in an impossible situation, and Alec Devereaux was rubbing her nose in it as though it was her doing. She rose abruptly. ''Excuse me,'' she said, ''I have to speak with my sister.''

Alec continued staring out the window.

Chapter Two

Jenni sat on the stairs, her eyes glued to the library door. Everyone had come out except Tess and some man she'd never seen before. She could hardly stand it! What was going on? She'd left the bathroom too soon.

Closing her eyes tightly, she crossed her fingers and then crossed her arms. "Come on, Tess."

"What are you doing?" asked Russell.

Jenni kept her eyes closed. "I have to concentrate."

"On what?"

"Making sure I get to stay with Tess."

"Oh."

"You cross your fingers, too, Uncle Russ. Every little bit helps."

He obligingly did as she asked, but kept his eyes on Jenni. "What are you going to do if it turns out you must stay with Cheryl?"

"That won't happen. Tess won't let me stay with Cheryl."

"She might not have a choice."

Jenni crossed her ankles. "I'm going to live with Tess."

The library door opened and Tess walked out. Jenni, her heart in her throat, stood up. "Tess?"

Tess looked at her little sister and smiled.

"I knew it!" Jenni whooped as she threw herself into Tess's arms. "I knew you wouldn't let me down!"

As Tess hugged her tightly, her eyes met those of Russell. "It was a little more complicated than talking her into it. In fact, it was nothing to do with Cheryl at all. Because of certain arrangements Father made, I'll eventually be your legal guardian."

Jenni's smile faded. "Eventually?"

"Our father set up some provisions in his will that have to be met before that can happen."

"Such as?"

Tess suddenly realized that she had no idea what to tell Jenni. She looked to Russell for help, but he didn't know what was going on, either. "It seems that our father chose a husband for me. After I've married him—which should be any moment now—you and I will go with him to England where we'll live for a year. After the year is up, I'll be granted legal custody of you."

Jenni still looked worried.

"What's wrong?"

"Nothing. I just..." She chewed on her lower lip. "Are you sure you want to do this? I didn't mean what I said earlier. I won't run away."

Tess smiled. "I know you won't. And I'm sure I want to do this."

Russell looked from Tess to Jenni, clearly shocked—but not so shocked that he didn't recognize where Jenni's questions about marriage had come from. Jenni looked up at him, pleading with her eyes for his silence.

He gave her a stern look, then turned his attention to Tess. "I can't believe your father would force you into something like this."

Tess shrugged. "There's nothing that can be done about it. Besides, it's only twelve months. I can get through anything for twelve months."

Russell squeezed Tess's shoulder. "I've been a very neglectful honorary uncle over the past several years. I'm sorry. And I want you to know that if you need me for any reason all you have to do is call."

"I know that," Tess said with a soft smile. "I've always known that."

He shook his head. "Your father and I were friends for more than forty years. I thought I knew him as well as one man can know another. But this . . . I never expected this from him. I can't imagine why he'd do this to you."

"In a strange way I don't think this marriage has anything to do with me. I'm merely the instrument of my father's revenge."

"I must say you're handling it well."

"That's going to be *my* revenge. I'll do what I have to in order to get Jenni, and after that, as far as my father is concerned, he won't be anything to me other than a bad memory. I don't think that's quite the legacy he had in mind."

Curtis Connack approached her with an older gentleman in tow. "Miss Parish, this is Judge LaMeer. Are you ready?"

She took a deep breath. "Yes."

Jenni grabbed her hand. "Tess . . ."

Tess smiled at her. "It's all right, honey. It's just a formality. You go pack some of your things. We'll be leaving soon."

As Jenni reluctantly disappeared upstairs, Russell moved closer to Tess. "What can I do?"

The attorney spoke. "You can witness the vows."

The four of them entered the library and closed the door behind them. "Judge LaMeer, this is Alec Devereaux, the groom," the attorney said as he moved quickly to the desk.

Alec nodded his head.

"Where do you want me?" asked the judge.

The attorney pointed to a spot in front of the desk. "There. And Miss Parish," he said pointing to a spot facing the judge's right, "you stand there and Mr. Devereaux beside Miss Parish."

They all took their places, with the attorney and Russell standing off to the side watching.

As the judge began speaking, Tess tried to listen, but her thoughts were in such turmoil that she couldn't sort through his words. It was as though none of this was real. In a few minutes she'd wake up and find that none of this had happened.

Alec stood stiffly beside her. He was furious, but it didn't show. The angrier he was, the cooler he appeared to others. He didn't like being manipulated. He didn't like being cornered. And if Tess Parish thought he was going to put on some charade of being married, she was mistaken. His life was going to go on very much as it always had. He was answerable to no one but himself.

When it was his turn to respond, he did so automatically, his voice deep but expressionless.

When Tess spoke, he was surprised to hear the tremble beneath the words. For a moment—just a heartbeat of time—Alec softened toward her. But he caught himself and his anger returned.

They had no rings to exchange, so even as they were pronounced husband and wife their fingers were bare. The judge, who apparently wasn't aware of the nature of the marriage, told Alec that he could kiss the bride.

Tess started to turn away, but Alec whipped her around and with his fingers dug into her shoulders, held her in place while he kissed her hard on the lips. There was a violence behind the kiss that frightened Tess—but more than that, it infuriated her. As soon as he let her go, she raised her hand and gave him a stinging slap on the cheek. "Don't you ever touch me like that again."

He raised his fingers to his cheek where red was already beginning to show. She was trying to read his expression, but couldn't.

And then her new husband surprised her. "I apologize," he said. "It won't happen again."

He turned to the judge, who was looking very, very confused. "What do I need to sign?"

The attorney shoved a paper across the desk toward Alec and handed him a pen. "By the *X* at the bottom. You, too, Miss Parish. I mean Mrs. Devereaux."

"Please," she said, "just call me Tess."

"Of course."

Alec signed the document and handed the pen to Tess. "I'll be going back to England tomorrow. When you choose to come is completely up to you."

Tess took the pen and watched him walk out the door. After signing where she'd been told, she took a deep breath and looked at the three men. "I'd like to be alone for a few minutes if you don't mind."

Russell squeezed her arm and herded the other two out ahead of him, finally closing the door and leaving Tess in blessed peace.

She looked around the library where she'd played as a child, seeing things she hadn't noticed earlier. Changes. There had been a portrait of her mother behind her father's desk. It was gone now, replaced by a huge painting of Cheryl. A framed picture of Tess as a young teenager holding a tiny Jenni used to be on the corner of her father's desk. The same frame now held a picture of her father and Cheryl.

It was as though she, her mother and Jenni had never existed.

Tess walked slowly to the window and looked outside. She couldn't get Cheryl's words out of her mind. Of course her father had had affairs. It made perfect sense. She remembered the time she'd found her mother sitting in front of her dressing table mirror, crying. When Tess had asked what was wrong, her mother had put on her brightest smile and told her it was nothing she needed to concern herself with.

How awful it must have been for her to have known that the man she loved had betrayed her over and over again. All these years later, Tess ached for her.

Her father had been her hero when she was a child.

But he wasn't a hero. He was just a man who'd cheated on his wife and abandoned his children.

This was his legacy.

Tess didn't hear the door open, but she knew it had. She could feel someone watching her. Straightening her shoulders, she dashed the backs of her hands across her damp cheeks before turning to find Alec Devereaux standing there.

Despite her efforts, it was obvious to Alec that she'd been crying. Once again, against his will, he softened toward her.

"What is it?" she asked quietly.

"I forgot to take a copy of the marriage license with me." He went to the desk, looked at several papers, folded one and put it in his inside suit pocket, his eyes on Tess. "Were you serious about wanting a job?"

"Very."

"I understand from Russell that you're a qualified teacher."

"That's right."

"Then I'd like to offer you a teaching job. I have need of a governess for my eleven-year-old daughter, Olivia."

"I didn't know you had a child."

"Why should you?"

"Are you divorced?"

"Widowed. Do you want the job?"

"I don't know. I need time to think it over. May I teach Jenni as well?"

"Of course."

It was a perfect solution. And yet, it was one more tie to this man she didn't know. This man who was her husband.

Alec took a business card out of his wallet and wrote something on the back of it before handing it to Tess. "You can reach me at this number until tomorrow evening. I'll need an answer by then one way or another so that I can make other arrangements for Olivia if necessary."

"What other arrangements?"

"Boarding school."

Tess accepted the card. "I'll call you."

There was a knock on the door. Russell opened it and looked inside. "Is everything all right in here?"

"Just fine, Uncle Russell."

Alec looked at his watch. "I have to go."

"I do, too," Russell said, his expression full of concern. "But I don't feel right about leaving you and Jenni."

Tess went to her uncle and hugged him. "You go on. Jenni and I are fine. We'll be going back to Boston as soon as we leave here."

"Call me when you get home so I know you've arrived safely."

"We will."

Tess could feel Alec's gaze on her and turned to look at him. "I'll call with my decision."

He inclined his dark head.

Tess followed the two men out of the library and watched as they both approached her stepmother. Cheryl, despite her mourning dress, made it obvious to anyone watching that she was attracted to Alec Devereaux. But it was equally obvious that, while courteous to her, Alec was disinterested. In Tess's experience, very few men weren't interested in that woman. She found Alec's reaction refreshing and intriguing.

"Tess, would you help me, please?" Jenni was at the top of the stairs with a suitcase so stuffed that the sides were bulging.

"What did you pack?" Tess asked with a laugh as she climbed the stairs and took the suitcase from her sister.

"Everything I could. I don't want to have to come back here. Where do we go now?"

Tess grunted as she lifted the suitcase and started carrying it down the stairs. "To Boston."

"For how long?"

"I don't know. A few weeks perhaps. And then we'll be moving to England. I might have a job at the home we'll be living in, as a governess to Mr. Devereaux's daughter. She's your age."

"What's a governess?"

"A live-in teacher."

"So you'd be a teacher in a house instead of a school?"

"That's exactly right."

They got to the bottom of the stairs and Tess all but dropped the suitcase. "Good grief, this thing is heavy."

"It has all of my treasures in it," Jenni said absently. "Now about this job, I'd still be coming with you, right?"

"Of course. I'd be teaching both you and this other girl."

"Ah!" She all but squealed with delight. "You'd be my teacher? My sister would be my teacher?"

"Right."

"It's perfect!"

"Don't think for a second that means you're going to have it easy, young lady. I'll probably be a lot tougher on you than your public school teachers. You're going to have to work hard for your grades."

Jenni wrinkled her nose. "All right. I suppose it was too much to hope for. So are you going to take the job?"

"I don't know. It's tempting for a lot of reasons."

"What did you tell him?"

"That I'd think about it."

"So now you've thought about it, and you're going to take it, right?"

"I've got to consider other available options."

"What don't you like about the job?"

"I didn't say there was anything I didn't like about it."

"There must be or you would have grabbed it."

Tess smiled as she shook her head. "You ask too many questions."

"I'm eleven. If I don't ask questions, nobody tells me anything. So what is it you don't like about the job?"

Tess sighed. "I guess I'm concerned about becoming entangled with the Devereaux family. Working in the house as a governess to Alec's child is more involved than I think I want to get."

"Why?"

"Because I'm only going to be there for a year. I want to be able to leave without any regrets when the time comes."

"Just because you teach the girl doesn't mean you have to like her," Jenni argued reasonably. "Besides, I don't know what you're so worried about. I like the guy. He's nice."

"You don't even know him," Tess said in exasperation.

"Yes I do. I told him where the library was when he came in. Besides, you're married to him now, right?"

"I guess you could say that."

"And that makes him my brother, right?"

"Brother-in-law. But that's only on paper."

"I know. But maybe some day it'll be a real marriage."

"No, it won't."

"Well, I still like him. And I think we can trust him."

"Now why would you think that?"

Jenni shrugged. "There are just some people you automatically know you can trust. It's a kid thing."

Tess rolled her eyes.

"I think you should take the job. It'll be cool having my sister for my teacher."

"You're incorrigible."

Jenni grinned at her. "But you love me, anyway."

"Indeed I do. Go say your goodbyes to Matilda so we can be on our way."

"All right. I won't take long."

Tess picked up the suitcase and dragged it to the elevator. While she stood there waiting for Jenni, she took out the card that Alec had given her and looked at it. Engraved on one side was his name, a London address, telephone and fax numbers. On the other side he'd printed a New York telephone number.

She ran the tip of her finger over that number.

Maybe Jenni was right. She was going to be living in the house anyway....

Tess sat on the couch in her small apartment watching Jenni who was lying on her stomach on the floor watching television and listening to the sound through remote headphones.

Her eyes moved to Alec Devereaux's business card lying beside the phone next to her. It should have been an easy decision. She needed the income. But she couldn't help feeling that working as a governess to his daughter would give Alec more control over her. Living in his house was going to be bad enough.

And if she didn't take the job? She wouldn't have any income, and his little girl would be sent to a boarding school.

Jenni laughed. Tess turned her gaze toward her sister and smiled. What the heck. It would be a good way to spend time with Jenni.

She reached for the phone and dialed. To her surprise, her call didn't go through a switchboard, but went directly to his room. She wasn't expecting him to answer.

"Hello," he said a second time, sounding impatient. "This is Alec Devereaux."

"Oh, hello. This is Tess."

There was a pause. "I take it you've made a decision?"

She cleared her throat. "Yes. I'm going to take the job."

"Good. When will you arrive in England?"

"I'll be able to leave here in about three weeks."

"Do you have enough money for airfare?"

"I will when the time comes."

"You're sure?"

"Yes."

There was an awkward silence. At least Tess thought it was. Her mind was completely blank.

"I have an appointment in a few minutes," he said. "Is there anything else?"

"No. I didn't mean to keep you. Goodbye."

At the other end of the line, Alec tiredly rubbed his forehead. Everything was such a mess. "Tess," he said, using her given name for the first time, "are you all right?"

She was surprised by his concern. And touched. "I don't know what I am at the moment. Numb, I think. How are you?"

"Fine." And just that quickly, whatever warmth had been in his voice was gone. "If you need anything, call my office. My secretary will be given instructions to help you any way she can."

Tess became equally efficient. "That's very kind of you. Good night."

"Good night."

Tess hung up the phone but continued looking at it. The man left her unsettled. Uneasy. One minute he was kind; the next cold. Twelve months was looking longer all the time.

Alec sat quietly after hanging up, staring at a blank wall, deep in thought. That woman affected him. She had from the moment he'd seen her at the cemetery.

And he didn't like it.

Chapter Three

Tess watched the English countryside slipping past the window of the train that was carrying Jenni and her to Gatesboro—and to Alec Devereaux. The rhythmic clack-ity-clackity helped to calm her jittery nerves.

It was beautiful country: green with gentle hills. They rolled through small, tidy villages with cobbled streets; past farmhouses with thatched roofs and low stone walls that separated pastures. Quite a contrast to New York and Boston.

She turned her head and looked at Jenni seated directly across from her, sleeping as though she hadn't a care in the world. A woman Tess didn't know had boarded the train two stops back, and she sat beside Tess doing her needlepoint.

"That's a beautiful design," Tess said.

The older woman looked at the pattern critically. "It's not one of my better ones, but it will match the rest of the pillows on my couch." She tilted her head and looked at Tess curiously. "American, are you?"

"Yes."

"What brings you to this part of England?"

Tess paused before answering. "I have a job as a governess."

"An American governess in England." The woman chuckled with evident enjoyment. "Now there's an interesting turnaround. Who hired you?"

"A man by the name of Alec Devereaux."

The woman cocked an eyebrow. "Alec Devereaux. Well, well, well."

"Do you know him?"

"I know of him. I think everyone in England knows of him. I understand he was recently married to an American."

Tess didn't say anything. She didn't want to admit she was the American he'd married. The more she could push it out of her thoughts, the happier she was.

The woman was undaunted by Tess's silence. "I imagine his mistress is kicking up quite a fuss."

"His mistress?"

She glanced at Tess. "You seem surprised. Men do have mistresses you know."

"Of course. I just didn't know that this particular man had one."

"Most wealthy men do. If the tabloids are to be believed, his come and go with some regularity."

Tess could picture the man with a mistress. She was having a little trouble picturing him married. "What was his wife like?"

"Elizabeth Devereaux was quite a socialite. You couldn't open a newspaper without reading something or other about her."

"What happened to her?"

"She died," the woman said bluntly. She looked toward the ceiling of their compartment, a frown crinkling her forehead as she tried to remember something. "It must have been three—no, four—years ago. I remember specifically because my granddaughter was born just a few days later."

"How did she die?"

"She drowned. I believe she was on a boat with her lover at the time. He drowned also."

"That's dreadful."

"Yes, it was quite a nasty business. An unfortunate scandal for the family." The woman looked at Tess sideways, her fingers still moving with lightning speed. "You didn't investigate your new employer very thoroughly before accepting your position, did you?"

"I didn't investigate him at all," Tess admitted with some understatement. "Everything happened without warning."

"Well, you can relax. You couldn't work for a finer or older family. Of course, it's had its share of scandals, as have all families in the public eye, but I don't think you have anything to worry about. I'm sure you'll be well taken care of."

The woman looked up as the train began to slow down. "This is my destination coming up." She packed her needlepoint canvas and threads in a clear plastic carryall with big painted flowers splashed on the sides. "It was lovely talking to you, dear. Best of luck with your new position."

"Thank you."

"Your stop, Gatesboro, will be the next one."

Tess watched her as she left the train and stepped onto the platform. The train pulled out again almost immediately.

Tess leaned back in her seat. What was she walking into? she wondered.

More scenery flashed by and then the train slowed. Tess reached over and touched Jenni's arm. "It's time to wake up," she said softly.

Jenni stirred but didn't wake.

"Come on, sweetheart, we're almost there."

Jenni blinked a few times, focused and leaned toward the window to look outside. The town of Gatesboro rolled past the window, small and quaint with its narrow, cobbled streets and low, centuries-old buildings.

"What do you think?" Tess asked.

"It looks old."

"And full of history, I bet."

"Whatever it's full of, even if it's boring history, I'd rather be here with you than in New York with Cheryl."

"Oh, Jenni," Tess said with a laugh, "I wonder if Alec Devereaux knows what he's gotten himself into."

"I don't think so," she said ingenuously. "I was on my best behavior when I met him."

The train slowed to a crawl, then stopped completely in front of a small, red brick station.

Jenni looked at Tess; Tess looked at Jenni. They smiled and simultaneously flashed each other a thumbs up.

Shouldering their carryon bags, they stepped off the train and looked around. Only two other people had gotten off with them. A trainman removed the luggage and set it on the brick platform. Tess and Jenni retrieved their four, large, wheeled pieces and attached the pull straps. Tess tugged on hers, and both suitcases listed to one side and fell over.

"I guess the bricks are too bumpy," Jenni said.

"We'll just have to carry them to the front of the station and hope we can catch a taxi to the house."

"Excuse me, ladies. Would you by any chance be Miss Parish and Mrs. Devereaux?"

Tess looked up to find a wool-jacketed old man with a large white mustache standing behind her. She straightened and smiled. "We would."

He offered the slightest of bows. "How do you do? I'm George Lindes, the caretaker at your new home. Mr. Devereaux sent me to fetch you. We don't have taxis here."

"That's very kind of him, and of you." Tess extended her own hand. "I'm Tess and this is my sister Jenni."

Jenni shook his hand as well and smiled. "Hi. Nice to meet you. Is the house far from here?"

"Perhaps fifteen kilometers." He looked at the suitcases and shoulder bags and quirked a bushy white brow. "Do all of these bags belong to the two of you?"

"I'm afraid so," Tess said apologetically, as she pushed her hair behind her ears. "We brought nearly everything we own. We'll help you with it."

"That won't be necessary. I can make two trips."

"Don't be silly." Tess and Jenni shouldered their carry-ons and lifted one suitcase each while the caretaker picked up the other two and carried them around the building to a hunter green Range Rover, which was the only occupant of a narrow, brick parking lot. They loaded everything into the back. Jenni climbed into the back and Tess in the front.

"How long have you worked for Mr. Devereaux?" asked Tess.

He put the car into gear and pulled away from the station. "My wife, who's the housekeeper, and I have been with the Devereaux family for nearly forty-five years."

"So you've known Mr. Devereaux his entire life?"

"Yes, ma'am."

"We just met him a few weeks ago," said Jenni. "He came to my father's funeral."

The old man's expression softened as he looked at her. "My condolences, young lady. And to you, too, Mrs. Devereaux."

"Thank you," Jenni and Tess both said at once.

"And congratulations, as well, on your marriage."

Tess was silent.

As the car crested a small hill, Tess saw acres and acres of rolling, lush, grassy grounds with an impressive speck of a house on a hill in the distance and a lake as blue as the sky beyond that.

"That's Devereaux Hall," the man said.

"That house?" Jenni asked.

"All of this."

Jenni's eyes widened. "Cool!"

"The house itself dates back to the fifteenth century. In those centuries it was continuously occupied by the Devereauxs until twenty years ago."

"What happened twenty years ago?" asked Jenni.

Tess could have answered, but didn't.

"No one is absolutely certain, but I believe the late Mr. Devereaux made some poor investments and lost the home as a result."

"Who lives there now?" asked Jenni.

"No one. It's remained unoccupied."

"So where did the Devereauxs move?"

"You'll be able to see their new home in a moment."

They turned down a narrow stone-paved road lined with trees and followed it for what seemed like miles. Leaves filtered the sun and dappled its rays on the stones and car.

Tess was struck by how peaceful it all seemed. Rolling down her window, she closed her eyes and leaned her face into the wind. It whipped her hair into a frenzy, but she didn't care.

When the car slowed down, Tess opened her eyes. There was the house—if indeed a structure so large could be called a house.

The caretaker parked in a cobbled courtyard. Tess opened her door and stepped out, her eyes never leaving the house. Jenni climbed out and stood beside her sister. "It's so big," Jenni said in what had to be the understatement of the century.

"Too big."

"But think how fun it's going to be to explore!"

Tess looked warningly down at her. "Just remember that it isn't your house. You only go where you have permission to go."

"Spoken just like a big sister," Jenni said with a smile. "Don't worry. I'll be good."

From the corner of her eye Tess saw the caretaker taking their luggage out of the back of the Range Rover. He was too old to be lifting things that heavy. Tess left Jenni and stepped around the car to help. Picking up one of the suit-cases, she started across the courtyard, her thoughts more on what lay ahead of her than where she was going at the moment.

She didn't see the Jaguar until it screeched to a stop less than a foot from her. She stood there, paralyzed. The suit-case slipped from her fingers and fell to the ground with a thunk. In the back seat of the car was a little girl. A red-headed, very beautiful woman was in the front passenger seat. But it was the driver who held her attention. Alec Devereaux's dark blue eyes gazed coolly back at her. "You might consider watching where you're going," he sug-gested politely.

That snapped Tess out of her trance. She picked up the suitcase and stepped aside. "So might you." Her cool po-liteness matched his note for note.

Tess saw the flicker of surprise in his eyes and couldn't decide whether she was pleased with herself for pricking him a bit or annoyed with herself for getting off on the wrong foot.

"I'll see you in the house. Good afternoon." The cool had moved all the way to cold.

She inclined her head and watched as he drove through the courtyard and around to the other side of the house.

The caretaker came up beside her. If he thought the greeting between the newlyweds was odd, he kept it to him-self. "Are you all right?"

"Fine, thank you. Who was in the car with Mr. Dever-eaux?"

"His daughter Olivia. And the woman was Mrs. De-Veere Guest."

Aha, Tess thought. "The Mistress," no doubt. She looked like a mistress. A sophisticated and expensive mis-tress.

"Mrs. Guest is a neighbor. She lives on an adjoining property with her brother."

"Does she spend a lot of time here?"

"When Mr. Devereaux is in residence, yes."

Tess didn't say anything.

Mr. Linde touched her arm. "Are you sure you're all right?"

Tess flashed him a quick, reassuring smile. "I'm fine."

She followed the caretaker across the courtyard and up the stone stairs to the double doors.

Jenni raced past them and through the cathedral-like door the caretaker had opened into a cavernous, circular entrance hall. She stopped just short of smacking into a petite woman with iron gray hair pulled softly away from her face into a French twist. "Hold on there, young lady," she said sternly.

"I'm sorry," Jenni said with a breathless laugh. "I didn't see you."

"Obviously. In this house we walk, we don't run."

"Yes, ma'am."

The woman looked her over very thoroughly. "You must be Jennifer."

"Uh-huh."

"I'm Mrs. Linde, the housekeeper."

Jenni, who didn't have a shy bone in her body, thrust out her hand. "Nice to meet you."

The housekeeper seemed taken aback by Jenni's forwardness, but responded well enough, taking Jenni's hand in hers. "It's a pleasure meeting you, Jennifer. We've been looking forward to your arrival." Then the housekeeper looked at Tess who'd stopped behind her sister. "And you, of course, are Mrs. Devereaux."

"Call me Tess, please."

"We're a little more formal around here, Mrs. Devereaux."

Tess's smile faded. Mrs. Linde was nothing like her husband. "I guess Americans tend to be more casual."

"Well, you're not in America anymore. I feel it's my duty to guide you in proper and acceptable behavior. Living in

England is a very different matter from living in the United States."

"I can see that," said Tess.

She turned to her husband. "Mr. Linde, I want you to deliver the luggage to the appropriate rooms."

"Of course."

"Thank you." She turned to Jenni with a smile. "Mr. Linde will show you where your room is."

Before any of them could move, Alec Devereaux strode into the foyer, Mrs. Guest on his right, his daughter on his left. Tess's eyes went straight to Alec. "I'm glad to see you made it the rest of the way to the house without incident," he said.

"As long as you don't drive inside I should be all right." She could have sworn he almost smiled.

"How was your trip?"

"Tiring."

"You'll have some time to rest this afternoon." He touched the little girl's shoulder. "This is my daughter, Olivia. Olivia, this is your new teacher and, for the next year, my wife."

Tess lowered her gaze to the little girl beside him. She was very pretty, with wide blue eyes as dark as her father's and a mane of strawberry blond hair brushed into a long ponytail and held in place with a large black bow. Olivia smiled shyly. "How do you do?"

Tess clasped the child's hand warmly in both of hers. "I've been looking forward to meeting you, Olivia."

Jenni, sensing a kindred spirit, walked right up to Olivia. "Hi. I'm Jenni, Tess's sister. This is an incredible house. Have you always lived here?"

"I was born here," Olivia said softly.

"I can't wait to look around."

Olivia brightened. "I'll show you if you like."

"First show Jennifer to her room with Mr. Linde, Olivia," the housekeeper said. "Then the two of you can explore."

Olivia looked up at her father for permission, which he gave with the faintest of nods.

"Well, let's go!" Jenni said as she unceremoniously grabbed her new friend's hand, dragging Olivia along behind her as she raced to the staircase.

"Alec," said Mrs. Guest as she rested her hand on Alec's suited forearm. "I'm not sure you want Olivia under the influence of that child."

Tess bristled. "My sister is a wonderful girl. Olivia couldn't ask for a better friend."

The woman studied Tess for a long moment and seemed to come to some sort of conclusion. "I'm sure you're right. Sometimes my mouth gets ahead of my brain." She held out her hand. "Since Alec doesn't seem inclined to introduce us, I will. I'm Blythe DeVeere Guest, a neighbor and friend of the family."

Tess warily accepted the offered hand.

Blythe looked Tess up and down. "So you're Alec's new American wife."

Tess was silent. She had no idea how much the woman knew.

"She's very pretty, Alec. You did well." She flashed him a mischievous look. "Aren't you going to give your bride a proper greeting? You've been apart for weeks. I should think the two of you would be falling all over each other."

"Knock it off, Blythe."

"Well, in arranged marriages I suppose these things take time."

Alec's eyes had been on Tess ever since he'd walked into the foyer. "Go to the stables, Blythe. I'll be down as soon as I've changed."

Blythe smiled at Tess, winked as though they shared an amusing secret and left. Alec stayed where he was, facing his daughter's new governess—and his new wife. "I trust," he said after a lengthy silence, "that you'll be more careful with my daughter's person than you are with your own."

It took Tess a moment to realize he was speaking about stepping in front of his car. "I'm afraid I wasn't paying attention. I can assure you that nothing like that will happen with Olivia."

"It had better not."

"I gather from what you said when Olivia was here that you told her about our arrangement."

"Yes. I didn't want her to think of you as her mother. It's important that she not get attached to you."

"I agree."

"In private we can behave as we would normally, but on those occasions when we're in public, we'll behave as a married couple. I don't want the reasons behind our marriage to become public knowledge."

"All right." Tess wasn't going to argue with him. He was going to have to live in England long after she was gone. "What about the people who work here?"

"The in-house staff has worked for my family for decades and their discretion is unquestionable. Olivia has been told not to speak of our arrangement, and my friends—those few who know—would never betray a confidence."

Jenni and Olivia came racing through the foyer. Jenni wrapped her arms around Tess and enthusiastically hugged her. "I love this place!"

Olivia stood there, out of breath and not nearly as well-groomed as she had been minutes earlier.

"And you should see my room! It even has a fireplace. And I can see the stables from my window. Did you know there were stables?" Jenni's words tumbled out. "Olivia and I are going down there now to see the horses. Is that all right? We're allowed to do that, aren't we?"

Tess laughed and ruffled her hair. "I think you should ask Mr. Devereaux."

She turned excitedly to Olivia's father. "Is it okay?"

Tess was fascinated to see that his expression softened. "You may go to the stables."

"Great!" Jenni grabbed her new friend's hand and started to drag her through the open front door. But Olivia pulled back this time. "Would you like me to go riding with you and Mrs. Guest, Father?"

It was obvious to Tess that Olivia really wanted her father to invite her to go riding, but Alec either wasn't hearing the plea in her voice or ignored it. "You play with Jennifer. Mrs. Guest and I have things to discuss."

The hopeful light in Olivia's eyes dimmed. "Yes, Father."

Jenni impatiently pulled on her hand. "Come *on!*" And once again Olivia was flying along behind Jenni, too busy trying to keep up to be sad.

Tess watched them disappear through the doorway feeling unaccountably sad herself. "Olivia wanted to go with you," she said.

"You disapprove of my saying she couldn't?"

"Well, yes. Surely nothing you and Mrs. Guest have to discuss is as important as your spending time with your daughter."

His eyes darkened. Tess thought that she'd never seen eyes that cold. "Let's get something straight right now. I will not have you telling me how to be a parent. When and how I choose to spend time with Olivia is my business, not yours, and your interference won't be tolerated. Is there anything in what I've said that you don't understand?"

Tess was furious. "I understand perfectly. And now let me tell you a thing or two. I'm not any happier about my being here than you are. But I *am* here, and I have opinions. If you think I'm going to live under this roof for a year without expressing those opinions, you are sadly mistaken."

"I won't have dissension in my home."

"Then you shouldn't have married me."

"If you recall, the ceremony wasn't exactly voluntary."

Tess took a deep breath and calmed herself before speaking again. "I'd like to go to my room now, please. I'm very tired."

"Mrs. Linde will take you."

"Thank you."

"After dinner this evening you and I will go over the course of study you've planned for Olivia. I assume you've come prepared to start immediately?"

"Yes, I have." It was becoming clearer by the second that Alec Devereaux was used to telling people what they would do, not asking. This time, though, she let it slide.

He inclined his dark head. "Until this evening."

Tess watched as he crossed the foyer and went up the stairs, presumably to change for his ride with Mrs. Guest.

"Mrs. Devereaux," the housekeeper said as she reentered the foyer, "I'll show you to your room now."

"Thank you."

"There was some confusion as to where your room should be. I initially had you in the room adjoining Mr. Devereaux's, but he had me move you to a different one between your sister and Olivia."

At the top of the stairs was another circular foyer with wide hallways radiating off in three directions. The housekeeper turned to the right and Tess followed her, taking in the huge oil paintings of past generations of Devereaux men and women.

"This is the schoolroom," she said, opening a door and standing aside for Tess to enter. It had desks, tables, bookcases and a chalkboard. Shutters were drawn over the bank of windows along one wall, sinking the room into gloom, but Tess could see that it could be made into a cheerful place.

"The next room," Mrs. Linde said as she closed the door behind them and led Tess down the hall, "is Olivia's."

She opened that door and Tess peeked inside. It was a not-so-typical young girl's room, immaculate and very grown-up except for the stuffed animals that rested against the pillows of her bed.

"Next," Mrs. Linde said as she closed that door and continued down the hall, "is your room, and after that is Jennifer's room. Both of the girls' rooms open into yours."

Tess walked into her room and looked around. The walls were papered in a rich teal—which just happened to be Tess's favorite color. Both the woodwork and the furniture were natural mahogany, a lovely contrast to the walls. The large four-poster bed was covered with a spread whose background was the same teal with a print that included a deep purple, gold and red. A huge armoire dominated one wall. One door led to a full bathroom. Another door led to Olivia's room and yet another to Jenni's. Mrs. Linde walked to the heavy drapes and pulled them back by hand. Tess's view, like Jenni's, was of the grounds with its incredibly green grass, perfectly manicured flower beds and the stables in the distance.

What Tess thought were windows turned out to be doors that led onto a balcony with a stone railing that ran the length of the second story. "All of the rooms on this side of the house open onto this balcony," the housekeeper told her. "It's quite safe around here, so you can feel free to leave your doors open at night if you want fresh air. This time of year, though, it tends to get a bit cool in the evening."

Tess stepped onto the balcony and stood quietly with her hands on the cold stone of the railing. As she looked at the grounds, she spotted Alec walking away from the house toward the tables. He'd changed into jeans, she was surprised to see, boots and a white shirt. Someone called his name and he turned around. A man about his own age came into view, brown hair, tall—but not as tall as Alec. Still, he seemed very handsome from what Tess could see.

Alec and he spoke for several minutes while Tess watched. When she raised her hand to push her hair behind her ear, Alec's gaze shifted to her. The movement must have caught his attention. Embarrassed at having been caught staring at him from afar, Tess felt color creeping into her cheeks. She turned quickly and went back into her room.

Mrs. Linde smiled kindly at her. "If you need anything, just ask. If we don't have it, we'll get it."

Tess smiled back. "Thank you."

"I think it'll do Olivia a world of good to have a young woman around the house."

"She's had governesses before, hasn't she?"

"Nannies, not governesses. And the nannies were invariably much older and far too stern, I'm afraid. Olivia needs to laugh and be happy. She's had too little of happiness in her young life."

"With Jenni around she'll have no choice."

The housekeeper nodded. "Yes, your sister seems full of high spirits all right, and more power to her. She'll be a breath of fresh air around here, I can assure you. It's wonderful that they took to each other so quickly."

Tess was beginning to think that Mrs. Linde wasn't so different from her husband after all.

"Is Olivia close to Mrs. Guest?" she asked, not sure whether to expect an answer or polite silence.

At first it seemed that polite silence would win the day, telling Tess that she'd overstepped her bounds, but then the housekeeper surprised her by answering. "Mrs. Guest has tried to befriend Olivia, but Olivia has been unresponsive."

"Why?"

"I'm not sure really. Perhaps it's because Mrs. Guest doesn't really care much for children and, despite her best efforts to keep it from showing, Olivia senses it."

Mrs. Linde hung up the last of Tess's clothes, fastened the suitcase and lifted it from the bench. "I'll put these in storage for you along with Jennifer's," she said as she picked up the second suitcase.

"Thank you, Mrs. Linde."

The housekeeper looked at her for a long moment. "I don't know the exact circumstances of your marriage to Mr. Devereaux except that it's in name only. Be that as it may, you're still Mrs. Devereaux and you'll be treated accordingly."

"I understand."

When she'd gone, Tess walked to the doors and tentatively looked outside. When there was no sign of Alec, she stepped onto the balcony and gazed at the stables.

This wasn't at all what she'd expected. It wasn't that she was intimidated by her surroundings, but by the situation. Olivia needed more than a teacher. She needed an emotional connection. It was obvious to Tess that she didn't have one with her father.

There was nothing worse than feeling as though you were all alone in the world; that there was something so lacking in you that your own father couldn't love you. No one knew that better than Tess. It had taken her years of heartache to figure out that it wasn't something lacking in her, but in her father. Maybe she could help Olivia to reach that understanding so she could be at peace with herself. Or better yet, maybe she could bring father and daughter together.

What a perfect solution that would be.

Tess smiled. She just loved happy endings.

Chapter Four

After Tess had rested for an hour or so, she showered and changed into jeans and a baggy sweater. Sitting with her legs crossed in the middle of the bed, she went over the school materials she'd brought from the States and her planned study schedule one last time and concluded it was as well done as it could be. Scooping everything into her arms, she left her room and headed downstairs. Mrs. Linde was walking through the foyer as Tess descended. "Hello," she called. "Do you know where Mr. Devereaux is?"

"In the library, I believe," the housekeeper replied.

"And where's that?"

"Down that long hall," she said pointing. "Second door on the right."

"Thank you."

Tess followed her directions to a closed set of double doors. Shifting everything to her left arm, she raised her right hand and knocked.

"Come in."

She opened the door and looked inside. "Hello. I hope I'm not intruding."

Alec rose from behind his desk. "What do you want?"

She stepped farther inside. "I know you said we should go over Olivia's study program after dinner, but if you decide to make changes, I'll need what's left of the afternoon to accomplish them. Would you mind going over the materials now?"

He looked something less than thrilled. "Take a seat. I'll be a few minutes."

Tess crossed to the desk and set everything down. As Alec returned to his chair, Tess sat down also and waited.

He had a file open and was making some notes on a pad next to it. Tess looked around the room—anywhere but at him—yet her eyes kept returning. After a few minutes she gave up trying to look elsewhere altogether and just focused on Alec.

He was, in a word, gorgeous. His hair, dark and inclined to waviness, was a little on the long side. It was under control at the moment, but looked as though it could be wildly out of control if he'd let it. His forehead was broad and intelligent, his eyebrows and lashes as black as his hair. His face, a sculptor's dream, was shadowed by late-afternoon beard. She was fascinated by the hint of a dimple in his chin.

And then there was his mouth. It was full and wide and as masculine as the rest of Alec Devereaux. She wouldn't have been human, or at least that's what she told herself, if she hadn't wondered what it would be like to be kissed by that mouth. Not like the kiss at their wedding. A real kiss. One intended to deliver pleasure.

Tess looked away for several seconds. These weren't the kind of thoughts she should be having. And yet....

Her eyes found their way back to him. Thoughts were harmless enough in and of themselves.

Emboldened by not having been caught looking, Tess allowed her gaze to roam leisurely over Alec. There was about him an aura of worldliness. And weariness. She tilted her head to one side. And sadness.

Alec tossed his pen onto the desk and leaned back in his seat, his eyes meeting Tess's. "All right. Start talking."

She was caught completely off guard. "Oh! I...I... well..."

"My daughter," he prompted. "Lesson plan."

"I know, I know. I momentarily lost my train of thought."

"Have you now recovered it sufficiently to continue?"

"Yes, of course." She went through the material she'd placed on his desk, found the lesson plan and handed it to him. "This is an outline for each subject and what I intend to cover for the next nine months."

He went over the plan very carefully, page by page, while Tess waited.

"You've done a very thorough job of preparation," he finally said as he slid it back across the desk toward her.

"I know."

"The only change I'd make in what you've set forth is the inclusion of some additional British history and literature."

"Any periods or writers in particular?"

"I'll leave that to your discretion."

"All right."

"I'll want weekly reports on Olivia's progress."

"Verbal or written?"

"Both. There shouldn't be any discipline problems, but if there are, I'll expect you to handle things as they arise." He looked at his watch as if to tell her he had to end their meeting. "Do you have any questions?"

"Not at the moment, but I'm sure I will."

"Very well." He rose to his full height, obviously waiting for Tess to excuse herself.

She rose, too. "Actually I do have one question. What time is dinner?"

"Seven o'clock for you and the girls."

"What about you?"

"I dine alone at a later hour."

Tess didn't say anything, but her expression gave her away.

"Do you have a problem with this arrangement?"

"Well, yes. I think we should all have dinner together—as a family."

"We aren't a family."

"We are for the next twelve months."

"On paper only."

Tess didn't want to let this go. It seemed somehow wrong. "Perhaps you'd consider having dinner with just Olivia. Jenni and I don't need to be included. It would give the two of you a chance to get to know each other better."

"Is this advice you bring to me from your own perfect childhood?"

"It's common sense," said Tess a little more sharply than she'd intended. "No child can thrive if it's ignored by its parents. You're all Olivia has and she needs you."

"You don't know anything about either my daughter or me."

Tess could tell that Alec was getting angry, but she didn't back down. "I know what I see."

Alec looked at her as though she'd crossed a boundary she shouldn't have. "I don't want to hear your American pop psychology. And I particularly don't want to hear it from the daughter of the likes of Thomas Parish."

He picked up the stack of books and papers, walked around the desk and handed them to her. "I want the classroom work to start tomorrow."

Suddenly the window behind them exploded. Glass flew everywhere. Alec knocked Tess to the ground and covered her body protectively with his.

When all was still, he raised himself over her. "Are you all right?"

Her eyes were wide with fear. "Yes, I think so. What happened?"

"I don't know." He raised his hand to her hair. "You're all full of glass. Are you cut anywhere?"

"I don't know." Her heart was pounding.

He started to rise but Tess caught his arm and held him down. "Don't go."

"I'll be right back. Just stay where you are." Keeping low, he went to the window and looked outside. When he was satisfied that there was no further threat, he went back to Tess.

"Everything's quiet," he said with surprising gentleness as he lifted her in his arms and carried her to the door.

"I can walk," said Tess.

Alec ignored her.

Mrs. Linde ran up to them. "What was that awful noise?"

"I think someone shot through the window," said Alec. "Get your husband. I want him to go with me to find out who it was."

"What about Mrs. Devereaux?"

"You just get your husband. I'll take care of Tess. And make sure the girls are all right."

"Yes, sir."

He carried Tess up the stairs to her room and into her bathroom. Setting her on the floor, he carefully lifted her sweater off over her head. She could hear little bits of glass hitting the marble. It didn't even occur to her to be shy as Alec turned her around, inspecting her for cuts.

Swearing under his breath, he dampened a cloth and dabbed at her back. "Does this hurt?" he asked.

"It stings a little."

He touched her more gently. "You just have a few cuts," he said as he rinsed the cloth in warm water. "None of them are deep. Just enough to break the skin." He put his warm hand on her bare shoulder and pressed her slightly forward so he could see her cuts more clearly.

Tess gradually became less aware of her fear and more aware of the man sponging off her bare back. Very aware.

Suddenly embarrassed, she crossed her arms over her breasts.

Alec was as gentle as he could be. Most of the cuts were tiny. If he was hurting her, Tess gave no sign. "I think your sweater protected you."

She nodded but didn't say anything. She just wanted him to stop touching her.

Alec's eyes involuntarily moved over her creamy skin. She was beautifully built, with shapely shoulders that tapered into a narrow waist.

"Are you finished?" Tess asked impatiently.

He tossed the cloth into the sink, pulled a towel off the rack and wrapped it around her shoulders as she straightened and turned to face him.

"Thank you."

He raised his hand to her hair. "You're going to need to brush the glass out of your hair."

Tess pulled her head away from him even as she clutched the towel more tightly around her breasts. "What do you think happened?"

"I don't know. If I had to guess, I'd say it was a gunshot."

Tess saw some blood on his face and forgot that she was trying to keep her distance. "You have a cut here," she said, automatically reaching out to touch a spot near the corner of his mouth.

He covered her hand with his and held it, his eyes on hers.

Tess was caught completely off guard by the warmth that flooded through her. Pulling her hand away, she tucked it safely under the towel.

Alec looked curious. He started to say something, but was interrupted by a knock on the door.

"Come in," he called.

The housekeeper came into the bathroom. "The girls were in the stables. They're fine."

"Where are they now?"

"In the house. They came back with me. And Mr. Linde found a man and his son in the woods. They were apparently poaching a deer. It was one of their bullets that shattered the window."

"Where are they now?" asked Alec.

"In your library."

"Thank you, Mrs. Linde. Help Tess get the glass out of her hair, please."

"Yes, sir." She looked at the back of his shirt, dotted with blood. "What about your cuts?"

"I'll take care of them when I've finished with the poachers," he said as he left, his anger clearly visible in the way he strode to the door.

Mrs. Linde, clicking her tongue, examined Tess's hair. "You are a terrible mess. Lean over the bathtub and let me see what I can brush out."

Tess absently did as she was told.

The housekeeper carefully pulled the brush through Tess's hair. "There must be hundreds of tiny slivers."

"Mmm-hmm."

"Nothing like this has ever happened before. I don't envy those men having to face your husband."

Her husband. What a strange thought. "Does he have a bad temper?"

"Not usually, but he doesn't tolerate fools either easily or politely."

She brushed Tess's hair several more strokes, then put the brush on the counter. "I think we got it all out. Now you go into the other room while I clean up in here."

Tess went into the bedroom and stood with her back to the dressing table. Slipping the towel off, she looked over her shoulder and examined herself. The cuts were visible, but not bad; red but not bleeding.

She gingerly slipped into an oversized chambray shirt and left her room to go in search of the girls. Hearing their laughter coming from the schoolroom, she opened the door and went in. Olivia and Jenni were sitting facing each other on the wide window seat. They were talking up a storm.

"What are you guys planning?" she asked with a smile.

"Nothing. We were just talking."

"About what?"

Olivia smiled shyly. "I was telling Jenni how glad I am that you agreed to be my teacher. If you hadn't, I would have had to go away to school."

"And I was telling her," said Jenni, "that we're broke and need the money."

"Jenni!"

"It's true," she said.

"Just because it's true doesn't mean it's something you should say." Tess smiled at Olivia. "I'm looking forward to being your teacher, regardless of what brought me here. I went over the lesson plans with your father this afternoon and he approved them. We'll be starting school tomorrow morning at eight o'clock sharp, so I want the two of you in bed early tonight."

"Yes, ma'am," said Olivia.

Jenni groaned.

"Do you ride horses?" asked Olivia.

"I'm afraid not."

"If you'd like, I can teach you. It's the only thing I do really well. Even Mrs. Guest says so."

"I imagine you do a lot of things really well. And I'd like it very much if you'd teach me. Perhaps you could help Jenni, too. I'm afraid we're both hopeless."

"You can say that again," said Jenni. "I already had my first lesson. It was all I could do to stay on the beast."

"You weren't *that* bad." Olivia was trying to be nice, but she couldn't hold on to the pretense. The two girls looked at each other and burst into gales of laughter.

"Well," Olivia amended, still giggling, "you *were* that bad, but you'll get better. It takes time."

Tess couldn't help but smile as she watched the two of them. A friendship was definitely in the making. They'd been there less than a day and already she sensed a bond growing between the girls. They were going to need it if they were going to be spending most of the next year together.

Mrs. Linde knocked on the open door and entered. "Mr. Devereaux requests your presence at the dinner table in twenty minutes."

"Whose presence?" Tess asked.

"All of you." She had the most quizzical expression on her face.

Olivia excitedly jumped off the window seat. "Truly? All of us? For dinner?"

"Truly, dear," Mrs. Linde said.

Tess smiled inwardly. Point to her. "Tell Mr. Devereaux that we thank him for his kind invitation and we accept."

"I'll do that."

When the housekeeper had gone, Jenni looked at Tess with a curious shrug. "What's all the fuss about having dinner with Olivia's dad?"

"What's the fuss?" Olivia asked, shocked that Jenni even had to ask the question. "My father never invites me to dine with him except on my birthday and holidays—when I'm here."

"Your family is weird."

"Jenni," Tess said sternly, "that's enough."

"We're quite normal, actually," said Olivia as she scrutinized her new friend. "Do you have any dresses?"

"Yeah. A couple."

"You'll have to wear one to dinner."

"A dress?" Jenni asked, horrified. "For dinner? And we're not even going out?"

Olivia laughed. "Mrs. Linde says that Americans live in jeans and sneakers. I guess it's true."

"They're comfortable," Jenni said defensively. "And if you ever wore them, you'd think so, too."

Olivia took Jenni by the hand and pulled her off the window seat. "Let's go to your room. I'll help you pick something."

The two of them left the schoolroom and walked down the hall, talking as they went.

Tess finished arranging things on her desk then went to her own room and searched through her closet. She decided on an Indian-print skirt that flared out at mid-knee, a rich blue silk tee and a wide brown belt at her slender waist. A quick brush of her hair and a touch of lipstick and she was ready.

And a little nervous, much to her surprise.

Jenni, in a navy blue-and-white polka dot dress with a split skirt, and Olivia, in a very proper, delicately flowered dress, walked into Tess's room via the balcony door. "We're ready," Jenni announced. "What do you think?"

Tess looked both girls over and smiled. "You look wonderful."

Olivia's cheeks were flushed with excitement. "Do you think my father will like this dress?"

"Oh, sweetheart, I'm sure he will. It's beautiful, and so are you."

Jenni tugged at the waistband of her dress. "Are we going to have to go through this every night?"

"Whenever we're invited downstairs for dinner. And stop pulling on it. You look fine."

"You'll get used to it," Olivia told her. "We should be going or we'll be late."

The three of them walked down the long staircase and into the dining room. The mahogany table could easily have accommodated twenty people.

Alec Devereaux, in a dark suit, came in behind them. His eyes met Tess's as though to acknowledge that he'd taken her advice, but she knew instinctively that he would never say anything out loud about it. He seated the girls, then moved behind Tess. His hands brushed her shoulders, sending a jolt of awareness through her. She looked up at him, unaware that her expressive eyes told him everything. "How is your back?"

"A little painful, but not bad. And yours?"

"I'm fine." He took his seat at the head of the table.

"What happened to the men who were hunting?"

"You don't need to worry about them. They won't be back."

The first course, a creamy chicken soup, was brought in by a uniformed maid.

"Would you care for wine?" he asked.

He'd asked Tess, but Jenni was the one who answered, the picture of serious consideration. "No, thank you. Milk would be nice, though."

This time when Alec's eyes met Tess's, there was a definite smile in their depths. "Of course," he said, his tone matching Jenni's in its seriousness. "And you, Olivia?"

"Milk also, please."

"Ellen," he said to the maid, "milk for the young ladies."

"Yes, sir."

"And what about you?" he asked Tess.

She touched her full water glass. "This is fine, thank you."

He poured himself a glass of red wine from a decanter on the table. "So, young Miss Parish," he said, "how are you enjoying your first day in England?"

"Well," said Jenni after swallowing a spoonful of soup, "I don't really know what I think of England, but I like it here. My room is so much bigger than the one I had in New York! And there's grass and horses and cats." She took another spoonful of soup. "I hope you don't divorce Tess even after the twelve months are up. I'd hate to have to go back to the city."

Tess's cheeks flamed. "Jenni!"

Ignoring her sister, Jenni looked at Alec. "Did you mind my saying that?"

"No. In fact I find your frankness refreshing." He glanced at Tess. "I think your sister's having a problem with it, though."

Tess wasn't amused and she didn't feel it was something she could just let pass. "You and I will discuss this after dinner, young lady."

"Don't be mad," said Olivia shyly. "I hope you can stay, too. It's fun having someone my own age around."

Tess relented. What was it about Olivia that touched her heart so? Perhaps it was because she reminded Tess of herself as a child. Olivia sat quietly in her chair trying to pay attention to her food, but irresistibly stealing glances at her father. She clearly adored the man. How could she tell Olivia not to adore him too much? She was startled when Alec actually spoke to his daughter.

"Are you looking forward to the start of school tomorrow, Olivia?"

Olivia set down her spoon and folded her hands in her lap before answering. "Yes, Father. I'm going to work very hard. You won't regret not sending me back to boarding school."

"Good."

"And if I do really well, would you allow Miss Parish—I mean Mrs. Devereaux—I mean . . ." She looked at Tess. "I don't know what to call you."

"Tess will be fine. I know it's confusing."

Alec didn't look as though he approved of the informality, but let it go. "Finish your thought, Olivia."

"Oh, yes. I wanted to know if I do really well, may Tess stay on to teach me next year."

"I don't know that she'd want to. By that time she'll be free to leave here."

Olivia looked at Tess. "Just because you can leave doesn't mean you'll want to."

Tess had no intention of staying a moment longer than she had to, but she certainly didn't want to hurt Olivia's feelings by saying so. "It's early yet. Why don't we wait until the time comes? By then you might not even want me around."

"I suppose," Olivia said quietly.

"Eat your soup, Olivia," Tess said gently. "It's getting cold."

Olivia picked up her spoon and began to eat.

"We're all looking forward to tomorrow. If it's a nice day, I think the girls and I will have our classes on the lawn by the lake."

Alec looked at her with those enigmatic eyes of his. "I'm sure the schoolroom would be more comfortable—and more conducive to learning."

"We'll be spending all of our time there as winter sets in. I think that for now, outside would be more appealing."

"Tess," he said with a hint of a smile in his voice, "you're the teacher. Do as you wish. I'm sure you will under any circumstances."

She nodded.

Alec studied Tess as he sipped his wine. "You're persistent."

"Thank you."

"I didn't mean it as a compliment."

Tess flashed him a charming smile. "I know."

Jenni and Olivia glanced at each other across the table as though the same idea had suddenly struck them both.

As the soup was taken away and the next course served, Tess listened and watched as the girls carried on an animated conversation with each other about the day's adventures.

Olivia turned to her father to describe something to him and flung out her hand. Her glass of milk went flying, spilling its contents in a white wave that soaked into the linen tablecloth. The silence was deafening as Olivia's cheeks flushed bright pink with distress.

Tess stepped quickly into the breach, drawing the attention away from Olivia. "Don't you hate it when that happens?" she asked as she rose to blot the milk with her napkin. "I did the same thing at a party last year—only my glass was filled with red wine and it went all over my date's tan suit." She glanced at Alec as she blotted. "When was the last time you knocked something over?"

"Three weeks ago in a hotel room in New York," he said as he looked at Tess. "But it was intentional."

She looked at him in surprise. "Really?"

"Really. Ellen," he said as the maid entered. "Would you get my daughter another glass of milk? She seems to have downed this one rather quickly."

For the first time since the accident, Olivia smiled, but it was a smile that broke Tess's heart. She knew exactly how the child felt; desperate to have her father love her and thinking she had to be perfect to earn that love. She reached over and clasped Olivia's hand, giving it an encouraging squeeze. The little girl looked at her with grateful eyes. In that moment a bond was formed between the two of them; a trust given and accepted.

The meal continued with Jenni regaling them with stories about America, school, her friends, her love of basketball—anything that came into her mind, it seemed. Tess loved listening to her. Jenni was such an unaffected, regular kid. It was nothing short of a miracle that she'd turned out that way—due in large measure, no doubt, to the fact that she'd had so little contact with Cheryl over the years.

Alec was charmed by Jenni, as well. He listened, asked questions and even laughed once. And Tess appreciated his kindness to her little sister more than she could say. Jenni was full of bravado, but Tess knew how hurt she still was.

As the dessert plates were being taken away, Alec looked at Tess.

And Tess looked at Alec, searching his eyes, wondering what he was thinking and searching for a hint.

But there wasn't any.

He rose. "Ladies, thank you for joining me. I don't know when I've enjoyed a meal more. But now please excuse me. I have some work to do."

Olivia waited until he was out of the room before she leaned toward Tess and whispered, "Do you think it went all right?"

Tess hugged her. "I think it went very well."

She let out a long, relieved breath and smiled. "Maybe he'll invite us again."

"He just might."

Jenni drained the last of the milk from her glass and wiped her mouth with her napkin. "What do you want to do now, Olivia?"

"My favorite television show is on in a few minutes. We could watch that."

"Okay. Where is there a TV? I haven't seen any."

"We only have one and it's in a little sitting room across from my bedroom. My father doesn't like television. I think he'd prefer it if I not watch at all."

"What does he think you should do instead?"

"Read."

Jenni pulled a face. "Oh, brother."

"I agree," said Olivia as she looked at Tess. "Would you like to join us."

"No, thanks. I think I'll go for a walk. But you two go ahead. Just make sure you don't watch too long. It's already late."

Jenni started to leave the dining room, but stopped, turned around and kissed Tess on the cheek. "See you later, Sis."

Tess's eyes were filled with love as she smiled at her. "Have fun."

When the girls had gone, Tess went to her room for a sweater, then left the house for the moonlit paths of the late-summer gardens. She loved to walk at night. The problem was finding a safe place to do it. But here it was like a world unto itself.

She moved slowly along the paths, stopping frequently to look at the flowers in the light of the moon or just to enjoy the peaceful sounds of the night. The crisp air was lightly perfumed with the scent of flowers Tess had no name for. Shoving her hands deep into her pockets, she followed the paths wherever they led, winding her way through the gardens, always within sight of the house.

Tess had been so busy for the past several weeks that she'd had very little time to think about everything that had happened to her. Her whole life had changed within a matter of minutes. There were times when Tess felt barely old enough to take care of herself, but now she was taking care of two eleven-year-old girls.

She stopped and fingered a silky blossom.

"You seem deep in thought," said Alec from a corner of the darkness.

Tess gasped and turned. He was standing beside a tree, leaning against it with his shoulder. "I'm sorry," she said. "I didn't know anyone else was here."

"I often come out here at night. The place lends itself to contemplation."

"Yes, it does. What are you contemplating?"

He looked at her for a long time before answering. "My thoughts are private ones."

"Of course. I didn't mean to intrude." She started to walk past him, but he reached out and caught her arm.

"Your living in my home is an intrusion."

"Need I remind you that it isn't by choice?"

"So you keep telling me."

Tess shook his hand from her arm. "What's that supposed to mean?"

"I find this whole situation odd."

"And you think I don't?"

"I don't know. You seem to have adjusted rather quickly."

"I do what I have to, to maintain some normalcy for Jenni."

"So this is all for Jenni?"

"You know perfectly well it is."

"I only know what you and your father's lawyer tell me."

Tess glared at him. "This isn't fair. You're behaving as though the marriage is my fault. You agreed to it and you participated in it."

"I wanted to get my home back."

"And I wanted to raise my sister." Tess was so angry that she hadn't noticed that she was crying. "Ohhhh!" she fumed as she dashed at her cheeks with the back of her hand. "I didn't want any of this! I didn't want to live in England. I didn't want to live in this house, and I certainly didn't want to be married to you!"

Alec was amazed at what his words had unleashed. "Take it easy."

"And don't tell me to take it easy!" She was shaking with an anger that had been building since her father's death. "I'm an honorable person. I would never, ever have... have...plotted what you're accusing me of. My father was a bastard and you're one, too." She started to storm past him, but Alec caught her in his arms and held her close.

"Let me go!"

"Not until you settle down."

She struggled against him. "I said let me go!"

He held her tighter. "And I said not until you settle down."

Tess was truly exhausted, both emotionally and physically. Just like that, she went limp in his arms. If Alec hadn't been holding her, she would have slid to the ground. His hold on her went from one of restraint to one of gentle support. Crying openly, she clutched his shirtsleeves and put her head on his shoulder.

After not quite knowing what to do with this bundle of emotions he was suddenly confronted with, he found himself stroking her hair. "It's all right, Tess," he said against her ear. "I shouldn't have said what I did. Your father manipulated both of us."

Tess tried desperately to get herself under control. Never in her life had she lost it like this. It was humiliating. "I'm sorry," she said as she weakly pushed herself away from him.

He kept his hands on her elbows to steady her.

"I'll be all right now."

Alec moved his hands up her arms and cupped her face. He wiped her tear-damp cheeks with his thumbs. "Better?"

She nodded.

He tilted her face up so that she was looking at him.

What was it about her, he wondered, even as he lowered his mouth to hers.

Kissing Tess was the most natural thing in the world for Alec. Like breathing. He pulled her closer and kissed her more deeply. After the briefest of hesitations, she opened herself up to him. Alec slid his hand down the curve of her back and pressed her body into his.

Tess gasped softly against his lips as she felt his unmistakable desire. Part of her wanted to pull away; but part of her wanted to be closer. She moved against him and he moaned.

Feeling him, hearing him, pushed her beyond thought. She raised her arms and tangled her fingers in his hair, pulling him even closer. Alec tugged on her hair, pulling her head back and exposing her throat to his lips' caress.

"Tess!"

She heard her name through a haze of passion.

"Tess! Are you out here?" It was Jenni.

She slowly opened her eyes and found herself gazing into Alec's. Both of them were breathing hard, pulled out of their fantasy and back into reality.

Alec touched her face. "No," he whispered. "Stay with me."

"I can't."

He kissed her again and she weakened.

"Tess! Where are you?"

She pulled away from him. "I have to go."

"You don't have to. Just don't answer."

Without giving him a chance to talk her into staying, Tess took a full step back. "I . . . I . . . can't do this."

Alec's hands fell to his sides.

Tess gazed back at him. Without saying anything else, she turned and walked away.

Alec's eyes followed her out of sight. Long after she'd gone he watched the darkness.

As Tess rounded the corner, she saw Jenni and Olivia standing in the doorway waiting. "There you are," said Jenni when she spotted her sister.

Tess took a deep breath and put a smile on her face. "Hi. What's up?"

"Nothing. You've just been gone for a long time, and we were worried."

"Everything's fine." Tess dropped her arms around the two girls' shoulders as they walked through the foyer and up the stairs. "You should be in bed."

"It isn't that late."

"It's late enough. I want both of you to get your night-clothes on."

"Okay." Jenni looked at her older sister curiously. "Are you all right?"

"Of course. Why?"

"I don't know. You look funny. Don't you think so, Olivia?"

Olivia stopped walking and looked at Tess, too. "You look as though you've been crying."

"I'm just tired. It's been a very, very long day."

Olivia tilted her head to one side. "I guess that could be it."

"Come on." Tess escorted Olivia to her door. "Get ready for bed. I'll be back in a few minutes to tuck you in. You, too," she told Jenni.

Tess went to her own room. Standing in the bathroom, leaning on the sink, she looked at her face. Jenni was right. She looked terrible. Turning on the tap, she ran cold water over her hands and dabbed it on her face. How was she ever going to be able to face Alec?

She just wouldn't think about it. It would be as though it never happened.

She absentmindedly dried her hands, picked up a brush and ran it through her tangled hair as she walked back to Olivia's room. The girl, already in bed, smiled.

Tess pulled the covers up snugly under Olivia's chin then sat on the edge of the bed beside her. "Tired?" she asked.

"A little. I've been too excited to sleep much for the last few days."

"Why?"

"I guess I was excited about you and Jenni coming here to live. And I was worried that I might not like you."

"And now that we're here?"

"I like you very much."

"I like you very much, too. So does Jenni."

"She's a lot of fun."

"But a little hard to keep up with."

"That's one of the things I like best about her."

"Me, too."

As Tess rose, she pushed Olivia's hair away from her face and smiled. "Get some sleep. I'll see you in the morning."

"All right."

"Do you want this closed?" she asked of the open balcony door.

"No, thank you. I like the fresh air."

Tess put her hand on the light switch. "Good night, Olivia."

"Good night, Tess."

With a click, the room sank into darkness.

Tess left via the balcony and went to Jenni's room. "Are you asleep?" she whispered into the darkness.

"No," Jenni whispered back.

Tess walked in and sat on the edge of her bed. "What do you think of your new home?"

"It's different but I like it. I like Olivia, too. She's really nice."

"Yes, she is."

"Tess?"

"Hmm?"

"Are we really going to leave here in twelve months?"

"Yes."

"Where will we go?"

"I'll apply for a job as a regular teacher in Maine and we'll go there."

"We won't have to see Cheryl, will we?"

"Not if you don't want to."

"I don't want to."

Tess leaned over and hugged Jenni. "I love you."

"I love you, too."

"Good night. Sweet dreams."

Tess went back to her own room, slipped into her nightgown and went to bed with a mystery novel.

She didn't hear the stealthy sound of bare feet padding along the balcony past her door.

Olivia peeked into Jenni's room. "Are you still awake?"

Jenni rose up on her elbows. "What is it?"

"You were right. Your sister's really nice."

"I told you."

Olivia flopped onto the bed. "I've been thinking about what we talked about earlier."

"You mean getting my sister and your father together for real?" Jenni asked.

"Exactly. I think we should do it. They're already married. All we have to do is get them to fall in love."

"Easier said than done."

Olivia was silent.

"Any ideas?" asked Jenni.

"Maybe it'll just happen naturally. You know, they'll do it on their own."

"We can't count on that. What we need is a plan."

"Well, we can throw them together as often as possible."

"That's good," Jenni agreed.

"We can put our heads together tomorrow," Olivia said as she got to her feet. "I better get back to bed before Tess notices that I'm gone."

"Okay. Good night."

"'Night."

Olivia sneaked past Tess's room and into her own. Jumping into bed, she pulled the covers up and lay back on her pillow with a big smile. She'd been searching for a way to make everything all right, and here it was.

Jenni lay on her pillow and stared at the ceiling. If she were really honest with herself, she had to admit that her dad hadn't been a very good one. She'd always thought that it was her fault, but Tess had told her it wasn't and she believed her. Tess knew about these things.

There was something about Olivia's dad that Jenni intrinsically trusted. She didn't know why; she just did. And that was something she'd never felt about her own dad.

She rolled over and pulled her covers up.

If Tess were to fall in love and stay married to him, it would be the perfect solution. Tess was already like her mother, and Mr. Devereaux would make a really cool dad.

Jenni, smiling, closed her eyes and within minutes was sound asleep.

Chapter Five

Tess wasn't aware of waking up. She just slowly realized that she had. It was still dark. Turning her head to look at the clock, she groaned when she saw that it was only four-thirty.

Snuggling under her covers, she tried to fall back to sleep. It was no use. After fifteen minutes she gave up. Kicking off the blankets, she padded into the bathroom, showered and dressed and sat at her desk to go over the first day's lessons. She had to admit that she was a little nervous. Her classroom experience up to this point consisted of assistant teaching in college and substitute teaching to support herself while she worked on her art. She wanted to do this right.

The morning flew by. The next time she looked at the clock it was time to get the girls up. And while they were getting showered and dressed, Tess went into the schoolroom to get it ready.

"Good morning, Mrs. Devereaux," said Mrs. Linde cheerily as she walked in with a tray of juice, tea, milk, croissants and sweet rolls. "This is what we have for breakfast here. I hope it suits you."

Tess eyed the mouth-watering pastries. "That's just fine. It looks delicious."

"You Americans usually have such big appetites at breakfast." She began transferring dishes from the tray to a large, round table surrounded by four chairs.

"This particular American is grateful for whatever she's given at breakfast."

"Not much of a cook, then?"

"Not at breakfast—but I get better later in the day."

"Food!" Jenni said as she walked in through the balcony door and sat at the table. "Thanks, Mrs. Linde, I'm starving."

"Not at all, dear." The housekeeper poured her a glass of milk. "What would you like?"

Jenni checked out the plate and pointed. "One of those." She continued looking as Mrs. Linde served her. "And one of those. And maybe one of those."

"Jenni," scolded Tess, "one at a time."

Jenni smiled disarmingly up at Mrs. Linde. "Sorry. They all look so good."

"Don't you concern yourself, dear. You may eat all you wish. I love to see a good appetite on a child."

Olivia came in from the hallway. "Good morning."

"Come sit down and have some breakfast," the housekeeper said warmly. "You've a very full day ahead of you and need your nourishment."

"It's just schoolwork, Mrs. Linde."

"Sometimes it's the work of the mind that's the most draining. I'm sure Mrs. Devereaux will agree with me on that."

Tess smiled at Olivia. "She's right, you know."

This morning Olivia was looking at Tess through new eyes: the eyes of a potentially real daughter. And just as she had yesterday, she liked what she saw. Tess was a genuinely nice person. There wasn't any way to phony something like that up without someone else being able to see through it.

Olivia sat next to Jenni and the two of them chattered as they ate.

Breakfast was over rather quickly. Tess gathered her things and turned to the girls while Mrs. Linde cleared the table.

"Let's go."

Mrs. Linde looked up in surprise. "Go where?"

"We're having our lessons outside today."

"But . . . are you sure it's all right?"

"We have permission."

Mrs. Linde still looked concerned.

Tess smiled and put her arm around the housekeeper's shoulders, something she wouldn't have dreamed of doing only the day before. "It's just outside, not to the ends of the earth."

"Well, I suppose it is a lovely enough day."

"I know the perfect spot," said Olivia.

"Then let's get to it."

With Olivia and Jenni in the lead, the three of them headed out of the house and across the grounds toward the lake.

As Tess was looking up at the cloudless sky and thinking about what a perfect day it was, Alec was watching the trio from his library window. Olivia said something and Tess, looking relaxed and happy, laughed.

As Jenni walked faster, Olivia slowed down and slipped her hand into Tess's. Their clasped hands swung back and forth in rhythm with their steps.

Alec felt a twinge. For just a moment—a flicker of time— he wanted to put himself in that picture.

And then it was gone.

The phone rang and Alec, his gaze lingering on Tess and Olivia, reluctantly crossed the room to answer it. He had work to do.

* * *

The air was just warm enough to be comfortable. Olivia took them to a spot under a huge old tree. If the thick trunk was any indication of age, it had been there for centuries, quietly watching over the lake, the house and its inhabitants.

The girls sat under the tree facing the house. Tess sat in front of them facing the lake. "What I'm going to do," she said as she removed texts and notebooks for the girls from her shoulder bag, "is review some of the work you both did last year and then move on to new things. We're going to start with math."

"How do you know what I studied already?" Olivia asked.

"I called the boarding school you attended, and they gave me all the information I needed about your scholastics, right down to the books you read. It turns out that you and Jenni are fairly equal in most subjects."

"Most?" Jenni asked, not trying to hide the dread behind the question. "Uh-oh."

"You, my love, are woefully behind Olivia in literature."

"Literature?" Jenni couldn't believe her ears. "Isn't literature something you have to take in college?"

"It's something you should be studying all the way through school. And I don't just mean English literature, but all kinds."

Jenni rolled her eyes.

"You'll enjoy it."

"Right." She didn't sound convinced.

"But I'm not going to force all of that enjoyment on you right now," Tess said, trying not to to smile. "First we're going to start with math." She handed each of them a textbook. "Turn to page five...."

The morning flew by. Both Jenni and Olivia were open to learning, and it made Tess's job a pleasure. Mrs. Linde brought them a mid-morning snack, and they took a lunch and exercise break at noon before returning to the tree for another couple of hours.

Tess was reading aloud some passages to them from Tennyson's "The Lady of Shallot," her voice dropping to a whisper. She didn't see Alec Devereaux approaching from behind her, but the girls did. They said nothing, even when he stopped just a few yards away to listen and watch.

"His broad clear brow in sunlight glow'd:
On burnish'd hooves his war-horse trode;
From underneath his helmet flow'd
His coal-black curls as on he rode,
   As he rode down to Camelot.

From the bank and from the river
He'd flash'd into the crystal mirror,
'Tirra lirra,' by the river
   Sang Sir Lancelot.

She left the web, she left the loom,
She made three paces thro' the room,
She saw the water-lily bloom,
She saw the helmet and the plume,
   She look'd down to Camelot.

Out flew the web and floated wide;
The mirror crack'd from side to side;
'The curse is come upon me,' cried
   The Lady of Shalott."

Tess looked at the girls. "You can feel the tension mounting, can't you? It's like a heartbeat that grows faster and louder, faster and louder."

Olivia looked past Tess's shoulder and smiled. "Hello, Father."

Tess turned to find Alec dressed in jeans and an oversize white shirt with the sleeves rolled up, his arms folded across his chest. "Checking up on me, I see," Tess said, charming him with her smile, determined not to let him see how disturbing she'd found last night.

Once again he almost—but didn't quite—smile back.

Olivia had noticed his casual clothes, too. "Are you going riding?"

He turned his attention to his daughter. "Yes."

"May I come with you?" Tess could hear the hope in her voice, and she held her breath while she waited for the answer.

"Yes, you may. I was about to invite you."

Olivia beamed.

"But not until you're finished with your schoolwork."

"We were just finishing for the day," Tess told him as she rose and brushed off her skirt.

Jenni elbowed Olivia and jerked her head toward the two adults. Not very subtle, but Olivia got the message. "And perhaps Tess and Jenni could come, as well. They haven't really had a chance to see the grounds yet."

Alec was silent, his expression difficult to read.

"So may they come?" Olivia asked again.

"Please?" Jenni asked.

He didn't look happy, and Tess tried to come to his rescue. "I know you didn't come here expecting to collect an entourage for your ride. Jenni and I have plenty of things to keep us occupied right here. Besides, I don't even know how to ride a horse."

"Then we should teach her, don't you think, Father?"

Alec's eyes were on Tess as she busily collected her books and paper and put them in her big, canvas bag. "Yes, Olivia, I think we should."

Tess stopped what she was doing and looked up at Alec. She really didn't want to go. "But you and Olivia..." Tess began.

"Would very much enjoy yours and Jenni's company."

Jenni made a motion with her hand like a train conductor pulling on a whistle rope. "All right!"

Tess was less than enthusiastic as she looked down at her skirt. "I'll have to change."

"Don't bother. We won't give you a lesson today. You can ride with me and Jenni can ride with Olivia."

The two girls looked at each other and smiled. This was working out very well indeed.

Tess, not at all happy with the way this was working out, finished packing her things and rose. Alec took the heavy bag from her and carried it to the stables.

Tess hadn't been inside the stables yet. It was a long, rather narrow building, beautifully maintained and painted a clean, bright white. It smelled like leather and hay and horses and burlap.

A horse, a very tall horse, was already saddled and tethered to the outside of one of the stalls. "John," Alec called out, "we'll be needing Olivia's horse saddled as well."

"Yes, sir."

A man Tess hadn't seen came out of one of the stalls, went to another one and led out a smaller horse. It was saddled in a matter of minutes, and the girls got in place on its back, Olivia in front and Jenni behind her.

"Your turn," Alec said as he put his hands at her waist and effortlessly lifted her onto the saddle. It was the first time Tess realized just how strong he was. Her skirt rode up, exposing her long, slender legs. She tugged at the material, but it was useless. There was just no way to straddle a horse in a skirt and expect modesty to prevail.

With equal ease Alec raised himself up behind her, his arms encircling her to grasp the reins. His muscular inner thighs hugged her from behind, the worn denim of his jeans smooth and warm against her bare legs.

Never in her life had Tess been so completely aware of another human being: his strength; the heat from his body; the clean smell of his skin. Tension grew in her as her body's very natural desire to get closer to Alec warred with her mind's resistance to any sexual feelings about the man.

Her mind won and she went rigid.

"Relax." Alec's mouth was close to her ear, his breath a whisper of warmth against her skin. "I won't let you fall."

Tess closed her eyes and swallowed.

His arms tightened around her as he turned the horse and guided it out of the stables to catch up with the girls.

Tess told herself that there was nothing personal in any of this. He hadn't even wanted her to come along. But that did nothing to dim her awareness of the man.

They started off slowly, then increased to a modest gallop. Tess's body fell into a comfortable rhythm with the pace of the horse—and with Alec. She tried desperately to concentrate on the scenery, but her thoughts—her senses—always brought her back to Alec Devereaux.

They rode for what seemed like miles, and every inch of the way she could feel Alec's legs against hers.

Olivia and Jenni were off in their own world, always staying well ahead of them, talking and giggling.

Alec reined in the horse and leaned forward until his chest pressed against Tess's back and his mouth was once again close to her ear. "This is where our property ends now and that which used to belong to us begins."

She turned her head slightly and found her lips almost touching his. Neither of them moved. "Do you mean the land you'll get back from my father's estate?" she managed to ask.

His blue eyes gazed into her golden ones. "Yes."

"Do you think we'll last the entire year?"

Alec climbed off the horse and reached up for Tess, his hands at her waist. "Yes." He let go of her as soon as her feet touched the ground, and started walking.

"Why?" She fell into step beside him.

"Because I won't have it any other way. That land is mine, and I'm going to get it back."

"What if you fall in love with someone in the meantime?"

"I won't."

"How can you be sure?"

"It's not an emotion I'm susceptible to."

"What about your mistress?"

A corner of his mouth lifted. "So you know about her, do you?"

"Everyone does. Don't you love her?"

"I enjoy her. I certainly don't love her. And she knows that. Love is a transient emotion, here today, gone tomorrow. It doesn't seem to be worth the effort."

"Didn't you love your wife?"

"I did not."

Tess was truly astonished.

"Don't you see how empty your life is?"

"In what sense?"

"In the sense of emotional fulfillment. Don't you want the woman you're holding in your arms when you wake, make love to and have children with to be the one person in the world you can't live without?"

"There is no such person."

"That's so sad."

"Sad for whom?"

"For the women who've loved you. But most of all for you, I think. You're missing out on a richness and texture in your life that nothing else can replace."

"You know this from your own personal experience, I presume?"

"Well, no. But it's the way I imagine it would be."

"You and your apparently romantic imagination are in for a rough landing, Tess. One of these days your unrealistic expectations are going to come face-to-face with cold reality. I hope there will be someone around who can pick up the pieces for you." He stopped walking. "Come on. Let's head for home."

He gave her a leg up and climbed on behind her. The horse restlessly stamped his feet, ready to run. Alec's arms tightened on the reins and in turn tightened around her, holding her body in place against his. Tess closed her eyes. Why did this man have to be so attractive?

His arms tightened around her even more as he pulled on the reins and wheeled the big horse around. "Come on, girls," he called to Olivia and Jenni. "Let's go."

Tess raised herself slightly in the saddle in an effort to keep her body from touching his, but the movement of the horse forced her back against him.

Okay. There was nothing she could do about it at the moment. She'd just try to relax, take deep breaths and it would be over.

Alec smiled. He knew exactly what she was doing and why. It was interesting to him that he felt he knew her so well. There was something about Tess that was so open and without guile—and yet not at all naive. He'd never met anyone quite like her.

When they arrived at the stables, Tess nearly fell off the horse in her hurry to get down.

Alec watched her with quiet amusement. "I would have helped you if you'd waited," he said, climbing to the ground and handing the reins to the stable hand.

"I didn't need any help."

The girls, laughing about something, rode in behind them and dismounted.

Tess forced a carefree smile to her lips. "You two seem to be enjoying yourselves."

"It was wonderful," Jenni said. "I can't wait to learn how to ride."

"I can give you a lesson now," Olivia said. Then she looked hopefully at Tess. "If that's all right with you."

Tess, avoiding Alec's eyes, took her book bag from the table where it had been placed and raised the straps over her shoulder. "The two of you can have free time until dinner, but after that you'll have to start on your homework."

She took a deep breath and turned to Alec with a coolly polite smile that she hoped masked her shaky knees. "Thank you for the ride and the tour. The grounds are truly lovely."

He inclined his dark head and followed her with his gaze as she crossed the lawn toward the house.

Tess was completely wrapped in her thoughts as she went into the house and blindly walked straight into the arms of a man she hadn't seen standing there.

"Well, hello!" he said with a cheery smile as he held her upper arms in his hands. "I was expecting Alec, but you'll do nicely. Very nicely indeed." His eyes moved appreciatively over her flushed face and windblown hair.

Tess looked at him blankly, her mind still on the man she'd left at the stables. "Excuse me?"

"Forgive my rudeness. I'm Trilling DeVeere, neighbor and brother of Blythe DeVeere Guest. And you must be the new Mrs. Devereaux I've been hearing so much about."

Tess shook the image of Alec from her thoughts and really looked at the man in front of her. He was the same one she'd seen speaking with Alec the day before—and he was even more handsome close up. She extended her hand. "How do you do? I'm Tess."

He raised her hand to his lips, his eyes never leaving hers. "You have no idea how delighted I am to meet you. And your name is Tess? What does that stand for?"

"Tess."

Laughter filled his eyes. "Of course. Well, Tess, welcome to England. How are you liking it so far?"

"Very much, thank you."

"Of course you haven't seen much of it yet."

"I've been to England before. Just not this area."

"Then it will be my pleasure to show you around."

He was as charming as he was handsome, and yet Tess wasn't attracted to him in at all the same way she was to Alec. "I don't know, Mr. DeVeere. I'm going to be very busy here."

"Please do me the courtesy of calling me Trilling."

"All right. I don't believe I've ever heard that name before."

"Nor has anyone else," he said with bored disgust. "My mother felt the need to honor some obscure relative by naming her only son after him. I've never quite forgiven her for it."

Tess's quick smile flashed.

"Much better," he said with a return smile. "You looked so serious when you came through the door. Problems on the home front already?"

"No, not at all," she said quickly. Too quickly.

Trilling's smile broadened. "I see."

Alec walked into the foyer at just that moment. "What are you doing here, Trilling?" His voice wasn't as friendly as it could have been.

"Flirting quite happily with your wife."

"Well, stop it." He put his arm possessively around Tess's shoulders. "She isn't used to your brand of flirting."

Tess moved out from under Alec's arm and extended her hand to Trilling. "It was a pleasure meeting you."

He held her hand in both of his. "We'll be seeing a lot of each other. As it happens, Alec is my best friend." He glanced wryly at Alec. "Quite possibly my only friend."

"Not for long if you don't leave my wife alone."

Tess looked at him in surprise. His wife? Since when did he think of her as his wife?

No one was more surprised than Alec at what he'd said. It was no doubt just a slip. And yet...

A frown creased his brow as he looked at her.

"This wife business aside," said Trilling to Tess, "I want you to know that I'd be more than happy to act as your escort in exploring the nearby villages and even if you go out riding. If you don't know your way around it's quite easy to get lost."

"Thank you. I'll keep that in mind. And now if you'll excuse me I have some things to do."

Trilling bowed deeply. "Until we meet again."

Tess smiled. She had a feeling he didn't mean half of what he said. In spite of that, she liked him. She started across the foyer toward the stairs.

"Oh, wait!" said Trilling. "I forgot to tell you what I came for. Blythe asked me to invite the two of you for dinner this evening."

"Tell her that we accept."

"No," said Tess, "we don't. You may certainly go if you like, but I have things I need to do."

"Will you excuse us, Trilling?" Alec said as he walked to Tess, gripped her firmly by the elbow and walked her down the hall, out of sight of their guest.

Tess shook herself free and turned to face him.

"I won't have you treating my friends in such a shabby fashion."

"I'm not going."

"Why not?"

"Why should I? Both Blythe and Trilling apparently know this marriage is a farce. There's no need for us to put on an act for them. And there's no need for us to be treated as a couple by them. You're their friend so you go to dinner and leave me out of it."

"Very well. If that's the way you want it."

"That's exactly the way I want it."

Alec was furious. Without saying another word he turned and left.

Tess leaned against the wall for support, her hand over her pounding heart. She knew she was being rude. It was kind of Blythe to include her in the invitation. But Tess had made up her mind on the walk from the stables to the house that she was going to spend as little time in Alec's company as she possibly could. And that meant not having dinner with him when she didn't have to. And not riding horses with him. And in general avoiding him whenever she could.

Rather than risk running into Alec in the foyer, she used the rear staircase to get to her room. Once there, she changed into shorts and a T-shirt, pulled her hair back into a ponytail and headed outside again. It was only six in the afternoon of a beautiful day and she wanted to go for a run before dinner. She suddenly found herself with a lot of nervous energy that she needed to work off.

Mr. Linde passed her in a car as she started off and gave a friendly wave.

It had been nearly a month since the last time she'd run so she took it slowly, not doing much more than a fast walk.

When she'd gone riding earlier, they'd crossed fields that contained animals in their natural habitat. Now, as she ran in a different direction, she passed pastures with cows and horses and one with sheep. She realized that it wasn't just a pretty piece of land, but a working property. Alec probably alternated pastures the way farmers alternated fields.

Tess gradually picked up her pace until she was running really fast. It felt good to release weeks of built-up tension. She must have run full-out like that for a mile or more and only stopped when she thought her lungs would burst if she took another step. Completely out of breath, she bent over, her hands on her knees, and painfully dragged air into her lungs.

She heard a car on the road behind her, but didn't bother to look since she was far enough on the side to be out of the way.

The car stopped beside her. Tess, still panting, looked up to find Alec in the driver's seat.

Tess sighed inwardly. Everywhere she went, he was there. And now, here she was, soaked with sweat. Her hair, where it had fallen out of the ponytail, was sticking hotly to her neck. Moisture, unseen beneath her T-shirt, was dripping between her breasts. She didn't bother to straighten, but remained bent with her hands on her knees, breathing hard.

Alec's eyes missed nothing as he looked at her. He was still angry. "Was this one of the important 'things' you needed to do this evening?"

"One of several."

He looked at her for a long moment. "I have to attend a dinner party in London in a few weeks. It's a formal affair, and we're invited to be the overnight guests of the hosting couple. You, as my wife, are expected to attend as well. Are you going to have a problem with that?"

"Of course not. I understand that I have certain social obligations. I just don't think dinner at the neighbors' house should be one of them."

The muscle in his jaw tightened. "It's going to be dark in another thirty minutes. I'll take you home."

"No, thank you. I'm fine."

"On the contrary, you look as though you're ready to collapse."

"I just need to rebuild my stamina. I'll take my time walking back. It won't take me that long."

Alec's eyes took in the wet tendrils of hair around her flushed and sweat-beaded face and the damp T-shirt that clung to her rounded breasts.

She was utterly beautiful.

Without saying anything else, he put the car into gear and drove off.

Tess straightened, still breathing hard, and headed toward the house at a normal pace. Suddenly her energy had left her.

When she got back, she looked in on the girls, who were sprawled across Olivia's bed doing homework, then went to her own room to shower.

Jenni and Olivia waited until they heard the water running in Tess's room. "We've got to do something," said Jenni. "I know time is on our side, but the two of them just aren't cooperating at all."

"What can we do?" asked Olivia.

"Something. We need to make sure they're pushed together as often as possible. If your dad ever really gets to know Tess, he'll fall in love with her."

Olivia nodded.

"And I think your dad is terrific. All we need to do is get Tess to agree."

"But how?"

"Don't keep asking how. Help me think of something."

The sound of water stopped. A few minutes later Tess, wrapped in a robe, her hair still wet, came into Olivia's room and sank into a nearby chair. "Is your homework done?"

"All of it," said Jenni.

"Good."

"Would it be all right if Jenni slept in here tonight?" asked Olivia.

"Kind of like a sleep over," Jenni said.

"I don't know." Tess was hesitant. "You have school tomorrow, and something tells me that the two of you will be up half the night talking."

"You have my word of honor that we won't," said Olivia. "Please?"

Tess relented. "All right, but at the first sound of giggles, Jenni goes back to her own room."

To Tess's surprise, Olivia leapt off the bed and threw her arms around Tess's neck. "Thank you."

Tess smiled and hugged her back. "You're welcome. And I want you both in bed early."

"We will be."

"Have you had dinner?"

"About an hour ago."

"I'm sorry I wasn't back in time."

"That's all right. We had fun."

"It's nice to be missed," Tess said dryly. She rose from the chair and gave Olivia another hug. "Good night, sweetheart."

"'Night."

She walked over to the bed and kissed Jenni on the forehead. "I never thought I'd hear myself saying this to you, but close the book and get ready for bed."

Jenni grinned at her. "I will. 'Night."

As soon as Tess was gone, Olivia bounced onto the bed beside Jenni. "What now?"

"We wait for your dad."

"And then?"

"By the time he gets home we'll have a plan."

Tess, unaware of the plotting, went downstairs to the kitchen to fix herself something to eat. She ended up with cheese and crackers and a glass of red wine.

In her room again, she put on a flowing, white Victorian nightgown. She loved old-fashioned clothes like that, but the only way she really indulged herself was with her nightgowns. They were charming rather than sexy, and that was fine with her. After a quick check on the girls to make sure they were in bed, Tess turned out all the lights in her room except the one on the desk. Sitting down at it with her plate and glass of wine, she reached for a pen and started a letter to Russell.

She paused in her writing at the sound of footsteps going down the hall. Alec was back. She heard his bedroom door close.

Russell was forgotten as she sat with the end of the pen lightly clamped between her teeth.

After a few minutes she gave up on the letter altogether, put down the pen and picked up her glass of wine. Suddenly there was a loud crash outside that brought her to her feet. With the glass still in her hand, Tess rushed to her balcony door and stepped outside. Alec was walking quickly toward her wearing black pajama bottoms tightened with a drawstring over his flat, bare stomach. "Are you all right?" he asked.

Tess reluctantly dragged her eyes to his face. "Yes. I just heard a noise. We'd better check on the girls. They're both in Olivia's room."

"I'll do it." Alec quietly opened their door and looked inside, then closed it just as quietly and returned to Tess. "They're sound asleep."

Jenni and Olivia grinned at each other in the dim light, flashed each other a thumbs-up for a job well done and curled up in their blankets to go to sleep.

"I wonder what it could have been?" Tess asked.

Alec went to the railing and looked at the ground. "A flowerpot."

"What?" Tess stood next to him, her arm touching his as she looked at the ground, too.

"One of the clay flowerpots fell from the outside ledge of the balcony and landed on the patio below."

Now Tess saw it. "I wonder how that happened?"

"A breeze perhaps. It happens every now and again." He took the glass of wine from her hand and drank from it, his eyes on hers. "What are you doing up so late?" he asked as he handed it back to her.

"Writing a letter to Uncle Russell," she said absently. "And it's not all that late."

A gentle breeze blew across the balcony, moulding the soft cotton of Tess's nightgown to the front of her body and billowing it out behind her in a cloud of white.

Alec's gaze made a slow journey over her body. "Oh, Tess," he said as he stepped in front of her, "I tell myself to ignore you, but you aren't the kind of woman a man can ignore."

Tess met his look with a direct one of her own. She knew exactly what was going to happen. Her mind told her to retreat, but her body stayed where it was.

Alec set the wine on the table. Then, cupping her face in both his hands, he gazed into her eyes. "Why do you have this effect on me?" he asked, more of himself than of her. He pushed her hair away from her face. "Part of me wants to run as fast and as far as I can, and the other wants to hold you close."

"Which part of you is here now?"

He lowered his lips to hers, kissing the left corner of her mouth and then the right. "This part," he whispered against her mouth just before his lips captured hers completely.

"And this part." He breathed warmly into her ear as he kissed along the side of her throat and lobe.

"And this," he said as he slid his hands down the curve of her back, pulling her body against his and leaving no doubt in her mind about the effect she was having on him.

Tess wound her arms around his neck and looked into his eyes. She didn't know what to say or think. She only knew that at this moment all she wanted was to be with Alec Devereaux, in his arms, his lips on hers. She was twenty-three years old and this was the first time in all of those years she'd ever let a man get this close to her.

Alec pulled her back into his arms and kissed her deeply. Tess drew her hands slowly down his leanly muscled back, loving the feel of his bare skin.

Twining his fingers through hers, he held her arms at her sides as he kissed her neck and shoulder. Releasing one of her hands, he drew his slowly down the length of her arm and side, cupping her breast through the soft material of the nightgown.

Tess's breath caught in her throat.

Alec raised his head and looked into her eyes. He wanted her. And yet something held him back.

Tess, sensing his hesitation, trailed her fingertips over his beard-shadowed face. "What's wrong?"

"I can't do this." Alec dragged his fingers through his thick hair as he stepped away from her. "I just can't do this."

Tess lowered her eyes, wishing herself invisible.

"Look at me," he said, his hand under her chin. "Look at me, Tess."

After a moment she did.

"You aren't the kind of woman a man has an affair with."

"Why not?"

He was taken aback by her question. "Because making love to you isn't something any man could do lightly." He

kissed her forehead as chastely as he would have a child's.
"Go to bed."

Tess swallowed hard. "I'm going to stay out here for a
while."

"I'll stay with you."

"No, please. I'd like to be alone."

Alec watched her for a moment to make sure she was all
right, then went to his room.

Tess leaned on the railing and stared into the darkness.
She should be used to rejection, but she wasn't. It hurt. She
hurt.

As she turned to enter her room, she spotted the wine-
glass on the table. Picking it up, she raised it to her lips and
downed the contents.

In her room, the desk lamp was still on, with the letter
visible beneath it. It seemed a lifetime ago that she'd started
it. Tess snapped out the light, and the room descended into
darkness except for the fire. She stood staring into the
flames, her arms wrapped around herself. She'd made a fool
of herself with Alec.

Again.

He must find her an endless source of amusement.

She took a deep breath and let it out in a long sigh. Some
things were harder to put out of her mind than others.

Alec lay on top of his covers, his hands behind his head,
staring at the ceiling. He wanted his life back the way it was
before Tess had burst into his world. Everything had been
simpler; more logical.

She was nothing to him. Nothing.

He'd wanted her in the way any man wants an attractive
woman, and he could have had her.

So why hadn't he?

She was nothing to him.

Chapter Six

"Hello there!"

Tess rose up on her elbow and saw Blythe walking along the lake bank toward her. "Hello," she called back and continued watching as the woman drew nearer.

As she sank onto the ground beside Tess, Blythe smiled at her. "I hope I'm not intruding."

"Not at all."

"It's a beautiful day. Probably one of the last, though. Despite the sunshine there's a chill in the air."

Tess studied the profile of the woman beside her. "I owe you an apology."

"Yes you do," Blythe agreed without rancor.

"I'm trying very hard to strike the right balance between Alec and myself because of the situation we're in, and I didn't think our having dinner with you as a couple was appropriate."

"I understand. No hard feelings."

"I'm glad."

Blythe wrapped her arms around her long legs and rested her chin on her knees. "How are you and your sister settling in? Alec never tells us a thing."

"Fine. It's been a few weeks now. Things aren't so new and strange."

"I suppose having Alec out of town helps."

"A little."

"When's he returning?"

"I don't know. He didn't tell me."

"Will you turn me down again if I invite the two of you to dinner?"

"I'd have to think about it."

"I don't think of the two of you as a couple. Truly I don't. Neither does Trilling. I'd just like to have a chance to get to know you." Blythe looked at Tess and smiled. "I find being in the country rather lonely at times. It would be nice to have a friend so close by."

"Why do you stay?"

She shrugged. "I guess because I began to feel even lonelier in London surrounded by people. I need some time to myself."

"I know what you mean. It's easy to lose track of who you are."

"Exactly right."

Tess closed her eyes and raised her face to the sun.

Blythe glanced sideways at her. "So how are things going between you and Alec?"

With her eyes still closed, Tess smiled. "I don't know how to answer that. I guess you could say we tolerate each other well enough."

"He's an attractive man."

Tess opened her eyes and looked at Blythe. "Yes, he is."

"I was madly in love with him when I was younger."

"How long have you know each other?"

"Always. Our parents were friends, so we were thrown together quite a bit as children. He and Trilling are more like brothers than neighbors."

"What was Alec like? I can't quite picture him as a child."

Blythe grew thoughtful. "He was quiet. Introspective. And a little sad, I think. He still is. That's why women find him such an irresistible challenge."

"I don't know what you mean."

"Every woman he meets thinks she's going to be the one to erase his sadness. No one has yet."

"What about his wife?"

"They couldn't stand each other. Elizabeth was..." Blythe searched for the right word. "She shouldn't have married. She was the kind of woman who couldn't be happy with one man."

"I imagine Alec gave as good as he got."

"He's not a promiscuous man, Tess."

"It doesn't matter to me whether he's promiscuous or not. Who Alec chooses to sleep with has nothing to do with me."

Blythe just smiled. She couldn't have given a reason, but she didn't believe Tess. Not that she thought Tess was lying. Just that she was unaware of her own feelings.

"I used to feel that way."

"About Alec?" Tess asked in surprise.

"My ex."

"Oh. I'm sorry."

"Don't be. I'm well rid of him." She looked at her watch. "I have to get going. Tell Alec hi for me when he gets back."

"I will."

"I can be a good friend, Tess," she said as she rose. "If you need someone to talk to, call me."

"Thank you, Blythe. I'll remember that."

With a wink and a wave, Blythe walked back the way she'd come.

Tess stayed where she was for another ten minutes, enjoying the sun and the quiet, before strolling back to the house. The girls were both spending the night at the home of a friend of Olivia's. As she entered the foyer, Mrs. Linde hurried up to her with Mr. Linde bringing up the rear. "Now remember what I told you earlier. Your dinner is in the refrigerator. Just two minutes in the microwave and it'll be ready."

"Thank you."

"We'll be back from my sister's by noon tomorrow. If you need us for anything, call the number I've left on the corkboard in the kitchen."

Tess smiled. "You don't need to worry about me. I'm a big girl."

"Yes, but you're going to be here all alone."

"I like being alone. Believe me, it's not a problem."

The housekeeper didn't look convinced. "Perhaps Mr. Linde should stay here. I can drive myself—"

"Please, Mrs. Linde, just go. It's a perfect time for the two of you to take a break. I'll eat the dinner you fixed for me, read a book and go to bed. The house will still be here when you get back tomorrow."

Before the older woman could say anything else, her husband took her gently by the arm and escorted her out of the foyer.

Tess wandered around the empty house. It was so quiet. It was so wonderful!

She ended up in the kitchen poking around the refrigerator. True to her word, Mrs. Linde had left her a plate covered with a clear wrap; chicken with a wine sauce, asparagus and rice. Tess popped it into the microwave for a couple of minutes and, while she waited, poured herself a glass of wine.

Carrying everything into the library, she put a match to the laid-out fire, browsed the shelves for a good book and settled onto the couch.

Of all the rooms in the house, this was her favorite. It was rich with wood and leather. And even though it was large, there was something quite cozy about it.

And it smelled wonderful; a combination of the apple wood that fed the fire, the leather, the books—and even a faint fragrance of expensive pipe tobacco.

The dinner was delicious, but she only picked at it as she read. The combination of the fire and the wine made her drowsy. Going upstairs seemed like too much trouble. She would just rest on the couch for a few minutes . . .

Lying down with her head on a throw pillow, the book hugged to her breasts, she closed her eyes and within minutes had drifted into a delicious sleep.

It was past midnight when Alec entered the library. He was surprised to find a lamp on, and even more surprised to find Tess asleep on the couch. After setting his briefcase on the desk, he crossed to Tess and stood looking down at her.

He hadn't realized until that moment how hungry he was for the sight of her.

She stirred but didn't open her eyes.

Alec sat on the coffee table and watched her. Again he found himself asking what it was about this woman that made him unable to dismiss her from his thoughts even when he was hundreds of miles away. She was beautiful, but he'd known women who were more beautiful. She was intelligent and capable of great charm, but he'd known women with those qualities in abundance.

It was this woman.

Tess slowly opened her eyes and found herself looking at Alec. She wasn't startled. "Hello," she said sleepily.

"Hello."

"When did you get back?" She struggled into a sitting position.

"A while ago. Where is everyone?"

"The girls are sleeping at Cassie Stanford's house and Mr. and Mrs. Linde are visiting her sister."

"And you're here."

"I hope you don't mind my using your library."

"Not at all."

Tess was still trying to collect her thoughts. They'd parted on somewhat hostile terms the last time they'd seen each other. Add to that the fact that this wasn't exactly the kind of man one made small talk with. "How . . . how was your trip?'' Tess inwardly rolled her eyes. Could talk get any smaller than that?

''Full of good news and bad, like most business trips. Since I didn't hear from you while I was gone, I assume things here went well.''

''Yes.'' Tess set the book beside Alec on the coffee table. ''Both Olivia and Jenni are doing good work.''

''And how are you doing, Tess?''

She looked at him in surprise. ''I'm fine.''

He tiredly rubbed his temples.

The nurturer in Tess surfaced irresistibly. ''What's wrong?''

''I have a headache.''

''Can I get you anything?''

''I could use some aspirin, but I'll get it myself.''

''Let me try something first.''

''Try what?''

''It's nothing drastic, I assure you. Sit on the couch.'' She patted the cushion beside her.

Alec did as he was told.

''Now face away from me and lean forward a little.''

He did.

Tess pressed her fingertips against his temples and began moving them in circles. She slowly worked her way down to the cords of his neck and the tight muscles of his shoulders through his suitcoat. After a few minutes she could feel him relaxing.

''That's wonderful,'' he said in a voice husky with fatigue. ''Where did you learn to do that?''

''It was one of the stranger courses offered during one of my summers in boarding school.''

''Just a minute.'' He took a cushion from the couch and tossed it onto the floor, took off his coat, loosened his tie and shirt collar and lay on the floor on his stomach with his head resting on the cushion.

Tess knelt beside him, her fingers kneading the muscles of his shoulders and back, moving down his arms inch by inch.

She took one of his hands in hers and massaged it a finger at a time. He had nice hands, strong with long fingers. Placing that hand on the cushion beside his head, she worked on his other hand.

Alec was so still. It took her a moment to realize that he was asleep.

She rose and turned out the lamp, then poked at the fire until it burned brightly. She should have left and gone to bed, but she didn't. She lay on her side facing Alec, her elbow on the carpeting, her head resting on her hand as she watched him sleep.

All kinds of thoughts crowded their way into her mind, none of them particularly clear. While he was gone, she'd imagined him with his mistress, even though she didn't have the faintest idea if they were together. What did he think? What did he feel? It was so hard to figure him out. Not that it really mattered. She was just curious.

Tess stretched her arm out and rested her head on it, still facing Alec. She would just close her eyes for a minute....

She stirred, somewhere deep in her subconscious aware that she'd been asleep. When she opened her eyes, it was to find Alec still beside her, awake, looking at her. "How's your headache?" she asked in a whisper.

"Gone."

Tess suddenly felt very self-conscious. She started to rise, but Alec put his hand on her shoulder. "Don't."

Their faces were only inches apart.

"It's late," she said.

"Or early, depending upon how you look at it."

"I should go upstairs."

His eyes moved over her face. "I don't want you to go."

"What?"

"And you don't want to go."

Tess knew exactly what he was talking about. "We can't."

"Why not?"

"Because we aren't in love."

"Since when did being in love become a criteria for having sex?"

"I...I..."

"I'm attracted to you. You're attracted to me. We're both consenting adults."

"I think it would be a mistake for us to get too close."

"I didn't say anything about getting close. I have no intention of falling in love with you. I just don't see why we can't enjoy each other without having to think beyond the moment."

A line from a song in *My Fair Lady* threaded its way through Tess's mind—about why a woman couldn't be more like a man. Why, despite everything Tess knew about men, did she still feel the need for a commitment before making love? Why couldn't she just "have sex" the way men could? Have it, enjoy it and move on.

Alec was right. She *was* attracted to him. She wanted him to touch her; *she* wanted to touch *him*. So what was holding her back?

Delusions.

The kind of man she felt she could fall in love with didn't exist. Saving herself while she waited for him to come along was pointless. And ever so slightly pathetic.

Why, indeed, couldn't a woman be more like a man?

In the dying light of the fire, Alec watched Tess's changing expressions and wondered what she was thinking.

She told him without speaking as she reached out her hand to touch his lips.

Alec moved Tess onto her back and raised himself over her. "You're a surprising woman. Every time I think I have you figured out, you do something or say something that sends me back to the beginning."

Tess looked into his eyes and Alec was lost. He covered her lips with his.

At first that was all they did. Alec couldn't have been more tender or patient. Just as he could feel the tension in Tess when they started, he could feel it drain from her as the kiss deepened. He stroked her soft skin, moving his hand down her back and the curve of her waist. Every time he moved, he could feel Tess's body get tense. Raising his head, he looked into her eyes. "You don't need to be afraid of me. I won't do anything to hurt you."

What Tess wanted to say was that she wasn't afraid of him. She was afraid of herself. Afraid of losing control.

"Close your eyes," Alec said as he kissed her ear. "Don't think about anything. Let your body relax."

Tess took a deep breath and slowly let it out.

Alec removed her clothing a piece at a time, exploring with his mouth everything he exposed with a slow deliberation that allowed him to know every curve; every hollow; every inch of her.

It was wonderful. Tess's control slipped away without her even realizing it was happening. Her body took over, responding of its own volition to each kiss, each caress.

Her own hands moved over Alec's smoothly muscled back, pulling his body closer to hers, wanting him with a desperation she never knew existed.

When he entered her, Tess inhaled sharply.

Alec grew still. "Are you all right?"

She nodded.

He kissed her tenderly and then began to move inside her with slow deliberation. Tess wrapped her arms and legs around him, holding his body against hers. Her entire body was moving toward something—something inevitable. She couldn't have stopped if she'd wanted to, and she didn't.

When the explosion came, it rocked Tess to her soul.

Alec held her long after it was over, smoothing her hair with his hand; kissing her cheek. As much as it had been a revelation for Tess, it had also been one for Alec.

If he'd thought that making love to Tess would get her out of his system, he couldn't have been more wrong. As Alec held her in his arms he could feel her tremble. He held her closer. He wanted to say something to her, but there were no words.

Alec rose from the floor to get the blanket from the back of the couch. He covered her with it, then wrapped her in his arms again.

Tess closed her eyes, though sleep was the last thing on her mind. She waited until Alec's breathing was deep and even before carefully moving out of his arms, slipping on her sweater, gathering up the rest of her clothes and quietly leaving the library.

Alec opened his eyes.

When Tess got to her room, she closed the door behind her, went straight to her bed and lay down. Tears streamed from the corners of her eyes and dampened her hair.

What had she done?

Chapter Seven

It was late in the morning when Tess awoke, more exhausted than if she hadn't slept at all. She sat on the edge of the bed, dreading facing the day—and Alec.

But she had no choice. She couldn't spend the day in her room, because it would look as though she were hiding. She was going to shower and primp and put a smile on her face, and no one would ever know about the turmoil inside her.

And she did exactly that.

An hour later when she went downstairs, she looked the way she usually did.

Alec walked into the house as Tess was in the foyer. Tess smiled at him as though she hadn't a care in the world, even though her heart dropped. "Good morning," she said.

"Afternoon. How did you sleep?"

"Very well, thank you." She didn't ask how he'd slept.

"Are you all right, Tess?"

"Fine." She gave him another smile. "If you'll excuse me, I was just going for a walk."

Jenni and Olivia burst through the door. "Hi, guys," said Jenni as she gave Tess a hug.

Olivia hugged Tess and then turned to her father. "Welcome home."

Alec did the unthinkable. He hugged his daughter. "Thank you, Olivia. Did you have fun at your friend's house?"

She was so flustered by his gesture that it took her a moment to collect her thoughts. "Oh, yes. We went to a movie and then stayed up late talking."

Tess looked at Alec in surprise. This time when she smiled at him, it was genuine. "Well," she said to the girls, "what are you going to do now?"

"Go riding," said Olivia. "It's time for Jenni to have another lesson."

"I'm going to walk into town a little later. Would you like to go with me?"

Jenni wrinkled her nose. "Not really. I have a lot of homework to get done." She flashed her sister a meaningful look.

"I didn't give you that much."

"Yes, you did," said Jenni. "I never had this much homework back at my old school. Especially not on weekends."

"That, my love," Tess said as she leaned over and kissed the top of her head, "is why you fell behind."

"Would you like to go riding with us, Father?"

He looked at his watch. "I'm afraid I can't. I have a friend staying at Mrs. Guest's house, and I need to get over there. I'll see you later."

"At dinner?" Olivia asked.

"I'm afraid not. I won't be back until late. I'll look in on you before I retire."

Tess refused to look at Alec again as she went outside with the girls. They took off at a run, their jackets flapping open, waving at her over their shoulders. She watched until they were out of sight, then, with her hands clasped behind her back, walked toward the lake. It had become one of her favorite spots.

She sat on the grass beside the water and listened to the relaxing sound of its ebb and flow. There was a chill in the air, but the sun was warm. Alec sat beside her. "We have to talk."

Tess continued looking at the lake. "No, we don't."

"You can't pretend last night didn't happen."

"Yes I can. I'm very good at pretending."

"Tess, things between us have changed."

She turned her head to look at him. "What exactly do you think has changed?"

"I'm not sure yet. It'll take time to sort through things."

Tess got to her feet. "You sort through them," she said, sounding a lot tougher than she felt. "But it's a waste of time. Nothing has changed between us except that we've had sex. It was a mistake and it'll never happen again."

Alec followed her with his eyes. There were a lot of ways he could have described what had happened. Mistake wasn't one of them.

Tess walked quickly back to the house. She needed to get away from there. She went up to her room, changed into jeans, a T-shirt with a regular shirt over that and a jacket. Taking some cash from a drawer, she tucked it into a pocket and headed outside.

Mr. Linde was walking across the courtyard and called out to her. "Good afternoon, miss."

"Oh, hello, Mr. Linde. When did you get back?"

"Hours ago. Mrs. Linde gets nervous if she's away from the house too long."

"And you?"

"This is my home. I miss it when I'm away. Where are you off to?"

"I thought I'd walk to town and look around. I haven't been there yet."

"That sounds fine, but it's a long way. You'd be better off driving."

"I'd rather get the exercise."

"It's too far for a walk." He thought for a moment. "A bicycle would be perfect. Do you know how to ride one?"

"Of course."

"Wonderful. I'll get one for you from storage."

"Thank you, Mr. Linde. I appreciate it."

Tess sat on the top step to wait, her eyes on the lake, looking for some sign of Alec and finding none.

Jenni and Olivia sat in the middle of Jenni's bed, a plate of cookies between them. "What do we do now?" Jenni asked.

"I don't know. We haven't been able to get the two of them together since that horseback ride."

"Your dad left right after that. We couldn't have gotten them together no matter what we did." Jenni smiled suddenly. "That ride went well, if I do say so myself."

Olivia nodded as she nibbled around the edge of her cookie. "I can't believe my father is going out with Mrs. Binford tonight."

"Mrs. Binford? Who's that?"

"The friend who came back from London with him."

"If she's your father's friend, why is she staying at your neighbor's house instead of here?"

"Mrs. Linde said that Mrs. Binford always stays with Mrs. Guest when she visits. It would be improper for her to stay here."

A light went on in Jenni's mind. "Ohh. In other words, she's more than just a friend."

Olivia nodded. "She's divorced."

"How do you know?"

"Mrs. Linde. Apparently my father's been seeing her for quite a long time."

"Have you met her?"

"Twice."

"What's she like?"

Olivia shrugged. "I guess she's pretty enough. And she seems nice. She can't lay a glove on Tess, though."

Jenni let out a long breath. "I wish we could do something that would keep your dad home tonight. How are we going to get them together for real if he's never home?"

"I know." Olivia lay back on the bed, her long ponytail hanging over the edge. "I could pretend to be ill."

"Would he stay home with you?"

She thought for a moment. "I don't think so. Mrs. Linde always knows when I'm faking, and she'd probably tell Father. Then I'd really be in trouble. And even if I were really ill, he'd probably have Mrs. Linde take care of me."

"So that's out."

Silence fell between them as they thought.

"What if we were to get Mrs. Linde on our side?" asked Jenni. "She adores Tess."

"I know," Olivia agreed. "But she'd never do anything to anger Father. He's her first loyalty."

"Does she like Mrs. Binford?" Jenni asked.

"Can't stand her. But Father likes her, and he doesn't bring her here very often, so she bites her tongue."

Jenni sighed again. "Do you think your father's in love with her?"

"I don't know. He never talks to me about personal things like that. He barely talks to me at all."

"Doesn't Mrs. Linde have an opinion?" asked Jenni.

"Before Father came home with Tess she thought he might marry Mrs. Binford. And she overheard Mrs. Binford say at a dinner party here a few months ago that she expected to be mistress here in the not too distant future."

"Mistress here?" Jenni asked, unfamiliar with the term.

"You know, the lady of the house."

Jenni shook her head. "We may both speak English, but we sure don't speak the same English."

Olivia sat up, broke the last cookie in two and gave half to Jenni. "You'll get used to it. At least you'd better if you're going to be living here permanently."

"Which brings us back to square one—figuring out how to make your father and my sister fall in love for real."

"Right. But before we do any more of that kind of thinking we're going to need some more cookies."

"Ah," Jenni said with relish, "brain food."

Olivia grinned as she picked up the plate and slid off the bed. "Great minds think alike. Let's see where Mrs. Linde is and raid the pantry."

"What will she say if she finds out?"

"Probably that you're a bad influence on me, but she won't mean it. I can tell she likes you."

"I like her, too. She's a lot nicer than the housekeeper my dad had."

Arm in arm, their heads together, they went downstairs.

Tess was enchanted by the old bookstore. Shelves and shelves were filled with old books that would have been nearly impossible to find anywhere else. Some of them were priced so high that only serious collectors would have been able to buy them. But Tess found a few titles she could afford. It wasn't until she got to the front of the store that she realized it was getting dark outside. As she was being checked out by the patient old man who owned the store, she asked to use the phone. He brought one up from under the counter. The housekeeper answered. "Mrs. Linde, this is Tess. I'm sure I've already missed dinner. I lost track of time."

"Where on earth are you?"

"The bookstore in the village."

"Don't worry. I'll send Mr. Linde after you."

"No, please, I'd rather ride the bike back. I just wanted you to know where I was so you wouldn't worry about me. I'd appreciate it if you'd tell the girls I called."

"Of course. Are you sure you wouldn't like Mr. Linde to pick you up? The bicycle will easily fit in the car boot."

"No, really. I won't be long."

"All right. I'll save a plate for you."

"Don't bother, thank you."

As she hung up the phone, the old gentleman handed her the receipt. "Did I understand you to say you were riding a bicycle?"

"Yes."

He pulled a canvas bag out and began packing her purchases. "This will hold up much better for you than plastic."

"That's very kind of you. Thank you. I'll return it the next time I'm in the village."

"Just bring it in for more books."

As Tess went out the door, he locked it behind her. She hung the book bag on the handlebars, kicked up the stand and headed down the narrow road out of the village. It was a beautiful night for a bike ride. She went slowly, enjoying it, glad that she didn't have to worry about running into Alec when she got home.

About fifteen minutes had passed when there was a snap. Tess's feet were flying freely in circles, peddling madly, but the bike was going nowhere.

Jumping off, she held on to the old-fashioned handlebar with one hand while she bent down to look at the damage.

Great. The chain was broken.

It was dark out already. Tess straightened and looked down the road. It was about as deserted as a road could be. But that was all right. She knew where she was. It was perhaps seven miles to the house. She was just going to get home later than she'd planned.

A lot later.

Tess adjusted the book bag on the handlebars to make it more balanced. It didn't work. It just made the bike more difficult to wheel. She stopped again and slung the bag over her shoulder.

After a while her steps fell into a steady rhythm. It was a glorious evening with a midnight blue sky dusted with stars. There were no streetlights to intrude. Tess took a deep breath of the fresh, crisp air.

Humming softly as she pushed the bike along, Tess let her thoughts wander—but stopped short of allowing herself to think about Alec.

In all honesty, life had been pleasant since she'd come to Gatesboro. She couldn't imagine a more serene setting for a family. Jenni was the happiest Tess had ever seen her, and Olivia was opening up more with each passing day.

And Alec.

He was in her thoughts whether she wanted him to be or not. Perhaps he was different from other men. She had to admit that he fascinated her. Her every instinct for self-preservation told her to run in the opposite direction, as far from him as she could get.

Every other instinct drew her closer to him.

Good grief, the old bike was heavy! She'd only been walking for an hour, maybe a little longer, but she needed a rest. Laying the bike on the side of the road, she dropped her bag of books beside it and sat down, her arms wrapped around her bent knees.

She'd been sitting for perhaps five minutes when she thought she saw headlights in the distance. The closer the car came, the bigger and brighter were its headlights. She thought about flagging the driver down and asking for a lift, but he was going in the opposite direction. Getting wearily to her feet, she righted the bike, shouldered her books and started walking again.

As the vehicle neared, the glare of the headlights illuminated her. To Tess's surprise, the car stopped beside her and Alec Devereaux stepped out. His gaze moved from her to the bike and back to her. "Problems?"

She allowed a glimmer of her relief that he was there to show. "The chain broke."

He reached inside the car and pressed a button that popped open the trunk. In one smooth movement, he lifted the heavy bike and set it inside. "Get into the car," he told her as he secured it with a cord. "I'll take you home."

Tess looked at his suit. "I'm really sorry. You're obviously on your way somewhere."

"Actually," he said as he straightened, "I was already there. The girls were worried about you and called me at Mrs. Guest's home to ask me to look for you."

"Oh, no," Tess groaned. "They should have asked Mr. Linde instead of bothering you. I'm sorry."

Alec gazed at her in the moonlight. "It's no bother, Tess," he said quietly. "I was worried, too." He moved toward her and her heart caught. She took an involuntary step backward.

Alec looked at her with an amused smile as he reached past her to open the car door. The rear car door.

That's when she saw, for the first time, the woman sitting in the front seat. "Tess," Alec introduced, "this is a friend of mine, Diane Binford."

The woman was lovely. She looked Tess over very carefully before speaking. "How do you do?"

Tess climbed into the back seat and Alec closed the door after her. "Fine, thank you." She was furious and trying not to show it. This woman was clearly his mistress. She couldn't believe it. He'd gone from his mistress to her and back to his mistress.

Tess felt ill. She hadn't realized until that moment how very much she'd wanted him to be different from other men.

Oh, God.

Alec and his mistress carried on a quiet conversation in the front seat. Tess sat in silence, desperately wanting the ride to be over.

Diane turned slightly in her seat. "How do you like living in England?"

"I like it very much," said Tess, sounding as pleasant as she could manage.

"And Olivia is a delight."

"Yes, she is," agreed Tess.

"Still, it must be difficult being away from friends and family the way you are."

"My sister is my family."

"Oh, yes, Alec was telling me that your sister is living here with you."

To Tess's further dismay, Alec drove to Blythe and Trilling's house. It was a much more modest country home than Alec's. As he parked in front, Trilling came out with a drink in his hand. "Well, hello everyone," he said as he leaned in Tess's window. "And hello particularly to you. I'm glad to see you're safe. The girls were worried. So was Alec." Trilling looked at her more closely in the light of a nearby outdoor lamp. "What's wrong?"

"Nothing."

He didn't look convinced.

"Really, I'm fine."

Diane said something to Alec, and Trilling suddenly knew exactly what was wrong. He squeezed Tess's hand. "Don't always assume that things are what they appear to be," he said quietly. Then more loudly, "I hope all of you can come in for a little while. Blythe spent the afternoon preparing a dessert, and I'm never going to hear the end of it if there's no one but me to eat it."

"I was just dropping Diane off," said Alec.

"Please," Trilling pleaded. "Don't put me through this. You know how Blythe can be."

"Just for a few minutes," Alec reluctantly agreed.

Trilling opened Tess's door. "Come, my dear."

"Trilling," she said quietly, "I really don't want to do this."

"Of course you do." He all but pulled her out of the car, looped his arm through hers and guided her to the house. Alec and Diane brought up the rear.

Blythe was standing in the doorway watching the procession. She smiled when she saw Tess and gave her a hug. "What a lovely surprise."

"You're very kind, Blythe," said Tess, "but I feel terrible imposing on you like this when you weren't expecting me. This must be awkward for you."

"Not as awkward as you might think," she said dryly. "Come in. Have some coffee." She pried Trilling's fingers from Tess's arm.

"Blythe..."

"Back off, Trilling. She's taken."

"Temporarily."

"Maybe. Maybe not."

Blythe took Tess's hand and led her into a large living room where a fire burned brightly. A tray was already set up on the coffee table with a pot and several cups and saucers. "Trilling," said Blythe as she sat on the couch and patted the cushion next to her for Tess to sit on. "Get another cup and saucer, will you? And see if cook has the dessert ready to serve."

Trilling raised a ticked-off eyebrow at his sister, but did as he was told.

Alec sat in a chair across from the couch. His mistress sat in one beside him. Tess ignored both of them as best she could.

Blythe poured the cups of coffee and passed them out. When Trilling returned, it was with an intricate chocolate layer cake already sliced and ready to be served. He set it in front of his sister, and she passed out dessert plates and forks.

Trilling squeezed onto the couch next to Tess. "Pardon me, Alec," he said, "but if you're not going to sit next to your wife, I will."

Tess was frankly grateful for his nonsense.

"My wife is welcome to sit beside whomever she wishes," said Alec.

Diane began telling what she considered an amusing story. Something about an acquaintance of hers in London. Tess heard very little of it. She was more interested in watching Diane as she spoke; the animation of her expression; the way she touched Alec's arm for emphasis. She really was lovely.

Tess took a few polite bites of the cake and then put the plate back on the tray. She had no appetite.

Blythe leaned toward her. "We're definitely different. When I'm upset, all I want to do is eat. The more fattening it is the better I like it."

Tess smiled. "This cake certainly qualifies. It's delicious."

"Thank you. It's a special recipe."

Alec had declined the cake. He looked very uncomfortable and kept checking his watch.

Trilling was enjoying his friend's unease. "How about a game of charades?" he asked innocently.

Alec rose abruptly. "I have to go. So does Tess."

Trilling smiled at Tess. "Do you have to go, darling?"

She just didn't have the heart to play. Not that night. "Maybe another time, Trilling." She rose, as well.

As they headed for the door, Diane caught Alec by the hand. "May I speak to you for a moment, Alec?"

Tess, Blythe and Trilling continued on to the car while Alec went back into the living room with Diane.

"So what do you think of the competition?" asked Trilling.

Blythe elbowed him in the ribs. "Honestly, Trilling, you might consider coordinating your brain with your mouth at least once in a while."

"I think she's lovely," said Tess. "And your sister is right, Trilling. You're too old to be outrageous."

"Since when is being outrageous the sport of the very young?"

"Since people stopped inviting you to their parties," said Blythe dryly.

"Oh, dear sister, you're such a delight to have around. When are you moving back to London?"

"Ignore him," said Blythe to Tess. "I do."

Alec appeared in the doorway with Diane. She raised her hands to his shoulders as she spoke to him, then went up on her toes to kiss him. Tess turned her head away.

"Just so you know," said Blythe, "Alec didn't bring Diane back here with him voluntarily."

"Blythe, I appreciate your interest, but it's really none of my business."

"Of course it's your business. He's your husband."

"You know the circumstances of our marriage as well as I do. So does Diane, apparently."

Blythe looked a little sheepish. "I'm afraid that's my fault. It just sort of slipped out in a phone conversation."

"Alec didn't tell her?" Tess asked in surprise.

"He didn't tell anyone except us and the Lindes. I think he figured it would be impossible to keep the secret from us because we're neighbors and would eventually notice that the two of you aren't exactly close."

As Tess nodded, she glanced at the couple in the doorway. Diane still had her hands on Alec's shoulders. Whatever they were talking about, it appeared to be quite intense. Alec circled her wrists with his hands and removed her hands from his shoulders. He said something rather sharply and walked away from her toward Tess.

"Ready?" he asked her.

"Yes."

He opened the car door, helped her inside. "Thanks for dinner and dessert, Blythe," he said, as he walked around to the driver's side.

"Let's do it again next week."

"Maybe."

He started the engine and put the car into gear. Tess waved to Trilling and Blythe as they pulled away. She liked the two of them a lot and wanted the chance to get to know them better.

Both Tess and Alec were silent as they drove. Tess just wanted to get home and away from him.

But instead of going home, Alec once again had a different destination: Devereaux Hall.

He parked the car in front of the huge, dark house and sat staring at it.

"This was never a particularly happy home for me," he said after a long silence.

"Then why do you want to live here?"

"All of my family's history is here. It's not just a home, it's a responsibility. I want to maintain it for Olivia and whatever other children I might one day have."

"If you're going to live in it, you need to do more than maintain it."

"What?"

"If it wasn't a happy home for you, you need to work really hard to make it a happy home for Olivia. Make her memories different from yours."

"The home is what it is." He looked at Tess. "And I am what I am."

"A home is what you make it," Tess said quietly. "And if a person doesn't like the way he or she is, it's possible to change. It's not easy, but it's possible."

Alec turned his attention to the woman beside him. "What about you, Tess? Can you change?"

"I change all of the time."

"I don't think so. You're still carrying around the emotional baggage of your childhood just like the rest of us."

That didn't sound like something Alec would say. Pop psychology wasn't in his personality profile.

He sensed what she was thinking and answered her unasked question. "Blythe."

"Ahh," Tess nodded and then shrugged. "Perhaps. Who knows?"

Alec looked at the house a moment longer, then put the car into gear. This time they went home. He parked in front of the house and turned in his seat toward Tess. "I'm sorry about bringing Diane with me to pick you up."

Tess didn't know what to say, so she said nothing.

Alec, his arm along the back of the seat, fingered a lock of her hair. "I don't know what to do about you. We're in such a gray area right now."

Tess moved away from him, but some of her hair was still twined around his finger. "There's no gray area. We're married now, and in eleven months we won't be."

"I understand that. But can't we have some kind of truce for the duration of our marriage?"

"I resent the implication that I've been anything less than civil to you."

"That's not what I'm saying."

"At least I'm not parading my lovers in front of you."

With a long sigh Alec let the hair slip away from him strand by strand. "If it's of any interest to you, I haven't slept with anyone but you since our marriage."

Tess's cheeks flushed.

"And I certainly don't regret what happened between us last night."

Tess looked at him for a long moment. "Why?"

"Why what?"

"Why haven't you slept with anyone else?"

"I don't know." His eyes met hers. "I don't know, Tess."

She lowered her eyes.

"This is a little off the topic, but I'm giving a dinner party in a few nights. I'd appreciate it if you'd act as hostess. The people coming, except for Blythe and Trilling, aren't aware of our arrangement."

"All right."

"Thank you."

She climbed out of the car but looked back in through the open window. "I appreciate the rescue."

"Anytime. Good night, Tess."

Tess walked into the house, aware of his eyes following her. She heard the engine start and the car drive off. Now where was he going?

As she tiredly walked down the upstairs hallway, she knocked on Olivia's door.

"Come in."

Tess opened the door and saw Olivia in her nightgown, sitting at her vanity in front of the mirror brushing her long hair. Jenni, wearing a below-the-knee T-shirt was lying on her stomach across one of the beds reading a poem aloud.

"You two should be asleep. Do you know what time it is?"

Jenni looked up from the book and smiled at her. "I see Olivia's dad found you."

"He did." Tess walked over to Olivia and took the brush from her.

"What happened?" asked Jenni.

"The bicycle chain broke. I didn't think I was ever going to get back here." She ran the brush in long strokes through Olivia's thick hair.

Olivia looked at Tess's reflection in the mirror. "We thought you were lost. That's why we sent Father to look for you."

"I appreciate the thought, and I appreciate the rescue, but I wish you'd asked Mr. Linde instead of bothering your father."

Olivia's gaze shifted from Tess to Jenni. "I guess we didn't think of that," she said. "We just wanted to make sure you were all right."

Tess put the brush on the vanity, stood behind Olivia with her hands on the girl's narrow shoulders and looked at her in the mirror. "There. You look beautiful."

Olivia tilted her head to one side as she gazed at herself critically. "Mrs. Linde says I look precisely as my mother did at my age."

"Then she must have been beautiful, too."

"I guess." She didn't sound impressed one way or another. "I don't really remember much about her. She wasn't here very often." She turned on her seat and gazed up at Tess. "It bothers me sometimes that I don't miss her more than I do."

Tess hugged her. "Don't do that to yourself. We all feel what we feel. There isn't any right or wrong."

"I guess."

Tess headed for the door. "Get to bed, you two."

When Tess had gone, Olivia and Jenni looked at each other and shook their heads. "I don't know," Jenni whispered. "We get them together and then they don't do anything with it. What does a person have to do?"

"Keep thinking," said Olivia. "We can't give up."

Jenni nodded.

Just as Tess got to her door, Alec's voice stopped her. "Tess, you forgot your books."

"Thank you," she said as she reached out for the canvas bag. Their fingers brushed. It couldn't have been a simpler or more benign contact, and yet her heart slammed against her ribs. She raised her eyes to his in surprise.

Alec knew. He'd felt it, too.

"Good night," he said abruptly and walked away from her.

Tess went into her room, closed the door behind her and leaned her back against it.

No, no, no, she said to herself. She didn't want to be attracted to him.

She just wanted to get custody of Jenni and get out of this place as quickly as she could.

Chapter Eight

"Tess?"

Tess continued to stare blindly at the paper in front of her.

Jenni glanced at Olivia and frowned, then walked up to her sister and touched her arm. "Tess?"

Tess looked up, startled. "Yes?"

"I said it's two o'clock. May we play now?"

"Oh, of course. I'm sorry. I wasn't paying attention to the time."

"Is anything wrong?"

Tess smiled reassuringly. "No. Everything's fine. Where are you going?"

"The stables. There are some kittens living in a rain barrel. You should see them all! And they're so tiny."

"Just be careful. And don't go off on any adventures unless you tell someone about it first."

"Don't worry. We'll be fine."

Tess sat still for a moment after they'd gone, then wandered to the closed balcony door and gazed outside. The girls came into view as they ran out of the house and across the lawn to the stables. Jenni was the happiest Tess had ever seen her.

Now, she thought, on to other things. The dinner party was tonight. She wasn't exactly sure what her duties as hostess included. Blythe had come over several hours ago and was helping to get things ready while Tess finished out the school day.

A high-pitched noise penetrated the silence of the schoolroom.

Tess quickly reopened the balcony door and listened.

There it was again. Faint, to be sure, but it could have been a scream.

Tess rested her hands on the railing and leaned forward as she looked toward the stables, where the girls had said they were going. She didn't hear the noise again, but she was uneasy just the same.

Moving at a fast clip, she bounded down the stairs and headed across the lawn, still cold and wet from the heavy afternoon rain. Even as she ran, Tess heard the scream again. She ran faster, steadily picking up speed until she reached the stable and burst through the big double doors. "Jenni? Olivia?" she called. "Where are you?"

Horses stamped their hooves and snorted, but no human voice answered her.

Her breath steamed in front of her as she ran through the long building, stopping at each stall to look inside. "Girls? Are you here?" There was an edge of panic in her voice.

Then she heard Jenni's voice. It came from outside in the back of the stables. Without missing a beat, Tess threw open the first door she came to and saw a sight that was going to stay with her for years to come.

"There he is!" Olivia yelled as she stood alongside an enclosed pen, jumping up and down and pointing.

Tess's gaze followed the direction of Olivia's pointing finger. There was a little pig in a corner of a muddy pen that measured perhaps twenty by twenty.

And then she saw Jenni, covered with mud, as she made her way across the pen toward the pig. Her coat was ruined.

"Jenni!" Tess yelled. "What on earth are you doing?"

Olivia hadn't noticed Tess, but now she looked up at her with wide eyes that said "Uh-oh!" more clearly than words.

"Well?" Tess asked. "Answer me. What's going on here?"

"We have to catch the pig and put it back," Jenni said breathlessly. "Mr. Linde told us not to let the pigs out, but one accidentally got away and ran in here. I've been trying to catch it. Would you help me, please, Tess? I can't get it by myself. It's too slippery."

Tess looked at the cold mud and groaned. "Oh, Jenni."

"I'm sorry. I really am."

Olivia touched her arm. "We didn't mean to let the pig out, honestly, Tess. And please don't tell my father about this. He'll be furious."

Tess smiled at her reassuringly. "Everything will be all right. He's not even due back from London for two more hours. Don't worry about it."

"So you'll help?" Olivia asked hopefully.

Tess looked at the pig—and the mud—and sighed. "I suppose I have to." She opened the gate and walked into the pen. Her shoes immediately sank two inches into the mud. "Yeech!"

"I know," Jenni said. "It's really gross. But you'll get used to it."

Tess lifted one foot and then the other. The movement made disgusting sucking noises as the mud protested letting go of her shoes. And when she was about ten feet into the pen, the mud finally won. Tess lifted her feet one at a time and her shoes stayed behind. "Jenni," she said, "you go around to the right and I'll go to the left. He'll have to dash past one of us to get away. We can catch him then."

"All right."

Squelch, squelch, squelch.

The two of them got into position. The pig had his back
to the fence and was eyeing them warily. "I think he's going to make a run for it."

"I'm ready," Jenni said.

Suddenly the pig shot past Tess. She made a dive for him,
missed and landed facedown in the mud. For a moment she
just lay there, very still, completely disgusted.

She raised her head and pushed herself up with her hands,
away from the mud, until she was on her knees.

"You missed."

It was Alec. Tess closed her eyes tightly for a moment,
wishing him gone.

"You left too much space between you and Jenni."

"Father!" Olivia gasped, her eyes filled with happiness
and dread, both at the same time. "I'm sorry about the pig.
It was an accident."

Tess opened her eyes. It hadn't worked. He was still there,
standing next to Olivia, his coat suspended from a finger
over his shoulder.

Alec looked at her mud-caked face and grinned.

Tess, on the other hand, wasn't at all amused. She could
only imagine what she looked like—and she had a very good
imagination. "If you think you can do any better, you're
more than welcome to try."

To Tess's surprise, he accepted the challenge. "Come on,
Olivia. You might as well help, too," he said as he dropped
his coat on the ground, followed by his suit coat, tie and
shoes. Rolling up his sleeves and the legs of his trousers in a
futile gesture intended to keep his clothes from getting dirty,
he entered the pen with Olivia behind him. "You go over by
Jennifer," he instructed her. Walking to where Tess was still
on her knees, he offered her a hand up and she accepted.
The mud sucked at her as she rose. "Now," Alec said,
"we'll corner the little fellow where he is, but you and Jennifer will come down the middle and Olivia and I will approach on either side."

Tess was freezing. She wasn't even wearing a sweater and it was cold outside. But there was the small problem of the pig. She eyed the creature skeptically. "Are you sure this is going to work?"

"Positive. Girls," he called to Olivia and Jenni, "are you ready?"

"Ready!"

"Let's go."

They all took their places and slowly moved in on the pig. His eyes darted from one to the other of them. The poor little thing was terrified, and who could blame it? But it had to be caught.

It made another run for it, this time past Alec. He dove for it just like Tess had done, and landed the same way, facedown, arms empty, but he was on his feet almost instantly running after the pig. It was complete chaos, with all of them running and falling and yelling, and the pig squealing and dashing around, determined to get away. Tess was running behind Alec, going as fast as the mud would allow—which wasn't very fast at all. Alec lost his footing and went down. Tess couldn't stop in time and came down on top of him. The pig ran over both of them and the girls, still chasing the pig, crashed into them as well. They were all lying in the mud, gasping for air.

Tess peeled herself off Alec's back and sat in the mud beside him. When he sat up, their eyes met. Tess bit the insides of her cheeks in a desperate bid not to laugh, but it was hopeless. She couldn't disguise her dancing eyes. "You're a mess!" she blurted out.

Alec looked down at himself. "It's a good thing I took the time to roll up my sleeves."

At that, Tess burst out laughing. It was infectious laughter, and Alec, who couldn't remember the last time he'd laughed out loud, found himself laughing, too. Olivia and Jenni looked at the two grown-ups in their lives, then looked at each other and shrugged.

The pig, undoubtedly thinking he was locked in a pen with a bunch of crazy people, tried to dash past them again, but this time Alec saw him coming and grabbed him.

"Father, you got him, you got him!" Olivia cried delightedly.

Alec struggled to his feet with the pig wriggling in his arms. "Let's put him back where he belongs."

Olivia followed along behind him. "We didn't mean to let him out, Father. It just sort of happened."

Tess got to her feet and draped her arm around Jenni's shoulders as the two of them squelched their way out of the mud. "Do you suppose Mr. Devereaux is mad?" Jenni asked.

"He didn't seem to be. But then he's very polite. It could be that he's furious and just isn't showing it at the moment."

"I hope Olivia doesn't get into any trouble."

"You'd better hope real hard, because if Olivia gets into trouble, you get into trouble."

Alec and Olivia came back. "All right," he said. "The pig is secure—until, of course, someone forgets to latch the gate again."

"I'm sure I'm the one who forgot," Jenni said contritely. "Don't be mad at Olivia. She didn't do anything wrong."

Alec nodded. "Isn't that interesting? Olivia just told me that it was all her fault. That makes it difficult to figure out who to punish."

"You'll have to punish both of us." Olivia looked as though she was going to cry.

"Or neither of us," Jenni suggested hopefully. "Don't forget that that's an option."

Tess turned her eyes toward the sky to study the clouds.

"This is pretty serious business," Alec said, his deep voice adding weight to the words.

Olivia and Jenni clasped muddy hands.

"I think what I'll do is tell Mrs. Linde that neither of you may have seconds on dessert tonight."

Both girls beamed. "Yes, sir."

"And don't forget to latch the gate next time. Do I have your word?"

"Yes, sir," they said in unison.

"Get yourselves cleaned up."

They raced off to the house. He started to yell something after them, but stopped when he realized they wouldn't hear. "Mrs. Linde isn't going to be happy if they track through her front hall."

"What choice do they have?"

"The stable shower."

"The stable shower?"

"Come on." He took her hand.

"My shoes. They're stuck in the mud."

"So they are." Alec suddenly leaned over, put his shoulder to her stomach and lifted her in a fireman's carry.

"What are you doing?" Tess was too shocked to struggle.

"Helping you as any gentleman would help a lady who'd lost her shoes."

He carried her into a small room just off the stables, closed the door behind them and set her on the ground. "What's this?" she asked, looking around.

"A shower for very muddy people." They were facing each other. He reached around her. Tess inhaled sharply and backed up against the wall. Alec stopped for a moment and looked at her. Moving his body close to hers, he reached behind her to turn on the water. A burst of cold spray hit her on the back.

"Oh!" Tess gasped as she shot forward and straight into Alec. "It's freezing."

"It'll warm up in a minute." Putting his hands on her arms, he turned her away from the shower even as he put himself under it. Tess just watched as he rinsed himself off, his head back, exposing his strong neck. In just a few seconds, he began looking like a wet version of himself with his hair slicked back.

Alec tilted his head back down and caught her studying him. With a half smile he put his hands on her shoulders again and turned her backward into the spray. He moved her slowly so that the spray inched its way over her, then put his hand under her chin to tilt her reluctant head back into the water. She was cold, and the water was now warm. It felt good to let it flow over her, washing the mud away. She closed her eyes. "Why are we doing this?"

"Because that's what the shower is here for." He rubbed his hands over her shoulders, arms and back, and more mud went swirling down the drain. "If we were to show up in the house like this, Mrs. Linde would do to us what she's probably doing to the girls at this very moment. You'll thank me later."

Tess opened her eyes and found Alec looking at her. She parted her lips to speak, but Alec pressed his finger against them to silence her. His eyes moved over her wet face, his expression unfathomable.

"What's wrong?" she asked.

"What makes you think anything is?"

"I don't know, really. You're—different today."

"Is that good or bad?"

"Good."

"Well, for what it's worth, you're different, too."

And she *felt* different. She'd been upset for days—or was it weeks? Or months? But she was tired of being upset. Now, for a few minutes at least, she was almost having fun.

Alec reached behind her to shut off the shower. Then without warning he swept her up in his arms again.

"What are you doing?" she gasped.

"We're walking back to the house, and you still don't have any shoes."

"Oh," she said weakly.

"And don't blush."

"Right."

Alec carried her through the stables and across the lawn.

Tess wasn't sure what to do with herself except go along for the ride. Her arm had automatically gone around the back of his neck when he'd lifted her. She now let it dangle a little so it wouldn't seem so—intimate.

Holding Tess with one arm, he opened the door with the other and carried her into the house. They hadn't gone five feet when Blythe stepped in front of them.

"Well, well, well," she said with a smile, "I imagine there's an amusing little story behind this."

Tess struggled out of his arms and stood up. "Something about a loose pig, mud, disappearing shoes. You know. The usual."

Blythe laughed. "Happens to me all of the time."

"What are you doing here?" asked Alec.

"I'm helping your wife get ready for this evening."

"Mrs. Linde is doing that."

"Ah, but someone needs to check the final details. And if I do say so myself, everything looks lovely. There's been a slight hitch in the guest list, though. I know you hadn't included Diane on it, and she was supposed to leave for her own home this morning, but it turns out that she's staying over, and well, you know Trilling and I can't very well leave her at home alone."

"So you invited her," Alec finished for her, not sounding at all pleased.

"Yes." She looked at Tess apologetically. "I'm so sorry. I know this is terribly awkward for you."

"It's all right," said Tess. "You had no choice. Everything will be fine."

"I feel wretched all the same."

"Are you leaving now?" Alec asked, his mood considerably less cheerful.

"Yes."

"I'll see you tonight, then." He turned to Tess. "You should get out of those wet clothes."

"I will."

Both women watched him as he climbed the stairs.

"He's really, really, angry," said Blythe.

"No he's not. He didn't even raise his voice."

"Alec never raises his voice. Trust me. I've known him all my life. He's angry."

"Well, if he is, there's nothing you can do about it now."

"I'm dreading this evening."

"There's really nothing to dread. Diane and I aren't in competition. I'll be completely out of the picture in no time. She knows that."

"I think she's afraid you'll seduce him away from her."

"I don't think Alec can be seduced," Tess said quietly. "At least not emotionally. If he's in love with Diane, nothing will change that."

"He might fall in love with you."

Tess shook her head. "I'm not his type."

"And what exactly is Alec's type?"

"I'm not sure. I think the first criterion is that she not be the daughter of Thomas Parish, which pretty much leaves me out in the cold. I think I irritate him for the most part."

"That's not the way it looked a few minutes ago."

Tess laughed. "Oh, that. I think that was Alec's way of trying to lighten up things between us. It's been tense around here." She rubbed her hands up and down her wet sleeves. "I'm really cold. If you don't mind, I'm going to go to my room and take a hot shower."

"Get going. I'll see you—" she looked at her watch "—in about four hours."

"Okay. Thanks for all of your help. I'd give you a hug, but..."

Blythe took a step back. "I prefer your gratitude at a safe distance. 'Bye for now."

Tess closed the door behind Blythe, then ran upstairs to her room. She stripped off her soggy clothes and hopped into a wonderfully steamy shower.

When she was finished, she toweled dry her hair, put on jeans and a sweater and went downstairs to see if she could help with anything.

Mrs. Linde looked up from a bowl she was stirring and smiled at her. "Good afternoon."

Tess smiled back. There were two other people Tess didn't know in the kitchen. "That looks delicious. What is it?"

"A special lemon and ginger batter I'm using for dessert." She pulled a spoon out of a drawer, dipped it into the batter and handed it to Tess. "Go on, taste it."

She didn't need to be told twice. It was incredible. "Oh, Mrs. Linde, it's delicious. I could eat a bowl of it before it's cooked."

The housekeeper took back the spoon. "Look at the dining room and see how you like it."

Humming softly to herself, Tess made her way to the dining room. It was absolutely beautiful. There were place settings for twenty guests. Low but lush arrangements of vivid flowers alternating with tall, slender candles filled the center of the long table. The china, crystal, silverware, linen napkins—it looked like a photograph in a magazine.

As she turned to leave, she nearly ran into Diane.

"Oh!" said Tess, startled, "I didn't know you were here."

Diane wasn't in the mood to be charming. "What do you think you're doing?"

"I was just looking at the table."

"It's perfect. I've already checked it."

"I didn't know. How long have you been here?"

"Long enough. What do you think you're doing with Alec."

"Doing?"

"Leave him alone. He's mine."

"I don't want to get into this with you," said Tess as she tried to walk past the woman.

"You're already in it." Diane stepped sideways to block Tess's exit. "I know what you're playing at," she said, "and it's not going to work."

"What exactly are you talking about?"

"Don't tell me that you and your father didn't conspire to get you married to Alec."

The accusation was ludicrous. Tess didn't even bother to respond.

"You think you'll get him to fall in love with you, and then all of this will be yours."

"I don't want all of this. I just want custody of my little sister."

"Surely you don't expect anyone to believe that."

Alec walked into the room and stood beside Tess. "It doesn't matter what anyone believes but me."

"Are you saying you believe her?"

"It's none of your business, Diane." He took her by the elbow and turned her around.

"What are you doing?"

"Taking you back to Blythe's."

"But I came here to help with the preparations. Your wife clearly doesn't know what's expected of her."

"I'm sure Tess will do just fine without your help. And when you come this evening, you will treat her with respect, or it will be the last time you set foot in this house. Do you understand?"

Tess was amazed when Diane managed an absolutely charming smile despite the dressing down she'd just received.

"Alec, you know you can always count on me to do the correct thing."

"I know, Diane. It's one of your sterling qualities." He looked at Tess and—winked!

She smiled at the unexpectedness of it. In that moment she felt almost close to him.

Chapter Nine

Jenni ran into Tess's room, her face flushed. "We're invited to the party!"

Tess turned away from the mirror. "What?"

"Mrs. Linde just told Olivia and me that Mr. Devereaux wants us to come to the party."

"That's wonderful!"

"Olivia's really excited."

"Where is she?"

"Getting dressed."

"What about you?"

"It'll only take me a few minutes."

"Good, then you have time to help me with this." Tess handed Jenni a pearl necklace that had belonged to their mother, and Jenni fastened it around her sister's neck. "Are you going to wear the matching earrings?"

"Mmm-hmm." Tess put the cap on her lipstick and twirled around. "What do you think?"

Jenni critically looked over the classic black sleeveless dress with its jewel neckline and skirt that flared slightly to just above Tess's knees. "I don't know," she said, wrinkling her nose.

Tess looked down at herself. "What's wrong?"

"Don't you have anything made from spandex?"

"Spandex!"

"You know, something that'll show your figure a little more."

"For heaven's sake, Jenni, you don't wear something like that to a dinner party."

"Models do."

"The obvious answer is that I'm not a model. And even if I were, I wouldn't wear a spandex dress to a dinner party."

Jenni shook her head. "You're never going to keep your husband with that attitude."

"I don't want to keep him! And I certainly don't want one who'd reject or accept me on the basis of my clothing. Besides, this dress is very tasteful." Tess turned and looked at herself in the mirror, her head tilted to one side. "I like it."

Jenni raised her hands, palms up. "All right. I tried." She flopped across Tess's bed. "Olivia sure is excited about dinner."

"It's another chance for her to be with her father."

"I know. She loves him a lot."

Tess sat on the edge of the bed. "Are you still happy here?"

"Oh, yeah. This place is great. And Olivia's the best friend I've ever had. It's like having a sister."

"Hey!"

Jenni grinned at her. "You know what I mean. You're so much older than I am that you're more like a mother. Even when I used to visit you at college you were like a mother."

"That's true."

"Now I have a sister *and* a mother. And having Olivia's dad here is like I have a dad, too." She smiled. "He helped me with my math the other night."

Tess looked at her in surprise. "I didn't know that."

"He was real nice about it."

"Why didn't you ask me for help?"

"I could have. I just decided to ask him instead."

Tess was silent for a moment.

"What's wrong?"

"Oh, honey, nothing's really wrong. I'm just worried about your getting too attached to the people here."

"Why?"

"I don't want you to be hurt when we leave."

"What about you? You love Olivia, too."

"Yes, I do."

"Olivia and I have talked about this, you know."

"And what did the two of you decide?"

"That even if it happens that we move away, Olivia and I are never going to lose touch with each other. We're sisters as much as if we were born that way. Just because we have to live apart doesn't mean we can't still be close."

Tess leaned over and rested her cheek on Jenni's head. "You're something else."

Olivia flew breathlessly into the room. "I'm ready. How do I look?"

Tess moved her finger in a circle. "Give me a spin."

Olivia obliged. "Well?"

She was wearing a low-waisted, pale blue dress with a broad white collar edged with lace. Her hair was tied back with a bow. Everything she had on suited her perfectly. "You look beautiful."

She beamed and looked more closely at Tess. "So do you."

Tess turned to Jenni and said a triumphant, "Hah!"

"I didn't say you didn't look beautiful," said Jenni as she got off the bed. "I just said that you should be wearing spandex."

Tess rose also. "Run and get your dress on so we can all go downstairs together."

"Okay. I'll be right back."

"I'll help you," said Olivia, following quickly after her friend.

Tess put a final touch on her makeup, and by the time she was finished Jenni and Olivia were back. "Here," she said as she brushed Jenni's forest green skirt down and straightened the short-waisted jacket. "You look lovely." There was nothing flowery or frilly about Jenni. She preferred her clothes straight and simple. The style suited her.

"Would you like to wear my gold necklace?" Tess asked.

"The one with the heart?"

She nodded. "It would look perfect with that outfit."

"Sure. Thanks."

Tess dug into her jewelry box and came up with the necklace. Standing behind Jenni, she fastened it around her neck. Her eyes met Jenni's in the mirror. "I can't wait to see what you're going to look like when you're all grown up."

"Probably the same as I do now—only taller." She fingered the necklace. "Did this belong to our mother?"

"Yes. And now it belongs to you."

"Oh, Tess, you don't have to do that."

"I was saving it for you."

Jenni turned her head and kissed Tess's cheek. "Thank you."

"You're welcome. And now," she said, straightening, "we should go downstairs."

Olivia and Jenni each slipped a hand into Tess's—and Tess was grateful for the support. She felt strange about going to this dinner. Particularly as the hostess. It was awkward, to say the least.

At the top of the stairs Tess looked down and saw Alec speaking to someone. Tess barely noticed the other person except to note that it was a man. It was Alec whom she saw, tall and straight in his black suit. Alec sensed her presence and looked up at her. His eyes locked with hers for a long moment, then made their leisurely way over her body, drinking in each curve. Tess felt a sudden heat flood through her everywhere his gaze rested. It was as intimate as if he'd actually touched her.

Jenni, unaware of what was happening, tugged on Tess's hand. "Come on, let's go down."

Tess looked blankly at her little sister. "What?"

"You stopped walking," Jenni said with a frown. "Is something wrong?"

Tess managed a smile. "No, of course not. I...I was just looking at the guests." She fell into step with Jenni and Olivia, studiously averting her eyes from Alec's, but very aware that he was still watching her.

When they arrived at the bottom of the stairs, Alec was waiting for them. He took Tess's hand and helped her down the last step. "You look beautiful," he said quietly.

Tess looked up at him. "Thank you." She couldn't help smiling. "So do you."

The grooves in his cheeks deepened.

"I'm sorry I'm late. I don't know where the time went this afternoon."

"That's all right. Wives aren't really expected to greet guests at the door. I'll introduce you as we walk around."

"What exactly do you want me to do?"

"Act as though we're really the newlyweds we're supposed to be."

Blythe came up to Alec and slipped her hand through the bend in his arm. "Hello, Tess."

"Oh, Blythe," she said, looking at the shimmering, sequined dress that hugged her slender figure, "you look stunning."

"I know." She smiled at her. "You should have heard the whispers start as you made your way down the staircase."

"Is that good?"

"Better to be talked about than to be ignored."

"I'm not sure that's always true."

Blythe saw the girls standing with Tess and nodded her approval. "You both look exactly as you should. Olivia, I can't believe how grown-up you're getting."

Trilling came up behind Olivia and squeezed her shoulders. "And who is this gorgeous creature?"

Olivia giggled. "You know who I am."

He tugged her hair and turned to Jenni. "And you! I can see that you're going to be a heartbreaker like your sister when you're older."

"I hope so," said Jenni. "May we wander around, Tess?" She looked at Alec for guidance.

"Of course," he said. "Just make sure you behave."

"And don't spoil your dinner by eating too many hors d'oeuvres," added Tess.

As they turned to leave, Jenni muttered to Olivia. "Why are people always treating us like kids?"

"Maybe because we're eleven."

Jenni looked at Olivia in surprise. "You're starting to sound like me."

Alec disengaged himself from Blythe and put his hand at Tess's waist. "Come with me. There are people I'd like you to meet." He moved her across the room going from group to group— Tess noticed that the couples tended to separate after they came in the door with the men gravitating to other men and women gravitating to other women. She tried to pay attention to names as she was introduced, but it was difficult when so much of her attention was taken up by the way Alec's hand moved from her waist to the small of her back; how he pulled her close to his side when they stopped to speak to someone and the way he looked at her.

He stayed with her the entire time, listening to her small talk, smiling at her occasional joke. He watched her and found himself admiring—even drawn to—her natural warmth and charm. She would be an asset to any man.

But for tonight she was his, and he found that fact surprisingly enjoyable.

Tess turned her head and smiled at him. Alec's heart caught. It was a strange sensation.

Blythe elbowed her brother.

"Ouch!" he said with a frown as he rubbed his side. "What did you do that for?"

"Look at Alec and Tess."

Trilling did. "So?"

"I think we just might have a real match in the making here."

"Oh, please," said Trilling, "this is Alec we're talking about."

"I think he's in love with her."

"So are half the men in this room."

"I'm not talking about them. I'm talking about Alec."

Trilling watched more closely. In all of the years he'd known Alec, he'd never seen him behave toward a woman, whether she was his mistress or not, with anything other than proper formality in public. But with Tess he couldn't seem to stop touching her. Maybe Blythe was right.

Blythe elbowed him again.

"Would you stop that!"

"Don't be such a baby. Look, Diane is here."

"Uh-oh."

"Uh-oh is right. I thought she wasn't coming."

"She apparently had a change of heart."

"This could get ugly," said Blythe. "I wonder if I should warn Alec."

"Alec can handle Diane."

"But why should he have to? He's having a perfectly pleasant evening with Tess. Why don't you take care of Diane for him?"

"Me?"

"She likes you well enough. Just keep her occupied and away from Alec and Tess."

"You don't ask much, do you?"

"What are you complaining about? She's better than what you usually end up with at parties."

"You're a vicious woman, Blythe."

She kissed him on the cheek. "Thank you, dear. I knew I could count on you."

Trilling made his way to Diane, who looked wonderful in her own right in a plum-colored dress with a tasteful diamond necklace.

Tess saw her from across the room. She watched Alec's expression harden when he spotted Diane.

Blythe walked over to the two of them with a smile. "No need to worry. It's Trilling to the rescue. And not that I'm not enjoying all of this mingling and chitchat, but I'm famished. When are we going to dine?"

The more Tess was around Blythe, the more she liked her. "I'm hungry myself."

"Then we'll eat." He inclined his head toward them. "Excuse me while I make the arrangements."

As soon as he'd gone, Blythe leaned into Tess. "How's it going?"

"I'm having a delightful time."

"That's all?"

"What else is there?"

Blythe shook her head. "You and Alec are a perfect pair. You never tell anyone anything."

"There's nothing to tell."

"Oh, I think there is."

"Why?"

"Body language. Yours. His. Yours and his together."

"Oh, Blythe."

"I watch people. I know things because of it."

Tess smiled at her.

"Don't look at me like that. I'm serious."

"I know you are. That's why I'm looking at you 'like that.'"

Alec returned with Olivia and Jenni. "Shall we go to the dining room?" He held out both of his arms. Tess took one, Blythe took the other and the girls followed behind.

Chapter Ten

Alec seated Tess at one end of the table with Blythe to her right and Olivia and Jenni next to each other on her left. Alec sat at the other end of the table, perhaps fifteen feet away, facing Tess.

Dinner was one delicious course after another with a different wine for each dish. Lobster bisque, a light salad, tournedos of beef, asparagus, potatoes au gratin and, of course, the lemon dessert that Mrs. Linde had prepared.

Jenni leaned toward Tess. "Why don't they just put everything on one plate and serve it? This takes forever."

"Think of it as a new experience. Have you finished your dessert?"

"Yes. May Olivia and I be excused?"

"Are you sure you don't want to stay for the dancing?"

"Positive. I've pretty much overloaded on grown-ups for one night."

"Olivia?" Tess asked.

"I'd like to leave, if that's all right."

"It's fine with me, but you should check with your father."

Olivia left her seat and took the long walk to her father. She whispered, he nodded, Olivia gave Jenni the high sign and the two girls left the dining room.

Alec rose. "I'd like to ask everyone to adjourn to the ballroom."

As the guests began leaving the dining room, Alec made his way to Tess and helped her from her chair. "Do you feel like dancing?" he asked, his mouth close to her ear.

"Yes."

"Good." With his arm at her waist, he guided her down the hall to a small ballroom with a beautiful chandelier hanging from the center of the ceiling. The parquet floor was polished so brightly that it shone.

There was a four-piece orchestra at one end playing a waltz. No one danced until Alec turned Tess into his arms and began circling the floor.

Alec looked down at her with a smile. "You've waltzed before."

"Believe it or not, I learned in school. I feel as though I should be wearing a ball gown."

"You look beautiful just as you are."

"Even without the spandex?"

"I beg your pardon?"

"Never mind," she said with a smile. "It's just something Jenni said to me earlier."

The music slowed and so did they. Alec's hand, low on her back, pressed her body into his as they moved rhythmically in mirrored unison. They fit together so well.

Tess closed her eyes and put her head on his shoulder. Alec rested his cheek on her hair. "You smell wonderful. You always do."

He did, too, though she didn't say it.

That song finished and another began, this one also slow. Tess tilted her head back to look at Alec. She wanted to say something to him, but forgot what it was.

Alec stopped dancing. The two of them were just standing in the middle of the floor while other couples danced around them. To her surprise, he lowered his mouth to hers in a kiss that was achingly tender.

And then they danced again.

For Tess, there was no one else in the room.

Trilling danced by with Diane every few minutes, but Tess didn't notice. And Diane, for her part, seemed content to ignore the two of them.

Blythe danced, watched and smiled, convinced she saw things no one else did.

As couples began to filter out, Alec took Tess by the hand and they walked to the front door to say goodbye together. The last three to leave were predictably Trilling, Blythe and Diane. Trilling kissed Tess on both cheeks. "You were the perfect hostess this evening."

"I appreciate the compliment, but all I did was show up. Mrs. Linde did most of the work and your sister checked things out to make sure they were done right." She looked over her shoulder at Blythe. "Thanks again."

"Anytime."

Diane kissed Tess's cheek and said nothing.

Then she kissed Alec's cheek for real and whispered something in his ear.

He nodded. "What time tomorrow are you leaving?"

"One o'clock."

"I'll stop over before you go."

It shouldn't have bothered Tess and she knew it, but it did. When the door had closed behind the trio, she turned to go upstairs.

"Tess?"

She turned back.

"You did a beautiful job of pretending this evening. There may have been rumors about us before, but I'm sure everyone who was here tonight is convinced that our marriage is real."

"That's good, I guess."

"Very good."

"I'm glad it went well," she said sincerely. "See you to-morrow."

"Good night, Tess."

When she went upstairs, she checked on the girls. They were sound asleep.

When Tess got to her own room, she slipped out of her clothes, draped them over the back of a chair and put on her flowing cotton nightgown and robe. Then she pulled a chair close to the lighted fireplace, curled up in it with a book and started to read. She could get lost in books. They kept her from thinking too much.

As time passed, Tess grew deliciously drowsy. She let the book slide to the floor and settled herself more deeply into the chair.

"Tess!"

Jenni was shaking her shoulder.

Tess opened her eyes and blinked to focus. "What? What's wrong?"

"One of the kittens must have followed us from the barn. It's outside somewhere. We can hear it."

Tess left the warm comfort of her chair and opened the balcony door. The kitten's pathetic and frightened little mews drifted through the night air. She moved closer to the balcony railing and tried to see where the kitten was, but it was too dark. It sounded nearby, though, perhaps in a tree.

"Olivia," Tess said as she went back into her room and put on her slippers, "do you know if Mrs. Linde has a place where she keeps flashlights?"

"A cabinet in the pantry."

"Good. Get one and bring it to me outside without disturbing anyone."

"All right." She turned and ran out of the room.

"What are you going to do?" Jenni asked, following Tess as she hurried into the hallway, down the stairs and out the door.

"The first thing we need to do is figure out exactly where it is and then see about getting it down."

As they made their way around the side of the house, they could hear the mewing again.

Tess stopped under a tree near the balcony and looked up. "Do you see it?" Jenni asked, squinting as she tried to pick out the tiny animal.

"No."

"If it's one from the barn it's really small," Jenni said, near tears.

"We'll find it," Tess said as she squeezed her arm. "Don't worry."

"I hope it's all right." She moved away from Tess and started looking up at another tree. "Where are you, baby?"

The kitten, hearing voices, started mewing nonstop, allowing Tess to zero in on it. "It's here," Tess called to Jenni.

Jenni ran to her. "Where?"

"Up this tree. Listen."

The kitten was obviously crying for help. And it was just as obviously very high in the tree.

Olivia came running back with the flashlight. She handed it to Tess, and Tess trained the beam in the direction of the cry. The kitten, one of the tiniest, scrawniest little creatures Tess had ever seen, was more than halfway up the old tree, clinging to a limb with all four paws, too terrified to move.

Olivia gasped. "We have to get it down! It's going to fall."

Climbing had never been one of Tess's favorite things, but she could do it when she had to. Swallowing her fear of heights, she handed the flashlight back to Olivia. "Jenni, give me a leg up."

Jenni locked her fingers and made a step.

"All right," Tess said. "On the count of three I'm going to put my foot in your hands, and you give me whatever boost you can to that first limb."

"Gotcha."

"One, two, threeee!" Jenni was strong and got Tess up that extra twelve inches she needed to reach the limb. Swinging herself up, Tess made it to a sitting position on that limb and then stood. Hiking up her long nightgown, she moved to the next limb. "Olivia," she called down, "train the light on the kitten for a second and then bring it slowly down to where I'm standing so I can see where the best limbs are."

Olivia did as she was asked.

Tess sighed inwardly. It was a long way to the kitten, and some of the limbs didn't look very sturdy.

The kitten looked down at her and mewed. "It's all right, sweetheart," she said soothingly. "Don't be afraid. We'll get you down and take you back to your mother."

Tess made her way up one limb at a time, trying not to look down.

"I'm scared," Olivia whispered to Jenni. "What if she falls?"

"I know. Go get your dad."

Olivia handed her the flashlight and ran back to the house. If Tess had been looking through the living room windows, she would have seen Olivia walk up to her father and whisper something in his ear.

"I've almost got it," Tess said as she stood on her toes and stretched to reach the kitten.

"Be careful!" Jenni yelled.

"I am. Don't worry." The kitten was just out of reach. Tess moved up the limb in an attempt to gain a little more height, stretched a little farther and ran her hand down the limb above her until she felt the furry little thing. Wrapping her hand around its skinny body, she lifted it from the limb and lowered it to her chest. "I've got it!" she called down to Jenni.

"Is it all right?"

"Just scared." Even as she said it, the kitten dug its claws into her shoulder. "Oh, ow!"

"What's wrong?"

"Nothing. Don't worry about it. Can you move the flashlight beam over the tree? I need to see my way down."

Jenni did as she was asked.

"This is going to be a problem."

"Why?"

"Coming up I just had myself to worry about. Getting back down holding a kitten is something else again."

And she was shivering from the cold.

But she had to get down. Talking soothingly to the kitten, she nuzzled it to get it to relax and, holding it close to her breast with one hand, she began lowering herself to the next limb while balancing herself with the other.

It didn't feel right. She was afraid she was going to fall, so she stopped and leaned against the trunk of the tree.

"What is it?" Jenni asked.

"I just need to regroup for a minute." She suddenly realized she hadn't heard Olivia's voice for several minutes. "Where's Olivia?"

"She went to get help."

"Oh, good. I think I could use some." Of course, Tess was thinking of Mr. Linde. When she heard Alec's voice, she grimaced.

"Stay where you are," he called up to her. "I'll come up and get you."

Tess didn't say anything. What could she say? A pig and a kitten, all in one day. One minute she was covered with mud and chasing a piglet, and another she was up a tree in her nightgown rescuing a kitten.

Sigh.

Jenni trained the beam of the flashlight on the tree so Tess could see him coming, in his black suit, limb by limb. When he was just beneath her, he held out his hand. "Give me the kitten."

She gave the kitten a little kiss on the nose and then handed it down to Alec. He slipped it gently into his pocket and then reached up for Tess. "Back down. I'll make sure you don't fall."

"Now that you have the kitten, I can get myself down."

"Stop being so proud and accept my help."

Feeling more grateful than she cared to admit, Tess backed down onto the limb in front of him. Alec's arm came around her waist and held her in place against him. "See?" he said against her ear. "That wasn't so difficult."

She had to admit that she felt a lot more secure. They were still a long way from the ground.

"I'll go down to the next limb and then you follow and we'll do that the rest of the way down."

"All right," Tess said quietly.

It seemed like it took forever, but she was finally on the last limb. Alec jumped to the ground, took the kitten from his pocket and handed it to Olivia. Then he held his arms up to Tess. "Jump."

She did, and he caught her and lowered her gently to the ground.

"Thank you," she said without looking at him.

His hands were still at her waist. "You're welcome."

Tess took a step back, out of his reach. His words congratulating her for a fine acting job were still fresh in her mind. Well, they didn't have to act for the girls.

Alec reluctantly released her and turned to his daughter. "Give me the kitten, Olivia."

She handed it to him and Alec checked it over with gentle fingers in the beam of the flashlight. "This little fellow's all right. He's just cold and hungry. Do you know where he belongs?"

"His mother's at the stables."

"Make sure he gets back there right away. He's too little to be wandering around at night like this."

"Jenni and I will take him," Olivia said.

As the girls walked across the lawn cuddling the kitten, Tess brushed off her nightgown. Anything to keep from looking at him.

Alec took off his suit coat and wrapped it around Tess's shoulders. His eyes lingered on hers. "Go stand in front of your fire. You're freezing."

Tess took a shaky breath and slowly let it out. "I will."

His fingers brushed her cheek. "Good night, Tess."

Clutching the jacket, Tess walked quickly into the house. When she got to her room, she stood in front of the fire, still wrapped in his coat.

And still trembling.

It was several minutes before the warmth began seeping into her. Tess leaned her head to one side and brushed her cheek against the material of his jacket. It carried his scent—clean and masculine. She took a deep breath and slowly exhaled.

Still hugging the jacket to her, Tess sank into a chair.

Jenni knocked on the door and poked her head around the corner. "We got the kitten back to its mother."

"Good," Tess said with a smile. "I imagine there was quite a reunion."

"You can say that again. The mother licked it so hard she knocked it off its feet."

"It didn't follow you again, did it?"

"No. We made sure. I think the little guy learned his lesson."

"I hope so. If he gets stuck in another tree, he's on his own."

Jenni just smiled, knowing better. "Olivia and I are going back to bed."

"All right. Good night, sweetheart."

"'Night."

But Jenni didn't go to her room. She went to Olivia's. "Any other ideas on how we're going to get those two together?" she asked as she flopped on the bed.

"I thought having him help her get out of that tree would do it."

"Nope. Tess is in her room all alone."

"I can't think of anything else."

"Me, either. At least nothing out of the ordinary. And I'm beginning to think it's going to take something very out of the ordinary to get them together."

"Grown-ups can be so blind sometimes."

"Most of the time."

"They're perfect for each other."

"Maybe if we got them away from here..." said Jenni.

"That's easier said than done."

They both fell deeply into thought.

"What if we get them to take us on some kind of Christmas vacation?" suggested Jenni.

"That's still a long way off."

"Not that long."

Again silence fell between them.

"Do you think your father would rather be married to that Diane woman?"

"I don't know."

"He doesn't seem to be in love with her. I watched him tonight."

"Love doesn't have anything to do with it."

"Come again?"

"People who are in my father's station in life marry because they find someone whose lineage is at least as impressive as their own."

"That's awful."

Olivia shrugged. "Awful or not, that's the way it is and has been for centuries."

"That's weird. Was your dad in love with your mom?"

"No."

"How do you know?"

"I overheard Mrs. Linde say that it was his duty to marry Mother, and he did it. My father always does his duty."

"You overhear her a lot."

"She *talks* a lot."

Jenni smiled. "I know. That's what I like about her."

Olivia climbed under her covers. "I'm too tired to think anymore tonight. Let's figure something out tomorrow."

"Okay. I'm tired, too. 'Night, Olivia." Jenni turned out the lights and went to her own room.

Tess grew drowsy as she sat in front of the fire wrapped in Alec's coat. She was so comfortable that she hated to go to bed, but it was late. Very late.

Rising from the chair, she slipped the coat from her shoulders and started to drape it across the foot of her bed, then changed her mind. Alec was still downstairs. Otherwise she would have heard him go to his room. She would return the jacket.

Walking along the balcony, she stopped in front of his doors and saw in the firelight that his bed was still made. She entered without knocking and laid the coat across a chair.

"Hello, Tess."

She spun around with a gasp. Alec stood in front of the fireplace watching the glowing embers, his arm resting on the mantel.

"I'm sorry. I didn't know you were here," Tess said.

"And if you'd known?" he asked quietly.

"I wouldn't have come."

He didn't have to ask why.

She turned to leave.

"Don't go, Tess."

She paused before turning back to him.

"There's no need for you to be concerned. I won't do anything you don't want me to do. I just don't feel like being alone."

Tess stood with her hands tightly gripping the back of a chair.

"Sit down," he said, inclining his head toward the chair, "I won't bite you."

Tess moved to the front of the chair and sat. The folds of her nightgown spilled around her.

"You did something of a quick change on me earlier."

"I don't know what you mean."

"We were getting along so well at the party, and then you just changed back to the way you were before."

"With everyone gone, I didn't think we needed to keep up the pretense."

"Was it a pretense?"

"You knew that. You even told me what a good job I'd done."

Something flickered behind his eyes. "I see."

Tess busily rearranged the folds of her nightgown.

Alec pulled another chair in front of Tess and sat down facing her. Leaning forward, he took her hands in his and gazed at them. "Our—relationship—has gotten a lot more complicated than either of us intended."

"Yes, it has."

"The question is, what are we going to do about it?"

"What are the options?"

"To avoid each other."

"Or?"

"To take each day as it comes without connecting it to the one before or to the one after."

"I'm not quite following you."

"I would like to know that if we make love again it will mean nothing beyond the pleasure of the moment. We're both adults, living under the same roof and very attracted to one another. It happened once and it will probably happen again. But that shouldn't affect our basic relationship, which for the most part is adversarial. I'm not going to forget who your father was and what he did to my family and to me. And if the two of us have the occasional companionable day, such as today, it changes nothing."

"I understand. And I'm relieved, frankly. You're exactly the sort of man I could never fall in love with."

"You can't say something like that and not give your reasons. You have mine."

Tess looked at their twined fingers. "When, and if, I ever fall in love, it's going to be with a man who wants me and only me. I want to believe absolutely in his fidelity. I will not be put in the same miserable position as my mother.''

''What if you fall in love with someone who isn't like that?''

''I won't.''

''How can you be so sure?''

''I won't allow it.''

''Do you think you can control love?''

''You do.''

''I don't control it. I just don't feel it.''

''When all is said and done, I guess that's the same thing, isn't it?''

''You're not like me, Tess. You're full of love. I see it in your eyes every time you look at Jenni—and even my daughter.''

''That's different.''

''Love is love. Either you can control it or not. I don't think you can.''

There was a knock on the door.

Alec didn't respond right away.

The knock came again, louder and more insistent.

''Yes?'' he said.

''It's Linde, sir. There's a telephone call for you.''

''Have whoever it is call back at a decent hour.''

''It's Mrs. Guest, sir.''

Alec sighed. ''All right, Linde. I'll take it in the library. Go back to bed.''

''Yes, sir.''

They could hear him moving off down the hall.

''Stay here,'' Alec whispered to Tess.

She didn't say anything.

When he'd gone, she sat staring into the fire, thinking about what he'd said.

Could she control who she loved and who she didn't? Could she separate making love from being in love?

She wasn't as sure as she'd led Alec to believe.

And so she rose from the chair and left his bedroom.

Chapter Eleven

Tess, wrapped in a warm sweater, sat on the lake bank in her favorite spot, a sketch pad open on her lap. The weeks were fading into each other, and it was getting colder and colder. Dropping her pencil onto the grass beside her, Tess blew on her fingers to warm them and pulled the sleeve of her sweater over her hand. She and Blythe had been meeting here several days a week and going for a brisk hour-long walk. Tess had arrived early today so she could do a little sketching. She loved her art, but just hadn't had the time to work on it since coming to England.

When she spotted Blythe coming toward her, she set her sketch pad on a rock and went to meet her.

"Am I late?" asked Blythe, shoving her huge, dark glasses farther up the bridge of her nose.

"No. I'm early."

They headed around the lake, following their usual path. Blythe was a little slower than normal. Tess glanced at her. "Are you all right?"

She pushed her glasses up again. "I had a late night."

"Party?"

"Yes. I had a few friends up from London. I hope you're not offended that I didn't invite you and Alec."

"Don't ever worry about that. I want as few social ventures with him as possible."

"Back to that again, eh? I thought the two of you were getting along rather well."

"We were. Are. Everything is very awkward."

"I see," said Blythe, smiling.

"What do you see?"

"Tess, the man is gorgeous."

"Believe me, I'm aware of that."

"You're attracted to him, and he's attracted to you...."

"I'm aware of that also."

"I don't know why you don't just give in to it. You're married, for heaven's sake."

Tess started to tell Blythe that she already had once, but couldn't bring herself to reveal that bit of information. What had happened was between Alec and herself.

Blythe shook her head. "I don't understand why people take this sex thing so seriously. It's just not that big a deal."

"You don't mean that and you know it."

"But I do mean it, Tess. I do. That's not to say I live my life by those words, but I truly don't understand why, in this supposedly enlightened era of equality between men and women, casual sex still has to be taboo."

"For one thing, it's dangerous."

"Not if you take precautions."

"And for another, regardless of equality, there is nothing more intimate you can share with another person. You're giving away a part of yourself and accepting a part of him in return. It shouldn't be done lightly."

"I suppose you're right." She waved her hand in the air. "Oh, I don't suppose it at all. I know it. But most men don't think that way."

Tess nodded.

"It's so often a game."

"Which I don't want to play."

"Of course," said Blythe thoughtfully, "not all men are jerks."

"Name one."

"Alec."

"Oh, please . . ."

"I mean it. I believe that when and if Alec ever truly falls in love, there will never be another woman for him."

"What makes you think that?"

"Because betrayal isn't in his nature. Just as he would never turn on a friend—and believe me, he's had more than ample reasons to write Trilling off—he would never betray the woman he loves."

"I think you're naive."

Blythe laughed. "Goodness, no one has said that about me for years."

But Tess was serious. "My stepmother said something to me after my father's funeral that's stuck with me. She said that if a woman offers a man—let's say *pleasure*—he'll turn on everyone he loves. My father certainly did."

"I'm not going to argue about men being weak when it comes to their libidos. And I'm not saying that once he's in love, Alec won't be physically attracted to other women. What I'm saying is that, attracted or not, he won't act on his impulses. And I say this not out of any naïveté, but out of a personal knowledge of his basic character."

"Well, who Alec eventually falls in love with isn't any of my concern."

"Even if that someone is you?"

This time it was Tess's turn to laugh.

"What's so funny?"

"Alec might be attracted to me, but that's where his interest begins and ends."

"You sound very sure."

"Let's talk facts."

"Go ahead."

"Alec has nothing but contempt for my father, which has to color his feelings about me."

"I would think so."

"He believes that I'm partly responsible for this marriage."

"You agreed to it, didn't you?"

"Well, yes."

"Then you are. But so is he. Any other facts?"

"He spends as much time in London as he does here, clearly in an attempt to stay away from me."

"And you think that stems from his dislike of you?"

"Of course."

"Has it occurred to you that what he's trying to do is put distance between the two of you because he's afraid of becoming too involved?"

"No."

"Well, it's occurred to me. It's occurred to Trilling. Why hasn't it occurred to you?"

"Because Alec isn't the kind of man who runs from his problems."

Blythe stopped walking and turned to face Tess. "He's not superhuman. Maybe he's afraid of what's going on. Maybe he's confused. Maybe he thinks that by not being around you he can keep himself from falling in love. You don't know what he's feeling."

"Blythe, why are you so intent on getting the two of us together?"

She turned to look at the lake. "I love him," she said simply. "He's been like a brother to me—more so than Trilling. I've had a lot of ups and downs in my life. He's been there to rejoice with me, and he's been there to catch me when I'm falling. I've never ever seen him look at another woman the way he looks at you. He's not even aware that he does it. If you are what's going to allow him to be happy at last, then I want him to have you." She turned to Tess with a half smile. "And I confess I've grown very fond of you. I can't think of anyone I'd rather see Alec with. Besides, if you leave at the end of your year of marriage, who am I going to walk with?''

Tess was genuinely touched. But... ''What about Diane?''

''Trilling and I tolerate her occasional presence in our home as a favor to Alec, nothing more. She's never been on my list of favorite people.''

She slipped her arm through Tess's, and the two women started walking back toward the house. ''I hope I've given you some food for thought.''

''You have. But it isn't going to change anything. I don't want to fall in love.''

''You say that like you have a choice.''

''I do.''

Blythe glanced sideways at her. ''You really believe that, don't you?''

''With every fiber of my being.''

''Well, just remember that I'll be there for you when you discover there is no such thing as 'choice' when it comes to love.''

Tess grew thoughtful. ''This is interesting.''

''What is?''

''I had a conversation almost like this with Alec. I was more or less taking your position.''

''So you at one time agreed with me?''

''I'm not saying that. I was being—'' she searched for the words ''—a devil's advocate.''

''Right.'' Blythe clearly didn't believe a word of it.

As they approached the house, Blythe inclined her head toward the driveway. ''Look who's home.''

Alec's car was there.

She looked closely at Tess's face but her expression told her nothing.

When they got to the drive, Blythe dug in her pocket for her car keys. ''Tell Alec hello for me.''

''I will.''

''See you tomorrow, same time.''

Tess went into the house and started up the staircase.

Alec walked into the foyer and saw her. For a moment he said nothing. He just watched. He'd been deliberately staying away for longer and longer periods of time. It was getting so he couldn't be in the same house with her. He couldn't see her without wanting to make love to her. It wasn't really love, of course. It was sex. His eyes traveled down her body. He loved the fluid way she moved. "Tess?"

Tess stopped but didn't turn right away. She hadn't seen Alec for nearly two weeks. She would be pleasant, but not too pleasant. Taking a breath first, she turned with a smile that was more polite than friendly. "Welcome home."

"Thank you. Would you come into the library please? We need to discuss something."

She came back downstairs and followed Alec down the hall and into the library. Instead of sitting behind his desk, he sat in a chair and waved Tess onto the couch. "I need you to come to London tomorrow."

"Why?"

"We've been invited to dine at the home of the president of a company that's very important to my company."

"Can't you go alone?"

"No. He knows I'm married now and wants to meet you."

She still hesitated.

"It's important, Tess, or I wouldn't ask you."

"All right."

"And one more thing. We're expected to spend the night as their guests. It's a courtesy on their part, so that we don't have to make the trip back to the country late at night or stay in a hotel."

"I'd rather stay in a hotel."

"It's not an option."

"Why not?"

"Because it would be rude."

Tess didn't say anything.

"I've turned down several other invitations. I couldn't turn down this one."

"I know. It's all right." Then she asked the really important question. "What should I wear?"

A corner of Alec's mouth lifted. "The black dress you had on for the party here will do nicely."

"Good. When do we leave?"

"I'm going back tonight. You'll catch the train tomorrow afternoon. I'll meet you at the station."

"What about the girls?"

"They'll be fine here with the Lindes." He leaned back in his chair. "How have you been?"

Tess shifted her weight. She was usually so at ease in the company of others. Not with Alec, though. "Fine. Busy."

"And Olivia and Jenni?"

"I had their reports forwarded to you."

"I didn't mean their reports. I mean, how are they?"

"Oh, I'm sorry. I misunderstood. They're both fine."

"Good."

Tess stopped fidgeting and looked directly at Alec. "I wish you'd try to spend more time with Olivia."

"I've had obligations..."

"I know. What you need to remember is that Olivia is one of your obligations. How she's treated by you now, at this time in her life, will affect her forever. She needs to know you love her."

"Don't start this again, Tess."

"I have to."

"No you don't. My relationship with my daughter has nothing to do with you."

"Yes it does. I've grown to love her. I don't want her to go through the same kind of pain I went through because of my father."

"Olivia isn't you, and I'm not your father."

"Alec, please—"

He stood up. "That's enough. I don't want to hear another word on this subject."

Tess stood also. "Why are you being so stubborn?"

"No more!" He strode angrily out of the library.

"Ohh!" Tess picked up a pillow from the couch and slammed it onto the floor.

Jenni poked her head around the corner. "Tess?"

She took a couple of deep breaths to calm herself. "What is it, Jenni?"

"I found this by the lake," she said as she came farther into the room carrying Tess's sketch pad.

"Thank you. I forgot all about it."

"What were you and Olivia's dad fighting about?"

"We weren't fighting. We had a simple difference of opinion."

Jenni picked up the pillow and put it back on the couch. Tess cleared her throat. "Where's Olivia?"

"In the kitchen."

The front door slammed. A minute later there was the sound of a car door closing and the roar of an engine that grew gradually more distant until there was silence.

Jenni looked at Tess and shook her head. She'd just about given up on getting her sister and Olivia's dad together for real. Tess wouldn't cooperate. And Mr. Devereaux wasn't any better. She handed her sister the sketch pad. "Olivia and I are going to watch TV for a while. And yes, our homework *is* finished."

Tess felt terrible. She didn't want Jenni to be around fighting. "I'm sorry, Jen."

"Can't you just try to get along with him?"

"I do try, but I'll make more of an effort."

"We still have eight months to go."

"I know."

Jenni looked at her for a long moment. "Tess, we could have a real family here."

"Oh, Jenni, no. Don't even think that. I told you the truth about this from the beginning."

"Things could change."

"No." Tess wasn't going to hold out any false hope.

Jenni started to leave.

"Wait a minute."

She turned back.

"I have to go to London tomorrow night. I won't be back until the next day."

"What do you have to go there for?"

"A dinner with Olivia's father."

She brightened. "Oh?"

"It's a business dinner."

Jenni didn't care. It was better than nothing. Feeling considerably cheerier, she went to find Olivia. If Tess was going to be gone overnight it would give Olivia and her some time to work on cleaning up one of the third floor rooms for Tess to use as an art studio. Tess was really going to be surprised.

Tess stared out the window of the train, watching as the landscape went from pristine countryside to increasingly dingy cityscapes with the rusting hulks of old railway cars littering unused tracks.

When they finally pulled into the station after a three-hour ride, Tess took her overnight bag from an overhead rack and followed a small group of passengers down the aisle and out the door. Alec true to his word, was waiting for her.

"Hello, Tess." His fingers brushed hers as she took the bag from her hand. "I wasn't sure you'd come."

"I told you I would."

They fell into step as they walked through the station and out the door to a waiting car. Alec signaled the driver to stay behind the wheel as he opened the door for Tess himself and climbed in after her. "We're going straight to our hosts' home. You'll have some time to freshen up before dinner."

Their shoulders touched as they sat beside each other. Tess moved just far enough away so that there was no contact. She tried to be inconspicuous about it, but Alec noticed. It did no good, anyway. Every time the limo went around a corner either she leaned into Alec or he leaned into her. She could have moved farther away, but chose not to. She didn't want Alec to know how he affected her.

It was a silent ride through the streets of London. Neither Alec nor Tess attempted to make small talk.

The driver parked in front of a large row house that reminded Tess of Boston. He got out and opened the door for them. Alec got out on the same side as Tess and reached back in for Tess's overnight bag.

As they walked up the steps of the row house, the door was opened by a butler. "Good afternoon, sir. Madame. We've been expecting you." He took the bag from Alec. "Follow me, please."

They stepped into a small elevator off the foyer with scissored wrought iron doors, went up three floors, stepped into another foyer and were taken to a room just down the hall.

As Tess looked around the cosy room, she set her purse on a dresser.

"I trust you'll find these accommodations satisfactory. If you need anything, pick up the receiver of the bedside telephone and press four. Dinner will begin in approximately an hour."

"Thank you."

The butler left, closing the door behind him.

There was one bed. Tess looked at it and then at Alec. "So where will you be sleeping?"

He looked around the room. "The chair, I guess."

Tess lifted her overnight bag onto the bed and began taking out her things.

Alec watched her. His wife.

The fact that he was married to Tess was occurring to him more and more frequently.

She finished putting her things away, set the bag in the bottom of an armoire then turned to Alec. "What now?"

"We dress for dinner." He took off his jacket and tie and started unbuttoning his shirt. "I'm going to shower first."

Tess abruptly turned away from Alec while he finished undressing and didn't turn back until she heard him close the bathroom door. Working quickly, she stripped out of her clothes and dressed as quickly as she could. By the time she heard the shower shut off, she was finished with everything but her hair and jewelry.

Alec came out of the bathroom, a towel wrapped around his waist. A smile curved his mouth when he saw what Tess had done. "There's no need to be modest. There isn't an inch of you with which I'm not familiar."

Tess could feel her cheeks flush. But for all of her embarrassment, she couldn't prevent her eyes from traveling down the length of his strong body.

She turned away.

Alec went about getting dressed. Tess listened to his movements as she brushed her hair.

"You don't have to hide your head any longer," he said after a few minutes.

"I wasn't hiding. I was doing my hair."

Alec fastened the studs in the front of his tuxedo shirt. "How are you with bow ties?"

"I'm good."

He draped the tie around his neck. "Help me out."

Tess stood in front of him. Reaching around his neck, she tucked the black silk under his collar.

"Don't stare," she said without looking at him as she adjusted the ends of the tie.

"Does it bother you when I look at you?"

"When you look at me in a certain way."

"What would that be?"

She finished tying and adjusted the loops, then rested her hands flat on his chest. "In a way that makes me aware of what happened between us."

He touched her cheek.

Tess stepped back. "I think it's time to go downstairs."

Alec lifted his tuxedo jacket from the back of a chair, while Tess tried to fasten her pearls. He watched her as he shot his sleeves and adjusted his cuffs, then came up behind her, brushed her hands aside and fastened the necklace for her.

Tess closed her eyes as his fingers touched the back of her neck. When she opened them, she found herself gazing into Alec's eyes reflected in the mirror in front of her. "You look lovely," he said.

"Thank you." She touched her dress. "Little did I know when I bought this three years ago that it would be so useful."

Alec twined his fingers through hers and tugged her hand. "Come on. Put on your newlywed persona."

They took the elevator downstairs where dinner guests were already arriving. Still holding hands, Alec took Tess to their host and hostess. "Dominick and Clara Judson, I'd like you to meet my wife, Tess."

Tess charmed them with her smile as she shook their hands. "It's so kind of you to invite us for the evening."

The man, a fellow of generous proportions, squeezed her hand. "It's a pleasure to meet you. Alec told us you were a beauty and indeed, you are."

"Thank you."

Alec put his arm around Tess's waist and drew her close to his side. "I think I'll take Tess around and introduce her."

"That's a good idea. I've invited the heads of each of the corporations interested in this joint venture, along with their wives."

As they crossed the room, Tess leaned into Alec. "What kind of joint venture?"

"It's not anything that would interest you."

"Try me."

He looked down at her with a half smile. "Do you really want to know or are you simply being polite?"

"I'm already being polite, and I really want to know."

"Without going into great detail, it has to do with bringing together several corporations, all of which do one thing very well with regard to computers, chips, software, video game creation, etcetera, and creating a package under one label that is more innovative than anything else on the market.''

''I didn't know you had an interest in computers. You don't even own one.''

''Yes I do. I just don't have one at home. Until this year I didn't spend enough time there to bother with it. And I'm not particularly interested in computers. I happen to own a company that produces a chip that's then sold to other companies for insertion into their computers. My job, as I see it, is to find markets for the product. That's what we're doing here tonight. The more business I drum up, the more people I employ.''

''I see.''

He took her around the room, keeping her close to his side, and introduced her to everyone there.

Tess enjoyed herself. She had to admit she liked being with Alec like this. There was no tension, no arguing. She could relax and allow herself to enjoy his company, admire his ability to charm, and revel in his attention to her.

As they sat at dinner, Tess watched Alec, her eyes thoughtful. He was the most interesting man she'd ever met. If she could set aside all the mess that was between them— if she could let herself trust him . . .

Alec chose that moment to glance across the table at Tess. His smile faded as he looked into her eyes. He wanted to pick her up bodily, carry her upstairs and make love to her all night. He hardly knew there was anyone else around.

They sat like that for a long time, looking at each other. There wasn't a person at the table who wasn't aware that something was going on. They could feel the electricity snapping between the two of them.

Then the woman beside Alec leaned toward him and spoke. He was startled out of his reverie and had to ask her to repeat what she'd said.

Tess folded her hands in her lap and stared at her plate. Alec was the only person in the world who could make her tremble with a look.

It took her a moment, but she pulled herself together and managed to make small talk with the men seated on either side of her. The dinner went on until after ten. Then they adjourned to a living room for drinks and coffee. Alec sat on a couch beside Tess, his arm around her shoulders. His fingers unconsciously caressed her bare arm.

It made her entire body tingle.

After a while people started to leave. There were several couples who, like Alec and Tess, had been invited to stay at the home. After taking leave of their hosts, the two of them rode the elevator to the third floor in silence, not touching.

When they got to their room, Alec closed the door and turned to Tess. Without warning, he pulled her into his arms and kissed her long and hard. Tess's body strained against his. She couldn't get close enough. She groaned against his mouth as his hand traveled down her back to cup her rear and press her even closer.

Suddenly he pushed her away. "God," he said, breathing hard as he dragged his fingers through his hair.

Tess felt as out of breath as she did when she ran. She stood in the middle of the room staring at Alec, saying nothing.

He shook his head. "I've got to get out of here." Without another word, he walked out the door and slammed it behind him.

Tess sank onto the edge of the bed, her hand over her pounding heart. Intellectually she knew he'd done the right thing. But the part of her that wanted him so desperately she ached with it had nothing to do with her intellect.

Alec took a taxi to another house about ten miles away. He paid the driver and told him not to wait, then used his key to open the door.

Diane, still dressed for an evening of nightclubbing, walked into the hall and smiled when she saw him. "I was beginning to wonder if I was ever going to see you again."

They both went into the living room, where Alec poured himself a strong drink and sat on the couch. Diane poured herself one and sat beside him, snuggling against his shoulder.

He sat in silence, staring into the fire.

Diane had known Alec for years and had seen him in all of his moods. But not like this. Never like this.

She left his unresponsive shoulder and turned to look at him. "What is it?" she asked. "What's wrong?"

"Nothing. I just needed to get away."

"Away from what."

He didn't answer.

It didn't matter to Diane what had brought him. He hadn't come to her since his marriage.

She leaned forward and kissed the corners of his mouth. "Let me take your mind off whatever has you so angry," she whispered as she undid his bow tie with a single gentle tug. "You know I can."

Alec looked at Diane—really looked at her perhaps for the first time since he'd known her. He cared about her, about what happened to her. But he didn't love her. He didn't even want her anymore.

Diane moved closer, running her hands across the front of his shirt. She gently bit his earlobe and kissed her way down his jaw until her lips found his.

Alec kissed her back, but his heart wasn't in it. He pushed her away, picked up his drink and walked to the fireplace.

Diane watched him in surprise. "What's going on?"

He stared into the flames. "I shouldn't have come here."

"It's *your* house."

"I bought it in your name. It's yours." He took the key out of his pocket and put it on the mantel. "I won't be using it again."

"I don't understand..." But suddenly she did. "You've fallen in love with your wife, haven't you?"

"Don't be ridiculous."

"I'm not the one who's being ridiculous. Have you forgotten who this woman is? Have you forgotten what her father did to your family? How he forced this marriage on you?"

"I haven't forgotten anything."

"So what's going on? Have you decided to forgive her?"

"With Tess," he said quietly, "it's not a matter of deciding. Things just happen."

"Because she makes them. She has insinuated herself and her sister into your life. She's making herself indispensable to you and Olivia so that at the end of the twelve months you won't want the divorce. Marrying you is the most important thing she's ever done. Do you think she wants to see you and all you have slip through her fingers?"

"She's not like that."

"Oh, open your eyes, Alec. She's a woman, and I know women."

Alec set his glass on the mantel next to the key. "I'm sorry I bothered you, Diane. I'm going to leave and I won't be back. Do what you want with the house. I don't care. And if you ever need anything, I want you to call me." He walked to the door, but turned back as he opened it. "I'm sorry."

As soon as the door closed behind him, Diane picked up her glass and threw it as hard as she could into the fireplace. It shattered. The fire hissed as the liquid sprayed into the flames.

Alec, deep in thought, his hands jammed into the pockets of his trousers, walked all the way back to the Judsons' house. The door was locked so he rang the bell. A few minutes later the butler, dressed in a robe, answered the door.

"I'm sorry for waking you," said Alec.

"It's quite all right, sir."

Alec took the elevator to the third floor and quietly opened the door to his room.

It was a moment before his eyes could focus enough in the darkness to pick out Tess, asleep in bed. He carried a chair to the side of the bed and sat in it, his eyes on Tess. Diane's words kept ringing in his ears. *Had he fallen in love with his wife?*

She was constantly in his thoughts. It didn't matter where he was. He couldn't see her without wanting to touch her; make love to her.

He stayed away from home as much as possible because of her, and yet when he returned, it was her face he longed to see. Tess stirred and opened her eyes. "Hi," she said softly.

Alec leaned forward. "Hello. I'm sorry about running out on you earlier."

"Don't be. I'm actually glad you did. You saved us both some grief."

His gaze moved lingeringly over her face. "Go back to sleep."

"What about you?"

"I just want to sit here for a while."

"All right. Good night." Her voice was a sleepy whisper.

"Good night, Tess."

He leaned back in the chair, stretching his long legs out in front of him, his eyes still on Tess.

He was tired but he couldn't sleep.

Chapter Twelve

Tess came home from London alone, not sure what had happened. Alec had been different toward her than usual—at least for a few hours. But when it had come time for her to go, he seemed anxious to be rid of her.

Two weeks had passed since then. No one was more surprised than Tess when Alec opened the door to the schoolroom. Olivia beamed at him. "Hello, Father."

He went to his daughter and gave her an awkward kiss on top of her head. "Olivia."

"When did you get home?"

"A few minutes ago." He smiled at Jenni. "Hello."

She smiled back.

Then he focused on Tess. "I'd like to see you in the library for a moment."

"Of course." She looked at the girls. "Why don't you read the next chapter, and we can talk about it when I get back."

As soon as Tess was out of the room, the two girls shot out of their seats in hot and discreet pursuit.

Tess closed the library doors behind her without realizing that Jenni's ear was pressed against it a few moments later.

"What do you hear?" whispered Olivia.

Jenni waved her hand impatiently. "Shh."

Olivia managed to wait for a minute before she tugged again. "What's going on?"

"I don't know. Their voices fade in and out."

Olivia waited impatiently again. "Anything yet?"

Jenni listened intently, then shook her head. "They're talking, but I can't hear what they're saying."

Alec was seated at his desk. Tess sat across from him, her hands folded in her lap.

"I want to talk to you about going on a Christmas vacation with the girls."

"To where?"

"Switzerland for skiing. I've been thinking about what you said, about my spending more time with Olivia, and this would be a good opportunity for that."

"Perhaps you should just take Olivia and leave Jenni and me here."

"Olivia wouldn't have any fun without Jenni. And neither of them will have any fun without you."

"Can you hear them now?" Olivia asked.

"Your dad just said something about a vacation in Switzerland."

Olivia started to squeal, but clamped her hand over her mouth before it could get out.

"What about you? Do you want us to go?" asked Tess.

"I want Olivia to have a nice holiday."

"I see."

"Trilling and Blythe are going as well. That might make it more fun for you."

"May I think about it?"

"Of course."

Tess rose. "I should be getting back to the girls."

Alec rose also. "Tess, this is off the subject, but I want to thank you for what you did in London. You were a big hit with both of the Judsons."

"You're welcome. Is there anything else?"

"No. That's all."

Tess hated how cold she sounded, but it was her only defense against him. She knew he'd been to see his mistress the night she'd spent in London. She had smelled Diane's perfume on his tuxedo jacket the next morning. What he chose to do, and with whom, was none of her business.

And yet it hurt her.

She left the library without looking back and headed upstairs to the schoolroom.

The girls made it into their seats just ahead of her and were desperately trying to look engrossed in their texts and not out of breath when Tess walked in. *Casual* was the word of the moment.

Too casual. Tess looked at both of them suspiciously. "What's going on?"

Jenni was wide-eyed innocence. "Not a thing."

"What did my father want?" asked Olivia, trying to deflect attention from her friend.

"He wants to take a Christmas vacation in Switzerland with all of us."

"We're going, aren't we?" asked Jenni.

"I haven't decided yet."

"What's to decide? I love to ski. You love to ski. We're invited. Just say yes."

"Please," pleaded Olivia.

"Jenni, something you need to consider is that you've outgrown all of your ski clothes and even your boots."

"My father can buy her whatever she needs," Olivia said eagerly.

"Thank you, Olivia, but that wouldn't be at all appropriate."

Tess truly didn't mind if Jenni went. The problem was finding the money to pay for it. Tess had used most of what little money she had to pay the property taxes on the house her father had left her. Unless she could find another source of income, Jenni couldn't go. "Give me some time to see what can be done." She looked at her watch. "You two are in overtime. School's out."

They left, heads together, talking quietly. Tess went straight to her room and took the pearl necklace her mother had given her out of the jewelry box. She held it draped over her fingers, liking its coolness against her skin. The clasp was beautiful; gold set with tiny diamonds and pearls. Even now, all these years later, Tess could see her mother wearing it. Whenever she was nearly ready to leave for the evening, she would sit in front of her dressing table, lift her hair out of the way and ask Tess to fasten the pearls around her slender neck.

Sometimes they'd reverse the process. Her mother would help Tess dress in clothes that were far to large for her child's body. She'd let Tess sit at the dressing table while she knelt in front of her and applied makeup on Tess's baby-soft cheeks with a light hand. The finishing touch was always the pearl necklace. Her mother would stand behind her to fasten the clasp, then lean down and kiss Tess on her cheek. "I may be your mother," she would always say to Tess's delight, "but I still think you're the most beautiful little girl in the world. And someday this necklace will be yours. I hope you'll think of me when you wear it and remember how much I love you."

And Tess did. Now she knew that even as her mother had said those words to her, she was dying. And though the end didn't come until years later, Tess often wondered whether her mother sensed that there was something wrong; that she wouldn't be there to see her daughter grow up.

Tess rubbed her thumb over the clasp. She hated to give up the necklace. Her stepmother had, over the years, destroyed, sold or given away nearly everything that had anything to do with her mother. This necklace and a few other pieces that Tess was saving for Jenni were all that were left.

But, when all was said and done, it was just a necklace. And if selling the necklace meant giving Jenni a chance to spend Christmas with her best friend without making Tess beholden to Alec Devereaux in any way, then that's what Tess would use it for. She'd still have her memories; she didn't need a necklace for that.

The problem was knowing where to take it. Something told her that Trilling DeVeere would know where to sell jewelry. And she was sure he'd be discreet.

Still holding it in her hand, Tess grabbed her purse and hurried out the door and down the steps. She wasn't paying attention to where she was going. She was too busy looking at the necklace, and she slammed headlong into Alec Devereaux who was coming up the steps and not paying attention, either. Alec caught Tess in his arms and held her against him until she regained her balance. Her purse and the necklace went flying straight down to the foyer.

"Whoa!" said Alec. "Where are you rushing off to?"

Tess's heart flew into her throat. Even with a touch as meaningless as this, he had such power over her. All she could do was look into his eyes.

"Tess?"

"Yes?"

"Is something wrong?"

"Oh, no, no. I was just—" She couldn't think what to say.

Alec's eyes moved over her flushed face. "Yes?"

Tess stepped away from him. "I was wondering if I could borrow a car?"

"You know you're welcome to any of the cars anytime. The keys are in them."

"Thank you. I don't know how long I'll be gone."

A corner of his mouth lifted. "You don't punch a time clock, Tess."

"I know." She caught herself staring at him. "Excuse me," she said as she hurried down the stairs to pick up her scattered belongings.

Alec followed her, picking up her hairbrush and lipstick and handing them to her without comment. But when he picked up the necklace, he raised it to the light to examine it. "What's this?"

"Just a necklace," she said quietly.

"Just? It's a beautiful piece. You wear it with your black dress."

Tess gazed at it with eyes sadder than she knew. "It belonged to my mother."

He took her hand in his, palm up, and gently lowered the necklace into it. "Why are you carrying it around with you?"

She closed her fingers around the pearls and Alec closed his hand around hers. "I just am." She took her hand from his, dropped the necklace into her purse and zipped it closed.

Alec rose and helped Tess to her feet. "Is everything all right?" he asked.

Tess gazed down at her purse. "Yes."

He put his index finger under her chin and tilted her face toward his. "Are you sure?"

"I don't mean to be rude, but you'll have to excuse me. I really must go."

Tess quickly left the house and took the Range Rover straight to Blythe and Trilling's home. She parked in front, walked up to the huge door, lifted the shining brass knocker and let it fall. Within moments a servant Tess hadn't seen before opened the door. "Yes?"

"Hello. I was wondering if Mr. DeVeere was in?"

"Yes, he just arrived."

"Would you please tell him that Tess is here to see him?"

"Certainly. Come in."

"No, thank you," she said pleasantly. "I'll wait out here."

The maid looked at her strangely. "As you wish."

Tess paced back and forth while she waited. It was really getting cold. Suddenly the door opened and there was Trilling. "Hello!" he said with a smile. "What a wonderful surprise. What are you doing standing out here?"

"I don't want Blythe to see me."

"Why not?"

"She worries too much. May I ask you a question?"

He closed the door behind him. "Fire away."

"Where can I go to sell some jewelry?"

"Why are you asking me that question?"

"Because you just strike me as someone who'd know the answer."

"Thanks a lot," he said dryly.

"Am I wrong?"

"Probably not. What is it you want to sell?"

"A pearl necklace."

"I'd try Martine's, in the village."

"You've sold things there?"

"Yes, and René, he's the owner, has always been fair."

"Thanks, Trilling. One more question and then I'll let you go. Where would I find ski clothes and equipment?"

"The nearest place would be Ardenshire."

"Where's that?"

"Just follow the road out of the village and you'll roll right into Ardenshire in about an hour and a half."

"Ninety minutes," she said thoughtfully. "I should be able to do that."

Trilling's face suddenly brightened. "Are you going to Switzerland with us?"

"Jenni is."

"What about you?"

"No. I…have other plans." Before he could ask any more questions, she kissed him on the cheek. "I have to go."

"Do you want me to come with you?" he called after her.

"No."

"Tell René that you're a friend of mine."

"I will. Thanks."

Tess zoomed into the village. There was a parking space right in front of Martine's. It was a small shop. The front window was undecorated except for a few exquisite pieces of jewelry. Some were obviously antiques.

Reaching into her purse, Tess fingered the necklace. Then she went inside. A woman behind the counter looked up and smiled. "Good afternoon. May I help you?"

"Yes. I'd like to speak to René, please."

"Of course. He's in the back room. I'll get him. And you are?"

"Tess Parish." She deliberately didn't give her married name.

The woman seemed to be waiting for further information.

"I'm here on the recommendation of a friend of mine, Mr. Trilling DeVeere."

"Oh, of course. One moment, please." She disappeared behind a black curtain, and just seconds later a small man with thinning dark hair appeared and extended his hand. "I'm René Martine. What may I do for you?"

"I understand that you sometimes acquire people's personal jewelry to sell in your store."

"That's correct."

Tess handed him the necklace. "I'd like to sell this."

He went behind the counter, laid it on a cloth and examined it more closely. "It's fairly good quality," he said. "How much are you asking for it?"

"I really don't know its value."

"I see. Well, I'd say it's worth between seven hundred to one thousand pounds."

Her heart sank. "Is that all?"

"I'm afraid so. Are you still interested in selling it?"

"I don't really have a choice."

"I'll tell you what, Miss Parish. I'll pay you eight hundred pounds for the necklace right now. If I'm able to sell it for more than that, I'll give you the overage, less my commission."

Tess looked at him in surprise. "That's very kind of you."

He shrugged. "Don't be grateful yet. I think the odds of my getting more are slim."

"I appreciate the offer just the same."

The jeweler smiled at her. "Wait here for a moment while I write you a check."

Tess stared out the window while he was gone. She was doing the right thing.

When Tess got home, she went straight to the library and found Alec there, working. She tapped on the doorframe and he looked up. "Hi," she said with a tentative smile.

"Hello, Tess."

"May I come in?"

"Of course."

She sat in the chair across from him. "I've given some thought to the Switzerland trip."

"And?"

"And it's fine with me if Jenni goes. In fact, I want her to. Thank you for inviting her. Just let me know how much her plane ticket and room charges are."

"She'll be my guest. You both will be my guests."

"That's very kind, but no. I'd prefer to pay our way. In this instance, however, it's just Jenni. I won't be going."

"Why not?"

"I think it's best if I stay here. I have a lot to do. It'll give me a chance to spend some time on my art. I've done almost no painting since I came here."

Alec leaned back in his seat, his fingers steepled under his chin, his eyes on Tess. "You can bring your paints to Switzerland."

"I don't want to go."

"Because of me?"

"Because of us. It's too tense."

"We can avoid each other."

"I think my solution is best." She got to her feet. "Anyway, thank you again on Jenni's behalf."

She left the library and went searching for the girls. She found them in the kitchen having a snack. "Good news," she said as she sat at the table with them. "Jenni will be going to Switzerland."

Both girls threw their arms around her neck and hugged her.

Then something occurred to Jenni. "What about you?"

"I'm going to be staying here. I'm invited," she said quickly so they wouldn't think Alec was ignoring her, "but I have a lot to do here."

"But we can't have Christmas without you," said Olivia.

"Of course you can. We'll talk on the telephone. Besides, you won't be gone that long. I'll save a few presents for you to open when you get back and you save some for me." She ruffled their hair and left the kitchen. End of discussion.

Jenni looked at Olivia and shook her head. "I can't believe this. Every time there's an opportunity for us to get Tess and your father together, one of them does something to mess it up."

Olivia nodded in agreement. "What are we going to do?"

"Go on the trip and figure out a way to get Tess there for Christmas."

"How are we going to do that?"

"I don't know yet. But we're never going to get her and your father together if she stays here."

"True."

"So we'll just have to think hard and come up with something."

"What if we can't?"

"Don't be so negative. Of course we will. We always do."

"But not very successfully. It seems like the more we try to get them together, the farther apart they drift."

"Appearances can be deceiving," Jenni said wisely. "I think they like each other very much. They just don't want to admit it."

"That's silly."

"That's grown-ups for you. We just have to show them the light, so to speak. And we *will* think of something. I promise. Besides," she added quietly, "Tess is all the family I have left. I'm not about to let her spend Christmas alone."

"Nor I," said Olivia.

Chapter Thirteen

Tess wandered through the big, dark, empty house. She told herself she'd be all right spending Christmas Eve on her own, but for the first time since everyone had left nearly two weeks ago, she was genuinely lonely. Walking into the living room where she'd decorated a small tree, she went through Alec's music and decided on Vivaldi rather than Christmas carols. Mrs. Linde had left a fire going to take the chill out of the air.

Tess sank onto the couch and stared into the flames. Jenni had called earlier sounding teary and upset because they weren't together. She supposed she could have impulsively jumped on a plane bound for Switzerland, but despite Jenni's tears, Tess just couldn't do it. She couldn't afford to be impulsive either financially or emotionally at the moment.

But she missed her little sister.

Tess looked at her watch. It was only eight o'clock, but it seemed like midnight. She'd found plenty to occupy her days since everyone had left. She'd painted more than she had in months. But this day had dragged interminably. Wrapping herself in a blanket, Tess lay on the couch with a book.

Before long, the fire, the music and the words conspired to make her sleepy. When her eyelids began to drift closed, she just let them. There was nothing to stay awake for.

It was after midnight when Alec walked into the house. He shook the rain off his trench coat and headed through the dark house toward the music.

When he saw Tess asleep on the couch, his expression grew gentle. He sat on the edge of the big coffee table and gazed down at her for a long time before touching her shoulder. "Tess?" he said softly.

She moved but didn't open her eyes.

"Tess," he said again, his deep voice more firm. "Wake up."

She opened her eyes and blinked rapidly several times, trying to focus. "Alec?" she finally said in a surprise as she struggled into a sitting position. "What are you doing here?"

"I'm picking up Jenni's Christmas present."

She looked at him blankly. "I don't understand."

"Your little sister and my daughter have been miserable without you. And they've been quite vocal about expressing their mutual misery. You've had more than enough time to take care of any personal business you had, and now you're going to return to Switzerland with me for Christmas and make everyone happy."

When she said nothing, he touched her arm. "Tess, I promise that I'll do my best not to make this more difficult for you than it has to be."

This was so unexpected that Tess didn't have any time to think up a reason not to go.

"Good. It's nice not to be argued with for once. Let's get you packed. I have a plane waiting." He rose and hauled Tess to her feet. "Go on."

The blanket fell from her shoulders. "I'll just be a minute."

"Good. I want us back to Switzerland by the time the girls wake."

Tess just looked at him, trying to think of some way to thank him.

"Hurry up."

She jumped, startled. "I don't know what to take."

"Anything you have that's appropriate for snow and cold along with some evening dresses."

She nodded and quickly left the room.

Alec picked up the blanket and draped it across the back of the couch. Then he went to the fire and moved the logs apart with a poker until the flames began to die.

He stared into the glowing embers, deep in thought. Until the moment he'd seen Tess tonight, he'd told himself he was doing this for Jenni and Olivia. But now he knew he was doing it for himself, as well. No matter how he distanced himself from Tess, something about her drew him back again and again. He didn't want to spend Christmas without her. Something had been missing from the entire vacation for him.

Tess.

He heard her clunking down the stairs with her suitcase and went to help her. She was lugging the big bag in both hands, letting the back of it hit each step as she got to it. Alec ran up halfway and took the bag from her, easily lifting it clear of the stairs. "Do you have everything you need?" he asked.

"I think so," she said hesitantly. "I hope so."

"Passport?"

"Yes."

"If you've forgotten anything, you can always buy it once we get to Switzerland."

With what? she wondered.

"Where's your coat?"

Tess ran back up the steps and retrieved it from the floor where it had fallen. When she got downstairs, Alec took it from her and helped her into it, lifting her silky hair out from under the collar.

The intimate gesture made Tess uneasy, but she hid her reaction.

He looked at her for a long moment. "Come on," he said as he lifted the suitcase and headed for the door.

Tess turned out the lights. It wasn't until Alec closed the door behind them that Tess saw the helicopter sitting on the cobbled driveway, its blade slowly whirring, slicing through the rain.

They both ran toward it. Alec gave Tess a hand up into the back and then stowed her suitcase on the empty seat beside her while he climbed into the front and shut the door. The pilot looked at him inquiringly. Alec signaled with a raised thumb, and within seconds they were airborne.

Tess had never been in a helicopter before, and she wasn't crazy about it—particularly not in the rain and wind.

It was a mercifully short flight; less than half an hour. The helicopter landed near a private jet that Alec had chartered.

Alec got out first and then reached in for Tess, lifting her to the ground. While the pilot got her suitcase, Alec lifted his trench coat over Tess's head to protect her from the rain, and they ran to the jet.

It was a small jet—just six seats, three on either side of the aisle. The pilot was in a separate compartment.

Alec helped Tess out of her coat, took off his own and hung them both in a narrow cabinet.

"Where should I sit?" Tess asked, looking around.

"Anywhere."

She picked the first one on the right. Alec sat across the narrow aisle from her.

The pilot came on board, closed the door and sealed it and went up front, out of sight. Minutes later they were taxiing down the runway of the small airport.

Tess leaned back in her seat. Everything had happened so quickly that she hadn't really had a chance to think about it.

Alec looked over at her. "Is everything all right?"

She turned her head toward him and nodded. "Thank you. It's good of you to go to all of this trouble for Jenni."

He didn't say anything.

"Why are you doing this, anyway?"

The groove in his cheek deepened. "Are you asking if I have ulterior motives?"

"Just 'why?'"

He shrugged. "Blame it on the Christmas spirit. Jenni and Olivia weren't looking forward to Christmas morning without you there. So now you'll be there and they'll be happy."

"I see."

He reached around behind his seat and pulled out a briefcase. "I have some work to do. Did you bring something to read?"

"No. I didn't even think of it. That's all right, though. I'm content."

Actually, she wasn't content. She was about as tense as she'd ever been. If he'd turned to her and whispered "Boo" she would have flown out of her chair.

And he sat there working as though he didn't have a care in the world. She wondered if he was as calm as he appeared or if he was churning on the inside just as she was.

Staring at him wasn't going to help anything. Tess turned her head and gazed out the window, watching the darkness roll by.

Alec didn't speak to her for the rest of the flight. She would occasionally feel his eyes on her and every once in a while she'd look at him.

Whatever they were doing, Tess was deeply aware of Alec's presence.

She was always aware of Alec.

When the jet landed, Alec didn't even look up. He just put his things into his briefcase and unsnapped his seat belt. As soon as the outer door opened, a man stepped on board. Alec showed him his passport and Tess handed over hers.

When Tess had her passport back and the man had gone, Alec got her coat and helped her into it. Alec went out first, then held out his hand to help Tess onto the tarmac.

From there they climbed into a waiting car, Alec in the driver's seat, and headed away from the airport.

"How far from here are we going?" Tess asked.

"About an hour into the mountains."

It had been snowing a little when they'd started driving, but after a few minutes the air around them was a flurry of white. Alec brought his speed down.

Reaching across Tess, he tugged on her seat belt to make sure it was secure. It was a simple gesture, and he probably didn't give it a second thought, but it made Tess feel protected.

"Are you cold?" Alec asked.

"A little."

He turned up the heat for her.

The snow fell thicker and thicker. Tess snuggled more deeply into her coat, glad to be in the car rather than out in the storm.

Alec slowed to a crawl, but kept the car moving. A one-hour drive turned into three.

When they finally parked in front of the lodge, the sky was just beginning to lighten a little. Alec helped Tess inside with her luggage. When someone approached to take her suitcase, Alec waved him away and took her up the elevator to her fourth-floor room. He used a key from his pocket, which he handed to Tess as soon has he'd opened the door.

The room was a suite. She stepped into an old-fashioned sitting room, big and charming with interior rough-hewn logs, a massive fireplace and large windows. It was furnished with a roomy couch, chairs, desk and round table for taking meals.

She didn't look in the bedroom.

"Do you want to surprise the girls now or freshen up and get some rest first?" he asked as he set down her suitcase.

"Now, if that's all right."

"Good. They'll be up in a few minutes, anyway."

He took her down the hall. A few rooms away he stopped and quietly knocked on a door. He was answered by a young blond woman who'd obviously been sleeping. "Hello, Christine," he said quietly. "I'm sorry to wake you, but I have a surprise for the girls."

Christine looked at Tess, smiled and held out her hand. "I know who you are. Jenni's sister. They're going to be so happy to see you."

"Christine takes the girls skiing and stays with them at night," Alec explained.

"It's nice to meet you," Tess said softly. "Are the girls still sleeping?"

"I thought I heard voices a few minutes ago. They may not be up but they're awake."

Alec went into the room and Tess followed. Like her room, this was also a suite, but with two bedrooms. Alec went to the far one and signaled with his hand that Tess was to stand behind him. The door was slightly ajar, but he knocked, anyway.

"Christine?" asked Olivia.

"No, it's your father. May I come in?"

"Of course."

He opened the door, but didn't move. Both girls were in their beds, but wide awake. "Merry Christmas. I've brought your present." Then he stepped aside and there was Tess.

Both girls let out squeals and ran to her, throwing their arms around her and hugging her until she thought she'd break.

"When did you get here?" Jenni asked.

"Just now."

"How did you get here?" asked Olivia.

"Your father came and got me."

Olivia went from Tess to her father and hugged him around the waist. "Thank you."

He hugged her, too. "You're welcome."

Jenni just grinned at him. He winked back at her.

"Now," he said, "the two of you get dressed, and we'll meet downstairs for breakfast."

They both raced for the bathroom.

Tess was still smiling. "I'll never be able to repay your kindness."

"Are you happy?"

Her eyes met his. "Yes, I am."

"Then I've already been repaid." He inclined his head. "I'll see you downstairs."

Tess went back to her room to wash her face and comb her hair. The girls came out of their room at the same time as Tess, and the three of them walked down the wood stairs rather than take the elevator. Olivia and Jenni talked a mile a minute, telling Tess about their adventures. The two of them finished each other's sentences and laughed at the same things. Tess had trouble sorting out what they were saying, but she enjoyed listening nonetheless.

When they got to the bottom of the stairs, a man was waiting to escort them into the breakfast room. Alec was already there, seated at a table, staring out a window. He rose as they approached, his eyes on Tess every step of the way.

As they sat at the table, Tess across from him, a child on either side, she studiously avoided looking in his direction. If she was going to get through the next few days, or however long she was going to be here, she was going to have to put as much distance between them as possible. *Emotional distance.* She was good at that; she'd been doing it since she was thirteen.

But not with Alec.

She glanced at him as he looked at the menu. He had obviously managed to tune out Jenni and Olivia's chatter.

He looked up suddenly and straight into her eyes.

"What are you going to have, Tess?" Jenni asked.

Tess cleared her throat and looked away from Alec. "Oh, juice and toast, I guess."

"Oh, Geez," Jenni said in disgust, "you're never going to be able to ski on that."

"Then you order for me."

"Now you're talking."

She and Olivia consulted with each other about what Tess should eat.

Tess looked anywhere but at Alec.

"Which one of you wants to tell Tess about her Christmas present?" he asked, after everyone had ordered.

"You do it, Olivia," Jenni said, her delight evident in the smile that tugged at her mouth.

Olivia looked as though she could barely contain herself. "Well, Jenni told my father and me how much you love to draw and paint, and I know you do some in the schoolroom but you really should have a place of your own just for that, so Father let Jenni and me pick a room on the third floor with lots of natural light, and we spent days cleaning it ourselves. It's all ready for you, along with any kind of charcoal, paint, canvas and sketching paper we could think of. So, Merry Christmas."

Tess leaned over and gave each girl a hug. "I wondered what the two of you were up to. Thank you so much. I can't wait to see it."

Their breakfast was served. Tess was confronted with a plate of eggs, hotcakes, sausage, tomatoes, fried potatoes and toast.

"Oh, dear," she said, wondering where to start.

"Doesn't that look great?" asked Jenni. "I have that all the time."

Tess looked at Jenni's plate. There were only hotcakes and sausage. "But not today?"

"I'm too excited. It's Christmas!"

Alec made do with eggs and toast, and Olivia had the same as Jenni.

But the more Tess looked at her food, the more appealing it grew. And it was delicious. For someone who didn't like big breakfasts, she made quite a dent in the mountain of food.

As breakfast neared an end, the girls grew antsy, anxious to open their presents. Tess folded her napkin and laid it on the table. "Jenni, I wish I had something more to give you, but your trip and new clothes are it."

Jenni jumped up and hugged her around the neck. "That's plenty. Every day that I'm here is like a new present."

Tess looked at her suspiciously. "You're kidding."

"Well, laying it on a little thick, maybe, but I am grateful."

Tess shook her head. "And, Olivia, your present was too big to pack, but it's at home waiting for you in your room."

Olivia hugged her, too. "Whatever it is, I know I'll love it." Then she turned to her father. "Now may we open our other presents?"

A corner of his mouth lifted. "Go ahead. They're under the tree in the lobby."

And they were off and running. Tess rose to follow them, but Alec's voice stopped her. "Tess, just a minute. I have something for you."

"Oh, no, please..."

He handed her an unwrapped black velvet box. "Just think of it as my gift to you for taking such good care of my daughter."

Tess looked at the box and then at him. "You shouldn't have."

He shrugged. "Probably not. But it gave me pleasure."

Tess pressed the catch, and the lid sprang open to reveal her mother's pearl necklace. Her lips parted softly in surprise. "But how... where...?"

"Trilling can't keep a secret."

Tess ran her fingers over the pearls before closing the lid and holding the box out to Alec. "Thank you, but I can't accept this."

Alec rose and pressed her hand, still holding the velvet box, to her breast. "Tess," he said into her ear as he stood behind her, "it's yours. It could never belong to anyone else. And if you ever find yourself in need of money again, swallow that pride of yours and ask me for help."

And then he was gone.

Tess sat there for several minutes, holding the box.

"Are you finished?" asked a waitress.

"Yes," she said softly as she rose. "Excuse me."

Walking into the lobby, she saw the girls by a twenty-foot tree, already ripping into gaily wrapped presents. Alec sat nearby in a wingback chair, watching. Tess walked to the staircase and sat on the bottom step, the velvet box on her lap. She was amazed at how much like home the lodge was, right down to the fire roaring in the big stone fireplace.

Jenni looked so happy. She kept leaping up and hugging Alec for the presents he'd gotten her. Olivia did the same thing.

As Tess watched, her throat tightened, but she didn't cry. This was exactly the way she imagined a real family would be. Jenni had found the father she'd been looking for in Alec. And Alec was learning how to be a father to his own daughter.

But this family had a deadline. It would all be over in September.

Chapter Fourteen

Tess felt as though she was on top of the world. The village lay spread out at the base of the mountain, thousands of feet below where she stood. The air up here was crisp and clean and cold. She took a deep, pleasurable breath and watched the air steam when she exhaled.

She'd been in Switzerland for nearly a week—in fact it was New Year's Eve. Alec had been gone part of the time, back to London on business. But the time he was there he tried to spend with the girls. Tess stayed on the slopes as much as she could and spent time with the girls. Dinners with Blythe and Trilling were fun. All in all, it had been a lovely vacation.

"I'll race you to the bottom."

Startled, Tess jumped and turned. It was Alec. "I didn't know anyone else was here."

"Neither did I." He stood next to her and looked down the mountain. "You shouldn't make this run alone. If you were to get hurt, it would take a long time to find you."

"I do it by myself all the time and haven't fallen yet."

Alec's eyes met and held hers. He had a way of looking at her that made Tess's knees weak. "So are you going to race me down the mountain or not?" he asked.

"What are we wagering?"

"If I win, you have to come to the New Year's Eve party."

"And if I win?"

A corner of his mouth lifted. "You won't."

"It could happen."

He thought for a moment. "All right. If you win—I don't know. What do you want?"

"The book of Byron's poetry in your library."

"Done."

Tess smiled and she lowered her goggles. Without saying another word, she aimed her skis straight down the mountain and pushed off with her ski poles.

Alec was right behind her for part of the way, then caught up, skiing beside her, not really trying to pass.

Tess felt so alive with the cold wind whipping her hair and the snow kicked up by her skies stinging color into her cheeks. Until this past week, she hadn't skied in years, but it had come back to her with incredible speed.

She made short zigzags to increase her speed and took a quick glance toward Alec, all in black against the white snow. He was inching his way past her. Even at that, she had a feeling he was holding back just to be polite.

Tess tucked in and picked up a little more speed, but couldn't catch up with Alec. By the time they'd gone another thousand feet, he was nearly an entire hill ahead of her.

He got to the bottom first, zipping to a stop in a spray of snow and looking back up the mountain at Tess.

She saw him waiting, but refused to slow up just because he'd already won. Taking straight aim, she flew the last hundred feet and came to a precision stop right in front of him.

"You're good," said Alec.

"You're better." She raised her goggles to the top of her head. "So I have to go to the party."

"The girls want you to."

Tess sighed. The sigh turned into a laugh when she saw Blythe walking toward them perfectly decked out in skin-tight ski pants and a white jacket with a fur-lined hood. "I've been looking all over for you two."

"For someone who doesn't ski, you certainly have all the right clothes," said Alec.

"You like it?" she asked, giving a little spin.

"You look wonderful," said Tess. "I'm surprised you don't have an army of men following you."

"I will by the end of the day."

Tess unsnapped her skis from her boots, hooked them together and rested them on her shoulder.

"You don't mind if I steal Alec from you for a few minutes, do you?" asked Blythe. "I need to talk to him about something."

"Alec isn't accountable to me." She looked at him. "Right?"

"Unlike most married men, that's exactly right. Don't forget about tonight, Tess."

"What about tonight?" asked Blythe.

"Tess is going to the party."

"Oh, good! I was hoping you would."

Tess smiled at both of them as she turned to go. "See you later."

She hadn't walked more than twenty feet when she spotted Jenni and Olivia coming toward her. "Hi!" she called out. "Are you two finished already?"

"Yeah," said Jenni. "We're going back to the lodge. We have to get ready for tonight."

"Tonight?"

Jenni looked at her sister as though she'd lost her mind. "It's New Year's Eve, Tess. Olivia's dad said we could come to his party and stay up until midnight."

"And you have to start getting ready now?"

"You can't rush beauty," said Jenni.

"That's very true." Tess was proud of herself. She didn't even crack a smile. "What are you going to wear?"

"One of the new dresses I got for Christmas," said Olivia.

"And you?" she asked Jenni.

"My blue dress. The full one with the long sleeves."

"You're both going to look lovely," said Tess, starting to walk toward the car. The girls fell into step beside her.

"You're going to the party, aren't you, Tess?" Olivia asked. "I know you said yesterday that you weren't, but you really are, aren't you?"

"As a matter of fact I am. Your father made a bet with me. If he could beat me down the mountain, then I had to go to the party."

Olivia grinned. "He's very good."

"Very."

"What are you going to wear?" asked Jenni.

"I don't know. I haven't really thought about it. I suppose my black dress."

"But he's already seen you in that!" Jenni protested.

"Who has?"

"Umm—anyone who's ever known you."

Olivia admired her friend's quick recovery.

"So?"

"You should wear something new. Something brighter."

Tess narrowed her eyes, but there was a twinkle. "Are we back to the old spandex argument?"

"No. I know I'll never win that one. But surely you can at least get yourself a new dress. It can even be tasteful, if you insist."

Tess couldn't help smiling. "Forget it. That black one has a lot of life left in it." She didn't tell her sister that she couldn't afford a new dress, even if she were so inclined.

"You're hopeless. Absolutely hopeless." Jenni raised her hands to the sky. "You try to bring them up properly, but do they listen to you?" She shook her head and answered her own question. "No. They just go on making fashion faux pas after fashion faux pas, humiliating the rest of the family." She sighed dramatically. "Come, Olivia. We've done all we can for her. The woman is never going to learn."

"Uh, Jen, we need a ride back to the lodge."

Jenni wrinkled her nose. "You just blew a great exit. So may we have a ride?" she asked Tess.

"Of course, if you can bear to be seen with such a fashion disaster."

They all fell into step, the snow crunching under their boots. As they approached the rented car Alec had provided for them, Tess hit the button on the key chain that unlocked the doors. The girls helped her fasten the three pairs of skis to the roof. They kept their ski boots on while Tess sat half in and half out of the car changing into shoes. "Are you guys sure you want to go straight back to the lodge? It's only four. The party doesn't start until eight."

"I told you, we have to get ready," said Jenni.

"What on earth could you possibly do to yourselves for four hours?" she asked as she dropped the boots onto the floor of the car and swung herself around behind the steering wheel.

"Stuff," said Jenni.

Olivia nodded. "Hair, makeup. You know. The usual things girls do to prepare for an evening."

"Most girls," Jenni added with a meaningful look at her sister.

Tess rolled her eyes, but she was smiling. "You don't give up, do you?"

"Never."

"And since when do you two wear makeup?"

"Christine showed us how to put it on. But don't worry, Tess. We don't use very much."

"I hope not. You're both beautiful just the way you are."

"So are you, but you use it."

"Like you, though, not very much. And some days I don't use it at all. Which has nothing to do with what we were talking about. I still want to know what's going to take you guys four hours."

The two girls looked at each other. "We might take a nap," Olivia offered.

Tess looked at her in the rearview mirror. "You're kidding."

Olivia yawned—somewhat unconvincingly. Then Jenni yawned.

Tess laughed. "Look, if you don't want to tell me, just say so."

"We don't want to tell you," said Jenni.

"Are you going to be doing anything that you shouldn't be?" Tess asked.

"Like we'd really tell you if we were."

"Are you?"

"No, of course not. We'll probably listen to some music or watch television." The girls looked at each other again. Tess saw the look in her rearview mirror, but let it go.

When they arrived at the lodge, they took their skis off the car and carried them inside. The girls raced straight for the stairs and to their room. Tess followed along behind at a slower pace.

The girls closed their door and locked it. "All right," said Jenni, "we're going to be leaving Switzerland soon. Tonight is about our last chance to get my sister and your dad together."

"What's the plan?"

"I don't know. I just have a feeling that it's tonight or never with those two."

Olivia nodded. "I have the same feeling."

"Grown-ups," Jenni sniffed. "They can't see what's right in front of them."

"That's what Mrs. Linde says."

"Did she offer any solutions?"

"No."

"That figures."

"We'll have to think of something ourselves."

"That's easier said than done."

"All right. On the count of three, start thinking. And don't stop until you have a really good idea."

"All right."

"One. Two. Three. Start."

Both girls sank into chairs, their brows furrowed.

Tess, blissfully unaware of what was going on elsewhere in the lodge, changed out of her ski suit and into jeans and a sweater. With a book under her arm, she went to the large main room off the lobby and sank into a cushy corner chair, hidden away from the casual observer, and tried to bury herself in a mystery.

She didn't know how long she'd been reading—a long time—when someone walked past her. She looked up and saw Alec, unaware of her, stop in front of the fireplace and stare into the flames.

What was he thinking? she wondered. He looked as unhappy as she'd ever seen anyone look.

He turned his head and looked into her eyes.

He said nothing.

She said nothing.

They just looked at each other.

"Alec!" said Trilling as he burst into the room. "What a lucky thing you're here." He smiled at Tess. "Good afternoon, Tess." He looked from one to the other. "Am I interrupting something?"

"What do you want?" Alec asked, sounding a little impatient.

Tess got to her feet. "Excuse me."

"You don't have to leave," said Trilling.

"Yes, I do. I'll see you tonight."

"So you're coming after all!" Trilling said with a smile. "Wonderful. Save me a dance."

"Of course."

When Tess got to her room, she looked through her closet. The only thing suitable for a New Year's Eve party was her black dress, and she was heartily sick of it.

Maybe Blythe could help her out.

She went down the hall to Blythe's room and knocked. Blythe opened the door and looked uneasily at Tess.

"What's wrong?"

She opened the door wider so Tess could see inside. Diane was there.

Blythe stepped out of the room and closed the door behind her. "She just got here."

"To see Alec?"

"Yes. Apparently he broke off their relationship a few weeks ago. She's here hoping to patch things up."

"Oh."

"What did you want, Tess?"

It took her a moment to remember. "Oh! I wanted to know if you had a dress I could borrow for the party tonight."

"I brought several with me. You can take your pick, if you don't mind Diane being in the room."

"I don't. What she and Alec do is no concern of mine."

"If you tell yourself that enough, you might begin to believe it, but I certainly don't." She opened the door and ushered Tess inside. Diane, seated in a chair, looked up but didn't say anything.

"Hello, Diane," said Tess. "If you're looking for Alec, he was in the lobby the last time I saw him."

"Thank you. I'm going to talk to Blythe a little longer."

"I'll be out of the way in a minute." Tess followed Blythe into the bedroom, and the two women went through the closet item by item. Blythe finally pulled a bright red dress off the rack and held it against Tess. "This would look beautiful on you. It's a Greek style that leaves one shoulder bare. We're fairly close in size, so it should be a good fit."

"Thank you so much. I'll try it. The girls will be thrilled to see me in something other than the one I'd planned to wear."

"So I heard."

They walked into the sitting room. Tess inclined her head toward Diane. "I guess I'll be seeing you this evening."

"Yes, I'll be at the party."

Tess smiled at Blythe. "Thanks again for the dress."

"Anytime."

When Tess got back to her own room, she sat on the edge of the bed and took a deep breath. It did matter to her that Diane was there. It mattered a great deal.

More than she cared to admit.

Tess twisted this way and that to look at her reflection. The red dress was exquisite and fit her like a glove.

She poked through her jewelry, but decided not to wear any at all.

She was more or less on her own for the evening. She and Alec weren't here as husband and wife and as a result were free to do as they wished. She had kind of hoped he would ask her to go with him, but he hadn't.

Picking up her purse from the bed, she headed toward the door. Then changing her mind about the purse, she tossed it back. She was only going downstairs.

When she stepped into the hallway, she found Trilling sitting in a wingback chair. As soon as he saw her, he rose and executed a deep bow. "Hello, beautiful lady." He eyed her up and down appreciatively. "And I do mean beautiful. I'm your escort for the evening."

"I thought you had a date."

"So did I, but she apparently found someone more interesting at the last moment."

"Impossible."

"That's what I thought, but alas . . ." He shrugged.

Tess put her arm through his and sympathetically patted his hand. "I'm sorry. But to tell you the truth, I'm glad I don't have to go alone. I was feeling really awkward."

"Believe me, Tess, you wouldn't have been alone for long."

She smiled and squeezed his arm. "Thank you, Trilling."

"Don't thank me yet. I want you to be warned that if I manage to catch the eye of some available young thing, I intend to drop you like a hot rock."

Tess laughed. "With one hand you giveth and with the other you taketh away."

He looked at her with a raised brow. "Of course, if you can tell me that your feelings for me are other than sisterly, I might be convinced to stick around."

"I'm sorry."

Trilling sighed dramatically. "I tried. Years from now, when we're both too old to care—or to do anything about it if we did—you'll realize the error of your ways."

Tess didn't say anything.

"You could give a man a little hope."

Her smile grew.

"All right. Just remember what I said. Like a hot rock."

"Got it," she said agreeably.

They went down the stairs to the main room of the lodge, already packed with people. The men, without exception, were dressed in tuxedos. The women were splendid in their sequined gowns and jewels.

Jenni spotted Tess from across the room and elbowed Olivia. "She's here."

"Where?" Olivia asked, looking around.

"Near the door. Look at what she's wearing!"

Olivia narrowed her eyes but couldn't find her. "Which door?"

"Oh, for heaven's sake, I can't point at her." She stepped behind Olivia and turned Olivia's head toward the entrance. "Do you see her now?"

"Oh, yes. She's with Mr. DeVeere. Wow! She looks fabulous."

"Right," said Jenni, chewing her lip nervously. "What do you suppose she's doing with him?"

Olivia shrugged.

"He could ruin everything."

Olivia nodded. "We have to get rid of him."

"But how?"

"I don't know."

"We'll have to work on that."

"We have to work on a lot of things. That awful Mrs. Binford has practically attached herself to my father."

"Our father," Jenni corrected. "I have a stake in this, too." Olivia and Jenni looked at each other and grinned.

"What are the two of you up to?"

Both girls jumped and turned around to find Alec standing there with "that woman" beside him. "What makes you think we're up to anything? Did you hear something?" asked Jenni, wondering how long he'd been standing there.

"What could I possibly have heard? I only asked because you usually *are* up to something," he said with a smile as he affectionately flicked her cheek. "Are you having fun?"

"It's wonderful. Thank you for letting us come."

Alec smiled down at his daughter. "We couldn't possibly have rung in the New Year without the two loveliest eleven-year-olds in Switzerland."

Olivia beamed.

"Is Tess here yet, Jenni?" Alec asked.

The two girls looked at each other with barely suppressed smiles. "Yes. I saw her just a few minutes ago."

"She came with Mr. DeVeere," added Olivia, watching closely to see her father's reaction.

Alec's expression was frustratingly impassive. "Where's your companion?"

"Christine's here. She's getting us some punch."

"All right. Stay with the party. I don't want either of you wandering off."

"We won't, Father."

He and Diane moved into the sea of people.

"You keep an eye on your dad," Jenni said, "and I'll keep an eye on Tess. Remember, at midnight we have to have them in the same place, and Mrs. Binford and Mr. DeVeere somewhere else entirely."

"This is going to be so good," Olivia said with relish. "I just know this is going to work. Did you notice that he even asked about Tess?"

Jenni nodded. "A very good sign. A very good sign, indeed."

Trilling maneuvered Tess to a clear spot on the wood floor and swept her into his arms. "Would you care to dance?"

Her eyes sparkled. "I think you're supposed to ask first and dance after."

"I always get that wrong."

Usually party music was overpoweringly loud, so it could be heard over the voices, but this music was at just the right volume. It was easy to hear, but there was no need to shout to be heard above it.

Trilling was a skillful dancer. He moved Tess easily around the floor. Although she tried to keep her attention on him, she still found herself looking for Alec.

"I guess this is one way to get you in my arms," Trilling said with a lopsided grin.

Tess looked up at him and studied his face, her head tilted to one side. "I can never tell when you're joking."

"I'm joking. Sort of." His hand slipped from her waist to her hip.

Tess shook her head good-naturedly and moved his hand back to her waist. "Do that again and you'll be limping your way through the rest of the evening."

He cringed.

"I mean it," she warned.

"Hey, you can't blame a fellow for trying."

"No, but you can maim him."

He nodded. "Good point. Say no more."

And again her eyes searched.

And found.

Alec was so tall that he towered over most of the guests. He saw Tess at the same moment she saw him. Their eyes locked and held. Tess felt him tugging at her very soul, drawing her nearer and nearer, out of her own control and into his. She stumbled, but Trilling caught her and hardly missed a step.

"Are you all right?" he asked.

"I'm sorry. I guess I'm a little clumsy."

"Hmm." Trilling looked around to find what she'd been staring at and saw Alec watching the two of them. "Oh, Tess," he said sadly.

"What?" she asked, looking up at him.

He shook his head. "I know the two of you are married, but you're not really falling for him are you?"

"Don't be ridiculous."

"I mean I love him like a brother, but I'd hate to see you get hurt."

"Why do you assume I would?"

"Because every woman who falls in love with Alec eventually gets hurt."

Tess could feel Alec's eyes on her. It took every bit of self-control she had not to look back.

Across the room, Diane knew very well who Alec was watching. "Let's dance," she suggested, to distract him.

"Diane, I don't want to dance with you. I don't know why you came here, but I can tell you that I wish you hadn't. It isn't going to change anything. I told you from the beginning what our relationship was."

"You did," Diane admitted.

"I told you I didn't love you and never would."

"I know."

"So what's the point of this?"

"I thought I could change your mind."

"You can't."

Diane pushed her hair away from her face. "I must be a mess. Excuse me for a moment while I freshen up."

On the other side of the room, Trilling leaned over to whisper in Tess's ear. "You won't mind if I desert you in a few minutes, will you?"

A dimple creased her cheek. "I assume this is the 'hot rock' moment we've all been waiting for?"

"Indeed it is."

"Of course I don't mind if you go. I'll be leaving soon myself."

"Are you sure?"

"I'm sure," she said with a smile. "Which lovely lady did you manage to steer away from her date?"

His mischievous smile flashed. "You know me too well." He put his hand on her shoulder and turned her toward a statuesque blonde who appeared to have been poured into her dress.

"Nice choice," Tess said approvingly. "She's stunning."

Trilling nodded.

"Does she know she's leaving with you?"

"Not yet."

"Good luck." Tess reached up to straighten his bow tie, then patted his shoulder. "There."

Trilling kissed her on the forehead. "See you tomorrow. Late. Very late."

As he made his way to his woman of the moment, Tess turned to the man beside her and inconspicuously looked at his watch. It was nearly midnight. She'd had all the conversations she cared to. She'd spotted Blythe a few times. Her attention seemed to be focused on a man she'd met earlier in the day. Tess didn't want to intrude. All she wanted to do now was go to her room.

Tess began making her way through the guests in search of Olivia and Jenni and finally found them off to one side near an alcove with their heads together.

"Hello, there," she said with a smile as she approached. "Are you enjoying yourselves?"

"Enormously!" beamed Olivia. "And you?"

"It's been a lovely party, but I think I'm going to call it a night."

"Oh, but you can't!" said Jenni. "You just can't!"

"It's all right," she said with a reassuring smile. "The two of you can stay here with Christine. You don't have to leave just because I am."

The two girls looked at each other, panicked.

Jenni licked her lips. "I think she should stay here until at least midnight."

Olivia nodded, picking up her cue. "Yes, that's right. We should ring in the new year as a family." She all but batted her eyelashes as she looked at Tess. "Please? It's only a few more minutes. And it would mean a lot to me. Us."

"All right," Tess said, gently touching her cheek, "I'll stay a little longer."

The girls looked at each other again, then turned back to Tess. "We have a few things to do," Jenni told her. "Promise us that you won't move from this spot."

"Why?"

"Just promise!"

"All right, but does it have to be this spot?"

"Well . . . what did you have in mind?"

"The enclosed porch."

"The one right over there?" Jenni asked, pointing to a place just over Tess's left shoulder.

Tess nodded.

Jenni thought it over. "Okay. But don't go anywhere else until we get back."

"I promise."

"We'll be right back." Jenni grabbed Olivia's hand and dragged her along.

Tess, smiling, shook her head and walked toward the dimly lit porch. The girls were obviously up to something, but that was all right. It was part of being eleven, she supposed.

Jenni stopped in a corner and turned to Olivia. "We have to work fast. You're going to have to get Mrs. Binford out of here."

"How?"

"I don't know. Think of something, for heaven's sake. Tell her she has a phone call. And make sure she goes to her room instead of one of the downstairs phones. Just see that she's nowhere near your father at midnight."

Olivia nodded. "All right."

"While you're doing that, I'll get your dad to dance with Tess so that they're together when the clock strikes twelve."

"Do you really think this will work?"

"It has to, Olivia. Everyone kisses at midnight on New Year's Eve. It would be rude of him not to kiss Tess." Jenni looked at her watch. "What time do you have?"

Olivia looked at hers. "Eight minutes before midnight."

"Same here. Now make sure you don't distract Mrs. Binford too soon. We don't want to give her a chance to get back before midnight."

"Right."

They each took a deep breath, flashed each other a thumbs-up and went their separate ways.

Jenni found her quarry first. Alec was standing alone at a window, staring outside. She walked up beside him and looped her arm through his. "Hi," she said with a sweet smile.

Alec looked down at her, and his own mouth curved. "Hello, Jenni. Enjoying yourself?"

"Very much, thank you. Or at least I would be if only..." She paused and sighed dramatically.

"What's wrong?"

"I'm worried about Tess."

Alec turned to look directly at her. "Why?"

"She seems so unhappy at times." Jenni looked away from him and out the window. "Like tonight."

"How do you know she's unhappy tonight?"

"I can tell."

"Did she say something to you?"

"No. She doesn't have to. We're very close you know. I can sense when something's wrong."

"I see." Alec had a feeling he was being maneuvered, but that was all right. He was curious to see where this was going. "What do you think is the cause of her sadness?"

Jenni appeared to give this serious consideration. "Loneliness."

"She has you and Olivia."

Jenni nodded. "I think she needs a husband, though. A real one. Not just one on paper."

Alec had to force himself not to smile.

Jenni watched for his reaction. "She's wonderful, you know."

"Yes, she is," he agreed.

"Everyone who knows Tess loves her."

He didn't say anything.

Jenni bit her lower lip and cleared her throat. "May I ask you for a favor?"

Here it came. "Of course you can, Jenni."

"Would you please ask Tess to dance?"

"You think that will make her less sad?"

"It can't hurt." She swung her gaze to him. "And it would mean a lot to me. And to Olivia."

A corner of his mouth lifted. "You're too charming for your own good."

"So you'll do it?" she asked hopefully.

Alec didn't say anything.

"Please?"

He ruffled her hair. "Where is she?"

Jenni slipped her hand into his. "I'll take you to her."

"I had a feeling you might."

As she led him through the guests, she took a discreet look at her watch. Conversation had swallowed a lot of time. It was only three minutes until midnight. She looked around to see where Olivia was and spotted her near the doorway. Olivia nodded.

All right! Jenni moved faster, pulling on Alec's hand to make him hurry. When they got to the faintly lit alcove, Jenni had a moment of panic when she couldn't find Tess. And then suddenly there she was, walking toward them. She was smiling, until she saw Alec. As her eyes locked with his, her smile slowly faded.

"What's going on?" Tess asked.

"Mr. Devereaux wants to dance with you." She looked from one to the other. "And I have to find Olivia."

Tess looked at her in surprise. "I thought you wanted us all to see the new year in together."

"I know. But something has come up. You two just have your dance and forget about Olivia and me. As a matter of fact, I happen to know that Olivia is really tired, and I'm really tired, so we're going to get Christine and go to our room.''

"But it's nearly midnight!" said Tess.

"I know!" She put her hand in the middle of Tess's back and pushed her into Alec's arms. "Good night. And don't worry about the two of us."

Before anyone could protest, Jenni had disappeared.

Tess looked up at Alec. "I'm sorry. I don't know what's wrong with her.''

Alec's hand was high on her back. He slid it slowly down to the small of her back and pulled her body against his. But he didn't dance. He just held her, his eyes on hers.

All Tess knew was that at that moment this was the only place she wanted to be. There was a look in Alec's eyes she hadn't seen before.

The music stopped for the ten-second countdown to midnight.

Alec still didn't move.

Noise suddenly erupted as midnight arrived. "Happy New Year, Tess," he whispered as he lowered his mouth to hers. Tess's lips parted beneath his. There was no hesitation; no thought that they shouldn't be doing this. Just a desire to be with this man.

Alec raised his head and looked into her eyes. Wordlessly he put his hands at her waist and lifted her onto a ledge so that she was slightly above eye level. "Oh, Tess," Alec groaned as he cupped the back of her head in his hand and pulled her mouth to his. He kissed her long and hard, but he wanted so much more. He kissed her face and throat and the curve of her breasts. Tess tangled her fingers in his hair and bent her head low over his.

Suddenly his arm went around her waist and he lifted her to the floor. "Let's go." Taking her hand, he led her to some doors at the end of the alcove and outside into the cold air.

Jenni and Olivia were standing off to one side with Christine. "What do you think happened?" Olivia asked.

"I think they kissed."

"I wish we could see in there."

"Well, we can't. We'll just have to hope for the best."

They turned to Christine. "We're ready to go to our room now."

Olivia suddenly spotted something over Jenni's shoulder. "Uh-oh."

"What is it?"

"You mean *who*. Mrs. Binford."

Jenni's eyes grew round like saucers. "Uh-oh."

"That's what I said. Let's get out of here."

"What if she finds my dad and Tess together? It could ruin everything."

"Good point."

"What are we going to do?"

"I'm thinking, I'm thinking."

But their time ran out. Diane walked straight to them through the noisy crowd. "There was no one on the phone for me, Olivia," she said tightly.

Olivia looked at her with innocent eyes. "Oh?"

"Is that all you can say?"

"Perhaps the person who called hung up before you got to your room."

Diane smiled, but it didn't reach her eyes. "Where's your father?"

"I just saw him a moment ago over there," said Jenni, with a gentle elbow in Olivia's ribs.

"Over where?" Diane asked.

Jenni pointed in the direction exactly opposite where she'd seen Tess and Alec.

Diane didn't even bother to thank them. She just turned sharply and left them standing there.

"What on earth is going on?" asked Christine.

"Nothing," they both said at the same time. "We just want to go to our room now."

"But..."

Jenni grabbed one of the baby-sitter's hands and Olivia grabbed the other and dragged her from the room. "Come on!"

Chapter Fifteen

As soon as they were outside, Alec took off his jacket and wrapped it around Tess. Then, with his arm around her, he led her back in through the lobby and upstairs to his room.

Once inside the room, they turned to face each other. His jacket fell from her shoulders, landing in a heap at her feet, but Tess didn't notice. She only knew that Alec's warm, strong hands were on her cold arms. As he drew them slowly down, Tess closed her eyes and just let herself feel him touching her.

When she opened them again, Alec was gazing at her.

"What is it about you that touches something so deep inside me? You travel to places in my heart where no one's ever been before."

Tess touched his lips with her fingertip.

Alec kissed it, then lowered his head to hers. His mouth was warm and inviting and drew Tess willingly inside. Her body reacted instantly.

There was a thunderous knocking on the door that startled both of them. Alec, still holding Tess in his arms, kissed her on the forehead. "We don't have to answer it."

"It might be the girls."

He sighed. "Who is it?" he called out.

"Diane. I need to see you."

That brought Tess back to earth more than anything else could have. She stepped away from Alec and tried to straighten herself out.

"Tess," he said softly, "there's nothing between Diane and me. There hasn't been for a long time."

"Diane apparently doesn't know that."

"She knows it all too well. She simply hasn't accepted it yet."

"I watched her with you tonight. She's in love with you."

"But I'm not in love with her."

"Are you in love with me?"

"Tess . . ."

Tess hadn't realized until that moment how much she'd hoped he'd say yes. "You don't have to answer that. If you were, I wouldn't have had to ask the question." She smoothed her clothes. "I'll be going now. I think you need to straighten things out with Diane so she can get on with her life."

"Where are you going?"

"To my room." She looked at him for a long moment. "Alec, I'd like to return to England tomorrow."

"Why?"

"I can't do this anymore. I can't play this game."

"This isn't a game."

"It is for you. I thought it was for me for a time, but not any longer. I can't make love to you without being in love with you. And I don't want to be in love with you. I don't want to end up like Diane, knocking on a door pleading to be let in, knowing you're with another woman."

"In this case the other woman is my wife."

"In name only."

Diane knocked again. "Alec, I'm not going away, so you might as well let me in."

Tess's hand hovered over the handle. "When we get home, I think it would be best if we had as little contact with one another as possible." She opened the door. Tess's eyes were full of sympathy as she looked at Diane. Neither spoke. Tess left Alec's door open as she walked down the hall to her own room. When she got there she realized she didn't have her key. It was in the purse she hadn't bothered to bring with her.

She rested her forehead on the cool wood of her door for a moment, collecting herself, then went downstairs to the front desk and asked the woman there for a key. While she was waiting, Blythe walked up to her and put her arm around Tess's waist. "Hello, dear. How was your New Year's Eve?"

"Wonderful. Horrible."

Blythe looked at her more carefully. "What's going on?"

"Nothing. I don't want to talk about it."

Blythe took her hand and pulled her into the deserted sitting room. "Don't ever say that to me. It's like an open invitation to pry. What happened between you and Alec tonight?"

"Nothing."

"Oh, no you don't," she said with a shake of her head. "That isn't a 'nothing happened' face. That's a 'something big happened' face."

Tess looked utterly stricken.

Blythe dropped the bantering tone. "What is it, Tess? What happened?"

"I can't explain it."

"Well I can. You're in love with Alec."

"Don't be ridiculous."

"And what's more, you've been in love with him at least since the day you came to his home, and probably before that."

"That's not true."

Blythe squeezed her hand. "Yes, it is. I could see it in the way you looked at him."

Tess stared at a spot over Blythe's shoulder.

"Why would you consider falling in love with Alec such a disaster? I can think of worse things."

"I can't. What could be worse than loving a man who isn't in love with you? I watched my mother go through hell because she loved a man who didn't know the meaning of the word. I can't go through that. I won't."

"Alec isn't like your father. He's the most honorable man I've ever met. I trust him absolutely. And I'll tell you something else. When he loves, it will be with his whole heart."

Tess's eyes filled with tears.

"You could be that woman."

"What if I'm not? What if I let myself feel all that I can feel for Alec, and I'm not?"

"But what if you are? Isn't the reward worth the risk?"

Tess shook her head. "I just want this arrangement over with. I want to get custody of Jenni and get out of this with my life intact."

"You'd better be careful. You might get what you wish for."

Back in England Tess and Alec set up what amounted to separate households under the same roof. He changed his living quarters to a different wing. He saw Olivia when Tess wasn't around and spent as much time as he could away from the house on business. When it came to Olivia's and Jenni's academic reports, Tess put them neatly on his desk every Friday. If he had any comments, he wrote them in longhand, attached them to the reports and put them in the schoolroom. If they happened to bump into each other, which was rare, they were coolly polite.

The months dragged by. Winter turned into spring; spring into summer. The classroom work continued but on a modified schedule of mornings only, leaving the afternoons free for whatever Tess and the girls wanted to do.

Tess and Blythe were on one of their afternoon rambles on a late-summer day when Alec drove past them, no doubt headed for the train station. Blythe shook her head as she watched him disappear into the distance. "The two of you are worse than children."

"We're handling an awkward situation the best way we can."

"By ignoring each other."

"Things seem to happen when we pay attention."

"Doesn't that tell you something?"

"Blythe, we've made it this far. We only have a few more weeks and then we'll both be free to go our separate ways."

Blythe looked at Tess, truly distressed. "I can't believe you're really leaving. Who will I walk with when you're gone? Who will be there to listen to my unwanted and un-asked-for advice?"

"I'll be a phone call away."

"It won't be the same."

"No," Tess agreed quietly, "it won't. But we'll still see each other occasionally."

"When? You probably won't be coming here."

"No. But you can come to Maine. The house is on the small side, but the view is incredible. It's worth being a little cramped."

"What about Jenni and Olivia?"

"Oh, don't ask. They're both so mad at Alec and me they're barely speaking to either of us. I think they hoped we'd fall in love for real before the twelve months was up."

"You did."

Tess glanced sideways at her. "I got over whatever weak moments I might have suffered in the past."

"Are you telling me you'll be able to end this marriage without any regrets?"

"Yes."

"I don't believe you."

"You don't have to. It isn't your marriage."

"But you're my friend. Alec's my friend. I can't begin to tell you what a terrible mistake I think you're making. You're both so stubborn, so determined, that you won't give in to what's plainly obvious to everyone else."

But Tess wasn't as tough as she led Blythe to believe. She had months ago come to accept the fact that no matter how hard she denied it out loud, she had fallen in love with him. It hadn't been any kind of sudden revelation. It was a knowledge that had just slowly grown within her.

He was the one.

There would never be a man she loved the way she loved Alec.

And now that she knew how much she could love, she couldn't imagine settling for anything less.

Blythe was still talking. Tess tried to listen, but only managed to hear fragments. All she could think about was that in a few weeks she would be leaving England.

In a few weeks she would never see Alec again.

"So you'll come for dinner tomorrow night, right?" asked Blythe.

"What?"

"I knew you weren't listening. I want you to come to dinner at my house tomorrow night."

"What about Alec?"

"I'm not inviting him."

"Then I'll come."

"It's casual."

"How casual?"

"Slacks, sweater, that kind of thing."

* * *

Alec read a newspaper as he sat on a bench at the train station, his suit bag draped over the back of the bench. Trilling got off a train coming from London, spotted Alec and made his way over to him. "Alec, what a lucky thing to run into you. Where are you headed?" he asked as he sat next to him.

"London." He looked at his watch. "In about five minutes."

"How long are you staying?"

"Overnight."

"You'll be back tomorrow?"

Alec wasn't feeling too friendly toward Trilling lately. Or Blythe, for that matter. Every time he saw them they talked about Tess, and she was the last person he wanted to talk about. "Yes."

"Good. Blythe and I are having a small dinner party and we'd like you to come."

"What about Tess?"

"I'm not inviting her," he said, only too well aware that his sister was.

"Then I'll be there."

Trilling remained seated, staring at the tracks.

Alec looked over at him. "What is it, Trilling?"

"Are you really going to let her go?"

He looked back at his newspaper. "I don't want to talk about this."

"You know you're in love with her. That's why you can't stand to be in the same room with her."

"I always imagined love to be just the opposite," Alec said dryly.

"You can't hold against Tess what her father was."

"You don't understand."

"No, I don't. If I were married to her, no matter what the circumstances, I'd do everything in my power to make sure I stayed married to her."

"Don't you realize that's exactly what her father hoped for when he blackmailed me into this marriage?"

"Does it matter? The man's dead."

"It matters. I won't be manipulated. Not by anyone, but particularly not by the man who did everything he could to ruin my family."

"I never thought I'd say this to you, of all people, but you're a fool." He got to his feet as the train to London rattled to a stop in front of them. "See you tomorrow night."

Alec pushed the conversation from his mind as he shouldered his suit bag, tucked the newspaper under his arm and boarded the train.

Tess slipped the belt through the loops of her cream-colored trousers and fastened it in front. Walking to her armoire, she took the matching jacket from its hanger and put it on over the simple silk T-shirt.

Jenni knocked and poked her head around the door. "May I come in?"

"I thought you weren't speaking to me," said Tess as she poked through her jewelry box for some earrings.

"I wasn't. Now I am."

She picked out two small gold hoops and looked in the mirror as she put them on. "So talk."

Jenni sat on Tess's bed, her legs dangling over the side. "We're supposed to leave here in about ten days, right?"

"Right."

"What would you say to Olivia coming to Maine with us for the next school year?"

Tess turned toward her sister and leaned against the dresser. "I would say that I don't think it's a good idea."

"Why not?"

"Olivia belongs here with her father."

"Then how about if I stay here?"

Tess shook her head. "No. I want you with me." She crossed the room to Jenni and sat next to her. "Look, I know the two of you are going to miss each other. Especially at first. But you can write. You can talk on the phone occasionally. You might even be able to see each other once in a while. But you are not going to live with anyone other than me."

"What if Olivia's dad wants to send her away to school?"

Tess's heart caught. "That will have to be his decision."

"I thought you loved Olivia."

"I do."

"Then how can you just leave her?"

"I don't have a choice, Jenni. You knew that before we came here."

"You could stay married to her father."

"No I can't."

"Why not?"

"Because it wouldn't work."

"You mean you won't let it work."

Tess rose from the bed. "That's enough, Jenni. I'm not going to discuss this with you any further. We're leaving here in a week and a half and that's the end of it."

Jenni jumped down from the bed and ran to the door, slamming it behind her.

Tess tiredly rubbed her forehead. This was getting more and more like a "real" divorce. She hated to see Jenni and Olivia suffer.

Once they were away from England, everything would be better.

For tonight, frankly, she was looking forward to a quiet, friendly evening with Trilling and Blythe. When she got back, which would probably be early, she'd sit down with Olivia and Jenni and try to talk some sense into the two of them.

When she got downstairs, Tess found the housekeeper in the kitchen. "Mrs. Linde, I'm going to take the Range Rover to Blythe and Trilling's. I won't be late."

"All right, dear."

Tess kissed her on the cheek. "Thank you for not being mad at me."

"Don't worry. The girls will come around."

"I hope so."

Tess went out the kitchen door, down the stairs and around the house to the car. The drive took just a few minutes, but Tess went slowly, taking the time to really look at her surroundings. It was beautiful here. She'd grown to love the countryside and knew already she was going to miss it.

All of her good intentions to make it through the year without getting involved with the people or home or village had come to nothing.

Tess parked the Range Rover and went to the door. Trilling opened it with a friendly smile. "Give me your keys."

"Why?"

"I need to move your car."

"Why?"

"Oh, some silly idea of Blythe's about not cluttering up the front of the house with a bunch of brightly colored metal."

Tess blinked. "What?"

Trilling shrugged. "Go figure."

"The keys are in the car."

"Great. Go on in. Blythe's in the main room."

"Thanks."

Tess made her way down the hall to the big double doors of the main room. Blythe was alone, standing in front of a picture window. "I take it I'm the first one to arrive," said Tess.

Blythe turned with a smile and crossed the room to kiss Tess on the cheek. "So far. What can I get you to drink?"

"Nothing yet, thanks. Who else is coming?"

"Oh, just this person and that." She waved Tess onto the couch. "Things have been hectic today. I'm going on a cruise."

"How lovely. Where to?"

"That's the part I haven't quite decided on yet. I just need to get away from here. And from Trilling. He's driving me mad."

"Perhaps he's the one you should send on the cruise."

"The thought has crossed my mind."

There was some commotion in the hallway. Blythe, looking suddenly nervous, got to her feet. "Tess, whatever happens in the next few minutes, I don't want you to be mad at me. We're only doing what we think is best."

"What are you . . . ?"

Alec walked into the room with Trilling. He was smiling at something, but the smile faded as soon as he saw Tess.

Tess rose slowly to her feet. "Blythe, I can't believe you'd do this."

"It wasn't my idea," she said. "It was theirs."

Jenni and Olivia entered the room behind Trilling and Alec.

Alec was clearly angry. "I want to know what the—" He caught himself and started over. "I want to know what's going on."

"The girls want to talk to the two of you," said Trilling.

"They could have done that at home."

"No, we couldn't," said Jenni. "You're almost never there at the same time. And when you are, you avoid each other."

"So they asked us to get you both here so they could talk to you about the divorce," said Blythe. "And that's what we've done. And I hope you'll forgive us, but I, for one, won't apologize for my part in this. If anything, I think you should apologize to me for putting me through this. I'm a nervous wreck."

Trilling took Blythe's arm and tugged her out the door, closing it softly behind them.

"Please sit down," said Jenni, her voice quavering. "On the couch. Both of you."

Alec was still angry. Tess could tell by the way he held himself. But he crossed the room to Tess and they both sat down. Olivia and Jenni sat across from them.

"First of all," said Jenni, "neither of us wants you to go through with the divorce."

"Jenni, you knew when we came here that it was temporary," said Tess.

"Please just let us talk first, okay?"

Tess nodded. "Okay."

"But since you are, we think our feelings should be taken into consideration."

"Father," said Olivia, "I want to be able to live part of the time with you and part of the time with Tess."

"And I," said Jenni, "want to live part of the time with you, Tess, and part of the time with Olivia and her dad."

"In other words," said Olivia, "Jenni and I want to stay together all of the time, like real sisters, with both of us moving between the two of you."

"May I speak now?" asked Alec.

Olivia nodded.

"We're not talking about moving down the block. We're talking about transatlantic travel several times a year, changing homes, schools, environments."

Olivia nodded again.

"It would be a monumental task to make those kinds of arrangements."

"We know," said Jenni, "but it isn't impossible."

"Jenni, I didn't go through everything that this past year has involved to get custody of you just to turn it over to someone else six months of the year," said Tess.

"It isn't just someone else. It's Olivia's dad."

Tess and Alec looked at each other. The girls had put them right in the middle of a—situation.

"Tess and I will discuss this and let you know what we decide."

"We want you to discuss it now," said Jenni. "Here."

"Then the two of you leave the room. We'll call you when we're finished."

The girls stood up together and walked in unison out the door, closing it behind them.

Alec rose from the couch, as though he couldn't stand being that close to Tess, and walked to the window. "This is getting complicated."

"What are we going to do?"

"I'll tell you what we're *not* going to do. Their idea of six months here and six months in the United States is out of the question."

"I agree."

He dragged his fingers through his dark hair. "We could alternate vacations with Jenni coming here for one holiday and Olivia going to you for the next. I have friends who've done that."

"That sounds reasonable."

"I think eventually they'll grow apart and won't even want to do that."

"Perhaps."

Alec turned to look at Tess. Seeing her now, after months of avoiding her, he realized how much he'd missed her. He started to say something but caught himself.

Tess looked, also. She knew that after this meeting she'd never see him again. He wouldn't be around to say good-bye. In that moment she made a decision to be honest with him.

She rose from the couch but stayed where she was. "Alec, before the girls come back there's something I need to tell you. When I first came to England I was determined to make the best of a bad situation. I didn't blame you for it.

My father did the same thing to you that he'd done to me. But I was also determined that nothing here would touch me in any way that mattered. I intended to go home with Jenni at the end of the year with my heart intact. And I felt fairly safe in thinking that I could. You weren't at all the kind of man I thought I could love. And Olivia—well, she was your child, not mine.

"I was wrong. I've grown to love Olivia as much as if she were my own. And I fell in love with you."

Alec's expression didn't alter.

"I know that doesn't change anything between us. Nothing I can do will ever erase the fact that I'm the daughter of Thomas Parish. I can't change what he did to your family, and I can't change the way he blackmailed you after his death. I can only tell you how sorry I am. And I also want to assure you that as soon as our divorce comes through, I will cease to be a factor in your life. Except for the relationship between Olivia and Jenni, it will be as though I never existed."

Tess didn't wait for Alec to respond. She didn't expect him to. Crossing the room to the double doors, she opened them and called for the girls.

They walked in as they'd left, determination on their young faces. And a little fear.

Alec didn't say anything for a long time. The only movement he made was the tightening of a muscle in his jaw.

And then he spoke. "I'm going to tell you what Tess and I have decided. There will be no compromising and no argument. Is that understood?"

Both girls nodded.

"We can't let you stay together year-round and move from America to England every six months. But we can allow you to spend holidays together. Tess and I will arrange a schedule and give you each a copy so you'll know what to expect."

The girls didn't look happy, but they also didn't look surprised.

Alec walked past them and out the door without another word. They heard his car start and speed away.

Tess walked to the girls and put an arm around each of them, holding them close to her sides. "Let's go home," she said quietly.

Blythe and Trilling both came into the hall. "I take it that was Alec we heard leaving," said Trilling.

"That's right."

"I suppose this means you won't be staying for dinner," said Blythe.

Tess let go of the girls, walked over to Blythe to kiss her cheek and then kissed Trilling's. "You two are real pieces of work. I think you need hobbies."

"Are you angry?"

"No. Just a little sad. I'll talk to you tomorrow."

She walked out the door with the girls, her heart aching. It was over.

Chapter Sixteen

As Tess had known he would, Alec had left the same night Tess had told him she loved him and hadn't been back.

She took a last look around the schoolroom, then went to Jenni's door and knocked. "It's time to go. Mr. Linde is outside waiting to drive us to the station."

Jenni opened the door and stood looking at Tess with a tearstained face. Olivia, in much the same condition, was just behind her. Olivia ran into Tess's arms and hugged her fiercely. Tess held her just as tightly. "I'm going to miss you so much," she said, her voice choking on the words.

Olivia nodded into her shoulder.

"But I'll see you in a few months when you come to visit."

She nodded again.

Mrs. Linde came up behind Tess, her mouth drawn in a defensively tight line, refusing to show that she was upset. She took Olivia gently by the arm and pulled her away from Tess. "Come on, now. Put on your brave face and say a proper goodbye. You don't want them remembering you all wet and blotchy.''

Tess took a tissue from her purse and wiped Olivia's cheeks. "I love you, Olivia, and nothing is going to change that. Not distance or time.''

"I love you, too."

Tess turned to the housekeeper and hugged her. "Thank you for taking such good care of us. I don't know what we'll do without you.''

Mrs. Linde hugged her back. "It's going to feel like all the life's gone out of the place, without you and little Jenni around.''

The four of them went downstairs and out to the car where Mr. Linde, Blythe and Trilling waited. Jenni hugged them all and got into the car, her head turned away so no one would see that she was crying. Olivia stood in the circle of Mrs. Linde's protective arm as Tess hugged first Trilling and then Blythe. "Remember that you two promised to visit Jenni and me in Maine.''

"And we will," said Blythe. "I miss you already.''

"You could always marry me when the divorce comes through,'' joked Trilling.

"If I did that you'd never find the woman you really love.''

"I think I already have," he said quietly. "The lady simply doesn't return my affections.''

Tess kissed his cheek. "Take care of Alec and Olivia.''

She hugged Olivia one more time before climbing into the car. Mr. Linde closed the door after her and walked around the car to the driver's side.

Tess stared out the window as they drove away, watching until the little group disappeared from sight.

Her throat was so tight it ached, but she didn't cry.

That would come later, when she was alone.

* * *

The same day Tess and Jenni left, workers poured into Devereaux Hall to clean and repair the damage that twenty years of neglect had wrought. It was less than might have been expected because the place was so structurally sound.

Alec lost himself in the business of restoration. It kept him from thinking.

It kept him away from the other house.

He hated being there now. It was, he thought, the most desolate place on earth with Tess and Jenni gone.

Rather than hiring a new governess for Olivia, he was letting her attend school in the village. She was making new friends, and while she still missed Jenni and Tess, she seemed a little happier. And Alec was making an effort to spend time with her and be a real father.

Tess had taught him that.

The house was essentially ready in a matter of weeks. Alec had spent the previous year selecting furniture and carpets to replace what he knew would be too old to be saved. Carpenters replaced rotted wood and refinished the main downstairs rooms; there was fresh paint and new wallpaper. The kitchen was usable, but needed to be modernized. That would be done over time.

But for now the workers were done.

Alec arrived from London without, as usual, letting anyone know he was coming. He went to Devereaux Hall and let himself in.

It smelled new.

He went from room to room, checking on the work. It was exactly the way he'd wanted it. There were even sheets on the beds. All that was left was to move in.

The library at Devereaux Hall was larger than the one at the other house. The books that had been his father's, grandfather's and all of the Devereauxs through the centuries were still there.

He took off his jacket and built a fire, then poured himself a drink and sat in a newly covered leather chair, his feet propped on the footstool.

It was finally sinking in. Devereaux Hall was really his. He'd gotten it back for all of the Devereaux generations to come. It was what he wanted. It had been his main focus for years.

Alec stared into the fire.

He should have been happy, but he wasn't.

This should have been one of the high points of his life, but it wasn't.

He finished off his drink and poured himself another, pacing as he drank it, and poured another.

The shadows of evening fell over the house, finally swallowing it altogether, but Alec didn't turn on a light.

For weeks he'd tried to avoid thinking about Tess by keeping busy.

He tossed another log onto the fire and stared unseeingly into the flames.

Tess.

Tess. Tess. Tess.

He drained the alcohol from the glass. Maybe if he drank enough he could stop thinking about her; maybe he could numb the pain. Pouring himself another one, he sank into the chair, his head against its back, his arms over the sides, the top of the glass hanging from his fingertips.

God help him, he didn't want to stop thinking about her. He remembered the first time he'd seen Tess. She'd been standing at her father's grave. There had been something about her that had drawn him to her even then—before he'd known whose daughter she was.

He thought of her with Jenni and Olivia, of how difficult the situation must have been for her, but how well she'd hidden it and how quickly she'd taken his daughter into her heart.

He thought of her chasing the pig and falling in the mud and rescuing a kitten from a tree.

He remembered what a joy she'd been to talk to on those occasions when they'd both managed to let their guards down at the same time. And how proud he'd been to call her his wife and introduce her to people who hadn't known the truth of their situation.

He remembered how her body felt pressed against his; how soft her skin was; how inviting her lips were; how perfectly they fit together.

He remembered the scent of her skin and hair.

It would haunt him for the rest of his days.

Alec finished his drink but didn't pour another one. He was as unaffected by the alcohol as if he hadn't drunk it.

For the first time in his life, he knew what it was to love.

It hurt him like he'd never hurt before. Tess had come to him to tell him how she felt and he'd just stood there, saying nothing. He'd let her go. Let her? Hell, he'd all but pushed her out the door.

And why?

He looked around the library. For this. This house. For the hatred of the man who'd taken it from his family and altered their lives forever. He'd let his hatred of Thomas Parish bleed into his feelings for Tess, when she was as much a victim of her father as he was.

How could he have been so stupid?

As he sat there staring into the glowing embers of the dying fire, the sound of the huge brass knocker hitting the door in the main hall thundered through the house. "Alec, are you there?" yelled Trilling.

Alec rose quickly and opened the door. "What's wrong?"

"We've been trying to find you since this morning," said Trilling as he pushed past him.

"What's wrong? Is Olivia all right?"

"She's fine. Fine. It's Tess."

Alec's whole body went cold.

"She called this morning. Jenni ran away. There's a chance that she's trying to get here. Her passport is missing and she apparently has been borrowing money from people for weeks."

"Did she call the airlines?"

"Yes, but they wouldn't give her any information from the passenger manifests. I guess they're afraid she might be some disgruntled noncustodial parent or something. She's working with the police now. I haven't spoken with her for a few hours, so I don't know what's happened."

Alec pushed Trilling out the door ahead of him. "Drive me to the house."

"What about your car?"

"Leave it here." Alec didn't feel drunk but he didn't want to take any chances.

The two men sped to the house. All of the outside lights were on. Mrs. Linde met them in the foyer. "Oh, thank heavens you're here."

"Have you talked to Tess?" asked Alec. "Is there any news?"

"Jenni called from the train station an hour ago. Mr. Linde picked her up and brought her here. She's upstairs in Olivia's room sound asleep. The poor child was ready to drop from exhaustion."

Relief washed over Alec. "What about Tess? Have you spoken with her?"

"Not yet. There hasn't been time. I was just going to call her when I heard the car pull up."

"I'll call." Alec strode into the library, found Tess's Maine number in his book and pressed the numbers that connected him first to the United States and then to Tess.

Tess answered on the first ring.

"Tess, it's Alec. Jenni's here."

Tess closed her eyes tightly.

"Are you still there?"

She nodded and then spoke. "Yes. Thank you so much for calling. Is she all right?"

"I haven't seen her, but Mrs. Linde says she's fine. She's asleep in Olivia's room right now. Would you like to speak with her?"

"No, no. Let her sleep. But when she wakes, let her know that she's in big, big trouble. Like nothing she's ever known before."

"I will."

Tess sank into the chair beside the phone, exhausted. She could barely form a complete thought much less make a decision. "I don't know what to do next. Should I come to get her?"

"No," said Alec gently. "Let me take care of things from this end. And don't worry. She's in good hands. I'll have her call you in the morning."

"Thank you, Alec."

"Get some sleep yourself."

"I will. Goodbye."

Trilling was standing in the doorway, his arms folded across his chest as he watched his friend. "You look like hell," he said when Alec had hung up.

"Thank you."

"Tess?"

Alec rubbed his beard-shadowed jaw. "It would appear that I'm in love with my wife."

"It's about time you figured that out. What are you going to do about it?"

"Bring her home."

Trilling smiled. Without saying another word, he turned and left.

Alec found Mr. and Mrs. Linde in the kitchen at the table having some tea. They both rose when he walked in, but he waved them back into their seats. "I'm going to clean myself up and then I'm going to Maine to get Tess and bring her back here. I'd appreciate it if the two of you would look after the girls."

"Of course," they both said at once.

"Will Mrs. Devereaux be staying long?" asked Mrs. Linde. "I mean should I make up her room?"

"I hope that my wife will be staying for a very long time. In answer to your second question, there will be no need to make up her room. She won't be sleeping there."

Mrs. Linde bit her lower lip to keep from smiling, but as soon as Alec left the kitchen, she turned to her husband and beamed.

Tess sat on a Maine cliff overlooking the Atlantic. The house her father had bequeathed to her was behind her. It was small and cosy, perfect for two people.

Jenni hadn't been crazy about her tiny room, but she would get used to it.

Jenni.

Tess had talked to her earlier and had been torn between telling her how happy she was that she was safe and blistering her ear for taking such a terrible risk and worrying everyone who cared about her.

She'd hoped to talk to Alec, but he apparently hadn't wanted to talk to her.

Wasn't it strange how things had turned out? She'd been so determined not to end up like her mother; but that's exactly what she'd done. She was in love with a man—and would always be in love with a man—who didn't love her. Their situations were different, but the results were the same.

The night was beautiful, warm for this late in the fall. She rose and started down the steep embankment to the beach below. It was a perfect evening for a midnight stroll.

She took off her shoes as soon as she reached the sand and dug her toes into it. The sand was cool on top and warm underneath.

There was no sound except for the wash of the waves. Tess walked into the ocean up to her knees and just stood there. It was as though there was no one else in the world. And to-night at least, on her own private stretch of beach, there wasn't.

She wanted to swim.

She could have dived in with her clothes on, but she wanted to really feel the water against her skin. It took her only a minute to strip off her clothes and toss them onto the sand. For someone who had never done that before, she was oddly unself-conscious as she walked back into the water completely nude and dove into the first large wave that rolled toward her.

She experienced an incredible feeling of freedom.

Tess dove again and again, swimming a little way out, but not too far.

Alec knocked on the front and back doors of Tess's house, but no one answered. He knew she was home be-cause her car was in the driveway. At least he assumed it was her car. And he knew she wasn't asleep because the lights were on inside despite the fact that it was past midnight.

As he stood on the porch looking around, he was drawn to the cliff. Standing on the edge, he looked at the spectac-ular view. Something in the water caught his eye. At first, because of the way it was diving, he thought it was a dol-phin. But when the clouds drifted away from the moon and let the full strength of its light shine on the water, he saw that it was a woman.

It was Tess.

He watched as she swam out and then let the waves carry her back in again and again.

He looked at the embankment to see if there was a way down and saw the steep footpath. It took him less than two minutes to get to the beach. He stood next to her clothes, watching.

Tess suddenly stopped swimming. Her back was to the beach, but it didn't matter. She knew Alec was there and slowly turned to face him.

Neither of them spoke.

A wave pushed Tess from behind like an invisible hand, moving her toward Alec. She stopped, but another wave pushed her again. This time she kept walking, rising out of the water naked and unembarrassed.

"Would you hand me my shirt, please?" she asked Alec as she stood in front of him. "I'm cold."

Alec picked up her shirt and helped her into it. "Your skin is freezing," he said as he stood in front of her, buttoning it. "We should get you inside where it's warmer."

"I didn't think I'd ever see you again," whispered Tess.

Alec, his hands working on the button just above her breasts, looked into her eyes. "I didn't, either."

"Did you bring Jenni home?"

"Jenni's already home. I came to get you."

"What?"

Alec trailed his fingers over Tess's damp cheek. "I love you. Never have I said those words to another human being. I never expected to say them." His eyes moved over her face. "Without you, everything else is meaningless. I've spent my life feeling as though something inside me was missing . . . as though a part of me that was supposed to be there wasn't. It wasn't until after you left that I realized *you* were the missing piece. You make me whole. I love you," he said again. "I want to spend the rest of my life showing you just how much."

Tess didn't move. She couldn't. What if this was a dream? What if she opened her eyes and he was gone?

"Will you marry me? For real this time."

Tess raised her hand to his face, touching him with her fingertips. He was warm. He turned his head and kissed her palm before covering her hand with his and holding it to his heart. She could feel it beating.

"Say something."

"Oh, Alec, I love you, too. Of course I'll marry you."

He pulled her into his arms and held her close. "God, Tess, I can't believe I ever let you go. Being without you these past weeks has been like death."

"I know."

"I'm so sorry for what I put you through."

Tess looked into his eyes. "It doesn't matter."

Alec kissed her, long and hard, and felt her instant response. He groaned and pulled back.

"What is it?"

"I want to make love to you here, now, all night long."

"I hear a *but* in there somewhere."

He kissed her again. "But I want to do it right this time. I want to take you home and marry you in front of the people we care about. And then I want the two of us to go somewhere where we can be alone to get to know each other inside and out."

"All right," she said softly. "But for now would you please hold me?"

Alec wrapped her in his arms.

Never ever again would he let her go.

Epilogue

Tess waited with Russell and Mr. Linde outside the little chapel attached to Devereaux Hall. The girls had unearthed a beautiful, antique, ivory silk dress from among the racks and trunks of clothes stored in the attic. It wasn't a wedding dress, but swept the floor in the style of its day. The high neck accentuated the graceful line of Tess's throat. It clung to her slender figure until flaring out just past her hips. The skirt back was slightly longer than the front. Instead of a veil, the girls had made her a crown of champagne-colored roses. Her bouquet was made of roses of the same color.

Their music selections were original. So far she'd heard everything from Handel—Olivia's choice no doubt, to Guns & Roses—definitely Jenni's selection.

Both girls poked their heads around the door of the chapel. "Ready?" Jenni asked.

"Ready," Tess said with a smile.

Olivia sighed. "You look beautiful."

"Thanks to you two."

They both beamed. Jenni looked back into the chapel. "Oh, we're ready in here. Don't come until you hear the music."

"Which music?"

"'The Wedding March,' of course."

"The one by Guns & Roses?"

Jenni rolled her eyes and closed the door. A moment later she heard the music. Mr. Linde stepped ahead of them and opened the door.

That's when Tess saw Alec, standing straight and tall in his tuxedo, waiting for her to come to him, his eyes full of love.

Russell put Tess's hand on his arm. "Ready?" he asked softly.

"Oh, yes."

They walked the less than ten feet to the front of the chapel. Trilling and Blythe were there.

"Who gives this woman's hand in marriage?" the minister asked.

"I do," said Russell as he placed Tess's hand into Alec's.

Tess barely heard anything else. She somehow knew when she needed to speak, but it was more instinct than anything else. Her eyes were locked with Alec's and she couldn't—didn't want to—look away.

When it was time to exchange rings, Tess placed on Alec's finger a simple gold band she'd purchased in the village.

"You and no other," Alec whispered for Tess's ears only as he slid an antique gold band on her finger, then raised her hand to his lips and kissed it.

"I now pronounce you husband and wife," the minister said. "You may kiss the bride."

A corner of Alec's mouth lifted as he cupped Tess's cheek with the palm of his hand and lowered his lips to hers. As he raised his head, he gazed into her eyes. "Now you're well and truly mine,'' he said softly. "I'll never let you go again.''

The girls rushed forward to hug them. Mr. and Mrs. Linde stood in the background, beaming from ear to ear. Blythe and Trilling were right behind the girls with their congratulations.

"We have one more thing to do," Alec said as he removed some papers from the inside pocket of his tuxedo. "Russell, do you have a pen?"

The older man, smiling a smile that said he knew what was going on, uncapped a fountain pen and handed it to him.

Alec opened the first paper. "Olivia, I know how much you've wanted Tess to be your real mother. As soon as she signs this paper, she will be exactly that."

He handed the pen to Tess and she signed without hesitation.

He opened another paper and spread it on top of the first. "And Jenni, you've been looking for a father ever since you came to England. If you don't have any objections, and with your sister's permission, I'd like to take on that role in your life."

"I'd like that very much," said Jenni emotionally.

He took the pen from Tess and signed the paper. "You're now legally my daughter and Olivia is legally your sister."

The two girls squealed in delight and hugged each other.

Alec went to Tess and pulled her into his arms. "We have something of an instant family."

"I know. Isn't it wonderful?" she said with a trembling smile.

"I love you."

Her eyes moved over his face. Everything that had happened to her in her life had led her to this man, this moment. He was everything she'd ever dreamed of and more.

"Wait a minute," Jenni said to Olivia, "we're only sisters on your dad's side. Tess is my sister, not my mother. So what does that make us on Tess's side?"

Olivia thought for a moment. "I believe, technically speaking of course, that you're my aunt. Isn't that right, Tess?" she asked.

"Isn't what right?"

"Jenni is my aunt."

"Well, yes, I suppose in a way."

Jenni grinned. "Cool!"

Alec held Tess close to his side. He wanted to hold on to her and never let her go.

And Tess wanted to stay right where she was.

Everything was the way it should be. All of the fears she'd had about falling in love with Alec were gone. She knew with every fiber of her being that Alec would never do anything to hurt her. He was completely honorable—*and he loved her!*

Alec twined his fingers through Tess's. "What are you thinking about with such intensity?" he asked.

Her eyes met his. "How very lucky I am. How much I love you."

The warmth of his gaze embraced her. Alec had never believed in happy endings.

Until now.

The morning after their wedding day, Tess stretched her hand out to the other side of the bed. It was empty. She opened her eyes and rose up on one elbow. Alec was standing in front of the window, staring out into the night. Pushing back the covers, she slid out of bed and walked up behind him, wrapped her arms around him and rested her cheek on his bare back. "What are you doing up?" she asked.

Alec pulled Tess around so that she was in front of him, her back against his chest, his arms wrapped around her. "I was thinking."

"About what?"

"You. Us. I am the luckiest man in the world. If anyone would have told me it was possible to be this happy, I wouldn't have believed them. Whenever I think I couldn't possibly love you more, I find that I do. I can't imagine life without you."

Tess turned in his arms. She raised her hand to his face and stroked his rough cheek. "I know."

"You've become such a part of me that I don't know where I end and you begin. And when I think about how close I came to losing you..."

Tess went up on her toes and kissed him. "You could never have lost me. If you hadn't come for me when you did, I'd still be in Maine waiting. I knew before I ever left England that I would never love anyone the way I love you. And I could never have settled for anyone else."

"It's so strange how everything worked out. I think sometimes about your father unsuccessfully trying to arrange a marriage between us when you were born and then waiting all of those years before exacting his revenge. I spent so much of my life hating the man, and now all I feel is gratitude. He can't have been all bad if he had a hand in creating you. And Jenni."

He held her close in his arms, his cheek on her hair.

Tess felt so safe. There wasn't a doubt in her mind or heart about his love for her. She trusted him completely.

She loved him completely.

* * * * *

Get Ready to be Swept Away by
Silhouette's Spring Collection

Abduction
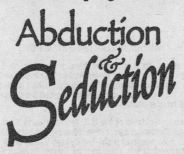

These passion-filled stories explore both the dangerous
desires of men and the seductive powers of women.
Written by three of our most celebrated authors, they are
sure to capture your hearts.

Diana Palmer
Brings us a spin-off of her Long, Tall Texans series

Joan Johnston
Crafts a beguiling Western romance

Rebecca Brandewyne
New York Times bestselling author
makes a smashing contemporary debut

Available in March at your favorite retail outlet.

ABSED

MILLION DOLLAR SWEEPSTAKES (III)

No purchase necessary. To enter, follow the directions published. Method of entry may vary. For eligibility, entries must be received no later than March 31, 1996. No liability is assumed for printing errors, lost, late or misdirected entries. Odds of winning are determined by the number of eligible entries distributed and received. Prizewinners will be determined no later than June 30, 1996.

Sweepstakes open to residents of the U.S. (except Puerto Rico), Canada, Europe and Taiwan who are 18 years of age or older. All applicable laws and regulations apply. Sweepstakes offer void wherever prohibited by law. Values of all prizes are in U.S. currency. This sweepstakes is presented by Torstar Corp., its subsidiaries and affiliates, in conjunction with book, merchandise and/or product offerings. For a copy of the Official Rules send a self-addressed, stamped envelope (WA residents need not affix return postage) to: MILLION DOLLAR SWEEPSTAKES (III) Rules, P.O. Box 4573, Blair, NE 68009, USA.

EXTRA BONUS PRIZE DRAWING

No purchase necessary. The Extra Bonus Prize will be awarded in a random drawing to be conducted no later than 5/30/96 from among all entries received. To qualify, entries must be received by 3/31/96 and comply with published directions. Drawing open to residents of the U.S. (except Puerto Rico), Canada, Europe and Taiwan who are 18 years of age or older. All applicable laws and regulations apply; offer void wherever prohibited by law. Odds of winning are dependent upon number of eligibile entries received. Prize is valued in U.S. currency. The offer is presented by Torstar Corp., its subsidiaries and affiliates in conjunction with book, merchandise and/or product offering. For a copy of the Official Rules governing this sweepstakes, send a self-addressed, stamped envelope (WA residents need not affix return postage) to: Extra Bonus Prize Drawing Rules, P.O. Box 4590, Blair, NE 68009, USA.

SWP-S295

THE SULTAN'S WIVES
Tracy Sinclair
(SE #943, March)

When a story in an exotic locale beckoned, nothing could keep Pippa Bennington from scooping the competition. But this time, her eager journalist's heart landed her squarely in, of all things, a harem! Pippa was falling for the seductive charms of Mikolar al-Rasheed—but what exactly *were* the sultan's true intentions?

Don't miss
THE SULTAN'S WIVES,
by Tracy Sinclair,
available in March!

She's friend, wife, mother—she's you! And beside each Special Woman stands a wonderfully *special* man. It's a celebration of our heroines— and the men who become part of their lives.

TSW395

Silhouette
SPECIAL EDITION ™®

WHAT EVER HAPPENED TO...?

Have you been wondering when much-loved characters will finally get their own stories? Well, have we got a lineup for you! Silhouette Special Edition is proud to present a *Spin-off Spectacular!* Be sure to catch these exciting titles from some of your favorite authors:

HUSBAND: SOME ASSEMBLY REQUIRED (SE #931 January) Shawna Saunders has finally found Mr. Right in the dashing Murphy Pendleton, last seen in *Marie Ferrarella*'s BABY IN THE MIDDLE (SE #892).

SAME TIME, NEXT YEAR (SE #937 February) In this tie-in to *Debbie Macomber*'s popular series THOSE MANNING MEN and THOSE MANNING SISTERS, a yearly reunion between friends suddenly has them in the marrying mood!

A FAMILY HOME (SE #938 February) Adam Cutler discovers the best reason for staying home is the love he's found with sweet-natured and sexy Lainey Bates in *Celeste Hamilton*'s follow-up to WHICH WAY IS HOME? (SE #897).

JAKE'S MOUNTAIN (SE #945 March) Jake Harris never met anyone as stubborn—or as alluring—as Dr. Maggie Matthews in *Christine Flynn*'s latest, a spin-off to WHEN MORNING COMES (SE #922).

Don't miss these wonderful titles, only for our readers—only from Silhouette Special Edition!

SPIN7

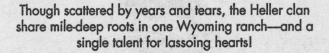

Silhouette SPECIAL EDITION™

A RANCHING FAMILY

Though scattered by years and tears, the Heller clan share mile-deep roots in one Wyoming ranch—and a single talent for lassoing hearts!

Meet another member of the Heller clan in
Victoria Pade's
BABY MY BABY
(SE #946, March)

The ranching spirit coursed through
Beth Heller's veins—as did the passion she
felt for her proud Sioux husband, Ash Blackwolf. Yet
their marriage was in ashes. Only the
unexpected new life growing within Beth could bring
them together again....

Don't miss **BABY MY BABY,** the next installment of
Victoria Pade's series,
A RANCHING FAMILY, available in March!
And watch for Jackson Heller's story,
COWBOY'S KISS, coming in July...only from
Silhouette Special Edition!

SSEVP2

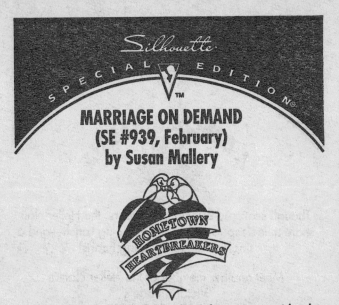

Silhouette

SPECIAL EDITION ™ ®

MARRIAGE ON DEMAND
(SE #939, February)
by Susan Mallery

HOMETOWN HEARTBREAKERS

Hometown Heartbreakers: Those heart-stoppin' hunks
are rugged, ready and able to steal your heart....

Austin Lucas was as delicious as forbidden sin—that's
what the Glenwood womenfolk were saying. And
Rebecca Chambers couldn't deny how sexy he looked
in worn, tight jeans. But when their impulsive
encounter obliged them to get married, could their
passion lead to everlasting love?

Find out in *MARRIAGE ON DEMAND*, the next story
in Susan Mallery's *Hometown Heartbreakers* series,
coming to you in February...only from
Silhouette Special Edition.

HH-2

A ROSE AND A WEDDING VOW (SE #944)
by Andrea Edwards

Matt Michaelson returned home to face Liz—his brother's widow...a woman
he'd never forgotten. Could falling in love with *this* Michaelson man heal the
wounds of Liz's lonely past?

A ROSE AND A WEDDING VOW, SE #944 (3/95), is the next story in this
stirring trilogy by Andrea Edwards. THIS TIME, FOREVER—sometimes a love
is so strong, nothing can stand in its way, not even time. Look for the last
installment, A SECRET AND A BRIDAL PLEDGE, in May 1995.

If you missed the first book in Andrea Edwards's THIS TIME, FOREVER series,
A RING AND A PROMISE (Silhouette Special Edition #932), order your copy now by
sending your name, address, zip or postal code along with a check or money order
(please do not send cash) for $3.50 ($3.99 in Canada) plus 75¢ postage and handling
($1.00 in Canada), payable to Silhouette Books, to:

In the U.S.	In Canada
Silhouette Books	Silhouette Books
3010 Walden Ave.	P. O. Box 636
P. O. Box 9077	Fort Erie, Ontario
Buffalo, NY 14269-9077	L2A 5X3

Please specify book title(s) with order.
Canadian residents add applicable federal and provincial taxes.

AEMINI-2

SILHOUETTE... Where Passion Lives

Don't miss these Silhouette favorites by some of our most distinguished authors! And now you can receive a discount by ordering two or more titles!

SD#05786	QUICKSAND by Jennifer Greene	$2.89	☐
SD#05795	DEREK by Leslie Guccione	$2.99	☐
SD#05818	NOT JUST ANOTHER PERFECT WIFE by Robin Elliott	$2.99	☐
IM#07505	HELL ON WHEELS by Naomi Horton	$3.50	☐
IM#07514	FIRE ON THE MOUNTAIN by Marion Smith Collins	$3.50	☐
IM#07559	KEEPER by Patricia Gardner Evans	$3.50	☐
SSE#09879	LOVING AND GIVING by Gina Ferris	$3.50	☐
SSE#09892	BABY IN THE MIDDLE by Marie Ferrarella	$3.50 U.S. ☐ $3.99 CAN. ☐	
SSE#09902	SEDUCED BY INNOCENCE by Lucy Gordon	$3.50 U.S. ☐ $3.99 CAN. ☐	
SR#08952	INSTANT FATHER by Lucy Gordon	$2.75	☐
SR#08984	AUNT CONNIE'S WEDDING by Marie Ferrarella	$2.75	☐
SR#08990	JILTED by Joleen Daniels	$2.75	☐

(limited quantities available on certain titles)

AMOUNT	$_____
DEDUCT: 10% DISCOUNT FOR 2+ BOOKS	$_____
POSTAGE & HANDLING	$_____
($1.00 for one book, 50¢ for each additional)	
APPLICABLE TAXES*	$_____
TOTAL PAYABLE	$_____
(check or money order—please do not send cash)	

To order, complete this form and send it, along with a check or money order for the total above, payable to Silhouette Books, to: **In the U.S.:** 3010 Walden Avenue, P.O. Box 9077, Buffalo, NY 14269-9077; **In Canada:** P.O. Box 636, Fort Erie, Ontario, L2A 5X3.

Name:_____

Address:_____ City:_____

State/Prov.:_____ Zip/Postal Code:_____

*New York residents remit applicable sales taxes.
Canadian residents remit applicable GST and provincial taxes.   SBACK-DF

Silhouette®
™